Borderlines

By K.L. Somniate

To people who're tired of straight dystopias.

"Has he recovered?"

Stumbling, falling, sliding down a hill, someone grasping at his shoulder, he gasps involuntarily on contact, because that is the shoulder they'd worked so carefully on, the one they had pulled and pulled and pulled and pricked and pricked-

"Yes. Adequately."

"Well, this will be the last time. He has no information to offer."

He's airborne again and being carried away.

The ground lurches over his head and in his disorientation, it becomes the sky.

He closes his eyes.

"He didn't really have any information to begin with though."

"No. No, he was a traitor. Disgraced. Or simply incompetent, perhaps. I can't imagine them sending a skilled or much beloved soldier on a suicide mission. That's grunt work, isn't it? Grunt work or disgraced work."

They sent him to die, they wanted him to cross the border and draw attention away from their probing of the southwestern border.

But it turns out he can't even accomplish this mission properly.

"It's sad. He wasn't even begging today."

Could barely breathe, much less beg.

"They make 'em tough over the border, huh?"

"No. Something about this one is just special."

Special, full of promise, full of dedication, abiding, obedient, unyielding, enduring, incorruptible, but men miscalculate, men are blind to themselves, men don't know one another anymore, don't want to, don't try to-

"You like this one, Doctor?"

"I like his spirit. I'd been looking for entertainment. More...*resilient* entertainment. It gave in the end, but they always do. Love for country notwithstanding."

"Love for country..."

Is there any other kind?

"Name?"

We don't need your name.

"Buddy?"

Look, my friend…look, we know you don't know anything.

"Alright, man."

You're barely a man. Let's see if we can make you even less than that, shall we?

Breathe. Breathe.

Eyes flickering.

Unseeing.

Someone's beside him.

He wants to move away, but he's so tired, everything hurts, it's so hard to breathe, something is holding him down, weighing him down, binding his aching bones to the earth. He's too tired to fight, and it's all the same anyway, whether it's Teacher or a stranger.

Briefly his vision clears and he catches a glimpse of himself (and a dark figure beside him, but he ignores this for now).

There's nothing holding him to the earth.

Just his own body, resistant to his commands, as distant and unreachable as home. He struggles to move somehow, in any way, but he might as well be looking at his body from a kilometer away, trying to move it without touching it.

His eyes roll up into his head and he no longer has to look at the pathetic mess of unresponsive limbs, gushing blood, and exposed bone that was once whole, that he had once identified as himself, but is now nothing more than…a stranger.

He has only this moment of peace before the nightmare begins again.

You almost died this time.

You're a tough one, aren't you?

But they didn't think you were worth keeping around anymore, did they?

I think you're worth something, Lieutenant.

You're entertaining at the very least.

He's screaming and someone else is screaming with him.

There's a terrible weight on him, perhaps the other person, whoever it is, and he pushes against it, crying out as his arm protests, his shoulder protests, his entire body, nothing but a splintered, shattered, repugnant lump of stripped flesh and weakened bones, protests as it's battered by a stronger, more solid body.

Eventually he can't do anything but lie back and accept his fate, the agony coursing through his veins like glass shards. His fingers can't stop trembling, his legs can't stop kicking as pain tears through his muscles, and spasms wrack his abdomen as he begins coughing up blood. He can see, feel that there is nothing on his chest, yet it feels tight, constrained, like something is crushing him, bearing down on his ribs patiently, sadistically.

Stay down, stay down, my friend.

You're going to hurt yourself, there's a good pet.

I wish they'd let me keep you.

You have this look in your eyes like you want nothing more than to live, and that's so different from what your mind is thinking, isn't it?

The eyes never lie. The mind might, but the eyes don't.

You want to live?

But what for?

There's nothing here for you.

There's nothing here for anyone like you.

He turns his head slowly to one side, trying to take advantage of these painful seconds of consciousness to get his bearings, some indicator of his location.

Where's home, my dear boy?

Dirty, bloodied rags on the floor.

The remains of a campfire.

He's alone.

But there had been someone here.

The embers aren't cold yet.

He shivers and curls slightly, instinctively.

Then screams out in pain.

They'll stop if I tell them. I control your body, my friend. I control everything you do, everything you feel. Everything you think, even. I've emptied out what little is in that cold, analytic brain of yours and filled it with myself.

Lovely, isn't it, what human beings can accomplish with just a little focus?

He's not in their dark room.

He isn't on their floor, his cheek grinded into cracked, stained tile, his back and sides and stomach mercilessly, unyieldingly the subjects of iron-toed boots and heavy belts and ringed fists.

He's lying on the ground, the taciturn, impartial earth.

And unlike in that room, he's wearing clothes.

Clothes which had been white, but seem to be red and brown now.

Red, from his blood, no doubt.

Brown from this dirt.

Brown from blood too, of course, because blood changes color when it dries.

Almost immediately, blood becomes dirt, nothing but a stain, indistinguishable from mud, from shit.

He touches it slightly, his fingernail carving a single line into it, and almost feels something in his empty heart.

Then he falls asleep once more, perspiration and something stickier, something more sinister soaking his brow.

"Not easy."

Can't have been easy. Growing up as one of their pilots. Plucked you right out of the cradle, didn't they? Trained you from childhood into adulthood.

Humans have always dreamt of flight. The ground merely feels...inadequate, for a species as lofty and accomplished as ours, isn't that right? How astounded and shocked we were to find that it was possible after all! What a marvelous world it is, and how simply marvelous humans are!

"You still in there, kid?"

Amusing, isn't it, how far we've come, far enough to detest the very thing we thought impossible.

Science will do that, won't it? Turn the miracle into the mundane.

"This is impossible. I should leave you behind."

Go ahead. Whoever you are, leave me behind. Let me die. I would rather starve or freeze or be eaten by something wild than continue doing...whatever you would call this.

Whatever it is that could possibly await me out there.

"Damn. Damn, this is fine and dandy while it's autumn, but it's going to be winter soon. We need to leave the area before then. Wake up. Wake up...please."

Leave me behind.

I am shackled to this earth, to this life, and I would rather die here and now than wither away in the chains of my own making.

I am a coward.

Let me go.

Let me die.

Let me...please.

He doesn't expect to wake up again, but he does.

He still hurts a great deal, but he can fight the exhaustion in his bones, the fire in his muscles, and struggle to sit up this time.

He fails, lying back down with a gargled yell as his back screams in protest.

He smells of piss and smoke and sweat.

"Hey!"

Someone blocks the light of the dark room (cave his mind thinks) he's in.

He flinches, closing his eyes, hand outstretched as if to protect himself.

"You're awake!" the man says.

Although, he's not sure if he can call him a man.

His face is rather round and youthful, energetic and not yet hardened by years of living. His hair, wild and defiant of gravity, brushes against the ceiling as he crouches and crawls in.

He flinches, but immediately regrets the involuntary action because it sends pain shooting from his side to his shoulder.

Which is sweaty and red and caked in mud and tied rather tightly with bandages.

"Why…?" is all he can croak in response.

His mouth feels full of cotton balls and he can't think of any other question.

This seems like the most relevant one anyway. Nothing else matters at this point.

The man shakes his head.

"Not important."

It's certainly not important enough for him to remain conscious.

He's strained himself too much.

He can feel blood leaking through his shirt, can hear the other man swearing, and then all he can see is darkness as the man leans over him again, blocking out the light.

The last thing he sees is the man's eyes, hazel or green or blue, looking down disgustedly on his pitiable, decaying body.

If it's not important, then let me die, please.

He's dimly aware of being carried the next time he's conscious.

He's very aware of it, actually, because it hurts.

Every rib seems to bend and lurch with every stride.

He opens his mouth to protest, but is not heard.

You've lost over 59 pounds, well, 27 kilograms by your scale. Congratulations.

You were already such a tiny little thing.

Blue sky.

Fluffy white clouds, the kind he'd stared at, earthbound, as an obedient little pilot-in-training.

A haze of green, grass and foliage.

Dizzying, sickening swirl of colors and light, too bright, just like-

He sits in a room bathed in blinding light for days. He can't sleep, not unless he passes out, and even then he wakes up to blinding light and it burns, it dries his eyes out, they itch, he wants to claw them out, and still they leave the light on him. Because he's nothing more than a specimen under a microscope, and there's nothing they cannot see, nothing they cannot expose.

He no longer wears any clothing.

They had deemed it unnecessary.

All he can think of, curled in the corner of a room bathed in constant, artificial light, are the rats of the Red Cluster base.

Cowering, timid, starving rats in their little test cages, naked and ugly, their revolting skin and tails writhing against one another. Their fur coming out in patches, leaving them bald and even more disgusting.

But he envies them, as he thinks of them, curled up in a cold white room with cold white lights and nothing at all to cover himself, to hide himself from their probing, judging eyes.

As wretched as they are, they have each other.

The light, blessed be the General, fades as his eyes roll to the back of his head.

The pain remains, but the light is gone.

They leave him with his arms tied over his head.

They leave him bent over, tied over a hard, cold, metal desk, the pain in his back almost splitting him in two when he's finally allowed to fall. Other times, he's simply left kneeling in a puddle of his own blood, his own skin, his hands tied together behind his back in a position that will ache for days.

He can only pray he will die before they come back.

When he falls over on his side, and they allow him to remain this way, he thanks them inwardly, for they are being merciful. The nights when it feels like they'd crushed every bone in his body, beaten every inch of his skin until it bled, are the nights he craves the most, because at least then, he knows they'll let him bleed on the floor the way he likes.

They'll think he's had enough, and that he would sooner die, lying in his own fluids, than get up and walk.

And they're right.

Even if they didn't tie him to something, he wouldn't have tried to run.

He would've rather done something more productive, like tried his damned hardest to kill himself.

It seems like the most desirable escape.

After all, there's no way out, out there.

But there's a way out, in here.

He can find it. He must.

"...?"

He opens his eyes slowly. Larger cave.

The man seems a little less huge and lumbering and more human-sized and mortal. He's knitting.

Something about that makes him feel something like hysteria burst to life in his lungs until he's breathless, choking. The man drops his project and seizes a canteen, but he merely lets out a huff of laughter and falls back down, still gasping. He licks the gap between his teeth where he'd lost molars in the beginning, where he'd had them smashed out of him as they didn't even bother with questions, just hitting and hitting and hitting for the hell of it.

What a shame it is, to ruin a pretty face like yours. Let's try and preserve that, shall we?

But lungs. Ribcage.

Kidneys. Spine.

They were fair game.

He'd pissed himself a few times.

Become immune to their taunts, but not their boots, digging into his genitals from time to time, and certainly not their laughter when they succeeded in forcing him to relieve himself in front of them.

Like a dog, on all fours, or on his back, as helpless as a child.

He smells like piss now.

Probably urinated all over himself sometime while he'd been unconscious.

He doesn't care.

What's one more person?

Trash the thing, trash the thing.

Useless body.

Can't move.

Can't control itself.

Isn't his anymore.

His hands shake. His vision goes in and out. Sometimes his urine is red. If he were to somehow survive this, he would be a broken, useless invalid, wouldn't he?

He'd rather not survive this.

An irrational hatred pulses in his throat.

He wants to lunge at this stranger.

Use every last ounce of energy he has left to scratch out his eyes, to tear out his throat with his still-intact incisors, to slam his fist into his face over and over and over again. But he does nothing but twitch feebly as the man touches him carefully, his callused hand on his shoulder.

"No strenuous movements," he says simply. "You need to get strong enough to walk on your own."

Fuck you.

He's awake when the man pulls his arms over his shoulders, hoists his body onto his back, and begins walking again.

He makes no indication of this, however, his eyes closed, his face in his shoulder.

The man is dressed like a civilian.

He smells earthy and musky and his clothes seem worn, but nothing gives him away as any profession in particular.

He opens his eyes briefly to see where they're going.

But all he sees are trees and grass and mountains on all sides.

The facility he'd been held in could've been in any direction, at the base or the summit of any of these mountains. Or it could've been somewhere else entirely, and this is merely where he's been brought.

He finds he doesn't care much.

He had accepted death inside the building.

Being outside of it changes nothing.

"I was born here."

He doesn't respond. He's not sure if the man knows he's awake.

"You were not."

Correct.

"You shouldn't be here."

No.

"But now you are," the man says thoughtfully.

Yes.

"You can help me."

Perhaps.

"I hope you will."

He has no answer.

He doesn't want to help anyone.

What if your spinal cord snapped?
What would your spinal fluid taste like, I wonder?
It would no doubt kill you.
But deep down, you don't mind that, do you?
You never minded.
Even when we first brought you here, you weren't afraid for your life, no, nothing as simple as that.
Did we *break you?*
Or did they?
"Do you want to know my name?"

The prisoner doesn't look up.

He's leaning against a tree. Or rather, he'd been leaned up against a tree, as he still can't move by himself, not without crippling pain.

He blinks.

Shakes his head.

Pain rattles dully against the inside of his skull.

The man nods.

"Alright."

We don't need your name.

"Do you want to know why I saved you?"

Not really.

But no harm in knowing that, I suppose.

This time he nods.

This time his throat aches and his head spins.

But he keeps his eyes open, despite his vision swirling and colors that shouldn't be there pulsing in his field of view.

The man eyes him, then turns and walks over to him. He tilts the prisoner's head back and slowly, he pours the water from his canteen to his lips.

He barely opens his mouth, letting the water trickle down his sore, dry throat. Cold rivers snake down his chin and onto his chest, but he barely notices.

The man feels his throat, making sure he swallows, then feels his forehead.

"You're still hot, but not as bad as yesterday," he says.

The news doesn't affect him very much.

The fever had been bad, the nightmares worse, and the constant sweating and unrest unbearable, but it might as well have happened years ago for all he cares about his condition now.

"…it's not because I think you're worth saving," the man says conversationally. "I don't know who you are. In fact, I don't think you do either. You're just one of their trained monkeys, aren't you? A flying monkey, haha. I doubt you were talkative even before they captured you. You guys just don't talk much, right? You shoot first, don't ask questions later."

He neither affirms nor denies this.

"But you're one of them, and that makes you valuable. I need you alive. I'm a member of the resistance."

The man puffs up as though proud. He then seems a little put out as the prisoner doesn't react.

"Well… your people have been in contact with us for some time."

This isn't news to him.

The prisoner closes his eyes.

"…well. You don't seem to care, so I guess it doesn't matter," the man says a little disappointedly.

Pride. Loyalty. Purpose.

These are things to hold onto.

"But I guess you should know that we're not going to get out of these mountains alive if you don't try to get better," the man continues.

As if he has any choice in that matter.

"Are you listening?"

What is there to listen to?

"If you die, they'll at least be grateful I got you out, won't they? Your people?"

Doubtful.

They wanted him to die.

He wants to accommodate them.

But this loudmouth rebel, this "political dissident" had come and "rescued" him from his duty.

No one would be happy about this.

His *government had lost a prisoner,* his own *government hadn't rid themselves of a useless traitor, and this resistance group would be entirely dissatisfied to find that he had no useful information, having been given none in order to ensure that when he was broken, he would say nothing of consequence.*

He can't summon the strength or will to shake his head. It hurts to move it. Nausea rolls in and he squeezes his eyes tightly shut, just wanting to sleep. Escape this pain, just for a while. Escape his own thoughts, this world. The foolish man who had taken him away from paradise, from blissful emptiness.

He sleeps fretfully, and the dissident has to tie him up to keep him from hurting himself.

Tell me about your mother.

The prisoner nods obediently.

"*Adrianna. Forty three years of age. Member of the Blue Cluster. Three hundred and fourth pilot of the second fleet of the third battalion-*"

"*No, no, no, no,*" *Teacher smiles.* "*I mean what was she like?*"

The prisoner opens his mouth.

But only blood seeps out, not words.

He can't force words to come out, no matter how hard he tries.

And he can't stop the blood.

"*That's a shame,*" *Teacher tuts.* "*All boys should love their mothers. Is that really what they teach you across the pond?*"

Metallic and filthy but soft as lips, it trails down his scarred throat, leaving behind burning wet red kisses. They linger at his collarbone.

"*You never hugged her? Kissed her? Held her hand as you walked through the market?*"

The prisoner can't even shake his head.

It makes him nauseous.

"*Well I can tell you a little about her, and about your father too.*" *Teacher smiles.* "*They were cold, heartless animals bred only to fly and to reproduce and to provide more animals to serve your beloved Battalion. They flew airships as ordered, and were killed in military skirmishes of no great significance. I'm amazed you know your mother's name. And that they give you names at all. Tell me, what does your name mean to you?*"

He seems to expect an answer.

But the prisoner's throat doesn't seem to be working.

Not even after the man slaps him hard, hard enough to knock him out of the chair and fall heavily on his side, eliciting a perfunctory scream as his ribs protest their rough treatment.

"*I expect to be answered...surely you have more than a number, a delineation, a label with which to process yourself?*"

"*I do,*" *he gasps.*

"*But it's meaningless,*" *Teacher pats his hip, noticing his flinch with relish.* "*Absolutely. Because a name means nothing if the person is nothing. A name has no power if its wearer has nothing attached to it but blood and bone. And as you know, or will know, if it still hasn't sunk in...blood and bone are breakable. They are not eternal. You have blood, bone, and flesh, but my dear boy, what you lack is something that cannot be given by any but God. My boy, you lack a soul.*"

The prisoner stays on his side, breathing heavily, tears welling up from physical rather than emotional pain.

"And that's not something a name can provide, I'm afraid."

He wakes up with his legs and hands bound, but is not particularly alarmed.

It's only logical, after all.

As his health improves, slowly but steadily, his captor must worry that he will try and escape.

But where does he have to escape to?

And what is there to escape from?

There's nothing in here, nothing out there that scares him.

He has no sense of purpose or aversion.

The dissident leads and he, for lack of anything else to do, follows.

"What are you afraid of?"

"...n-nothing."

"I don't believe that. They might've bred the fire out of your soul, the passion from your heart, but nothing can suppress human biology, the simple desire to live. As long as you are alive and fear death, you are afraid of something."

"I am not."

"I am not," the prisoner whispers aloud.

"What?" the dissident yells.

He's knee-deep in a freezing stream, trying to catch fish.

He does not reply, merely pulling his knees to his chest, feeling a twinge of pain, but nothing as extreme as it had been for weeks, and stares at the fire, his cheek pressed into rigid earth.

She is a somber woman.

She does not speak to him.

They merely wait in silence to be reviewed by the Commander.

She has not seen him since his birth.

It has been six years since then.

He had told himself that he would not be affected by her presence, that she was merely a high-ranking officer, and that he would treat her with nothing but respect as his superior.

But something stirs within him, a puzzling, impractical urge that compels him to speak.

"Mother."

She stiffens. He thinks she might reprimand him for not calling her Lieutenant. But she relaxes and seems to take it in stride as she turns to look at him directly, with a keen professional eye.

"Yes, cadet?"

"I...I will serve to the best of my ability," he says. The words have left his mouth many times, many times since he'd begun his training, but this time he puts as much conviction in his voice and mind as possible. It is not a meaningless morning chant, but a proclamation, from deep within his child heart.

She nods. "I would expect nothing less from...a child of my blood."

They enter the Commander's office and speak no more. After he is assigned to his next training camp, she does not look back as she walks away. He does not look at her either.

They do not meet again.

"You can walk?" the dissident asks.

The prisoner grits his teeth.

He clings to a tree trunk, his kidneys full, his back throbbing, his entire bottom half weak and wobbly. He can take a step, but it makes him want to scream and hit something, anything to distract himself from the pain, his legs burning as though his blood is made up of needles.

They give out.

The dissident catches him and lowers him gently to the ground.

"Not exactly," he says as he pats the other man's head almost absentmindedly. "Sorry."

The prisoner wipes the sweat from his brow and sighs.

"Careful or you'll break your teeth. You wouldn't like that, would you, having a tube stuck down your throat into your belly? Or me, ladling soup into your mouth for the rest of your life? Try not to bite down."

He can't help it. Every muscle seizes up and freezes as electricity sets his blood on fire. He bites and bites and bites and nothing can stop him.

"I was born in Springfield," the dissident says.

He's very strong, the prisoner thinks.

Carrying me. And talking.

"You've never even heard of it, right?"

Of course not.

"It's in the west. The sturdy, robust west. The frontier," the man says, smiling.

The prisoner stares at the endless sky. It looks so calm from down here. And so clear today. He blinks and sees the ocean, rushing at him, his wings ablaze, his stomach flipping as he falls.

"They say the south's nice, the flowers are always in bloom, the winters are mild, but I like snow. I like the ground frosted overnight. I like the smell of pine trees, don't you?"

I don't care for it.

"The mountains are nice. Not like these," the dissident groans, gesturing about them. "But beautiful, absolutely gorgeous. You could get lost in them and die feeling like you're in heaven, or at least, as close to God as you can get down here."

Still not close.

"Your people don't believe in God, do you?" the dissident says gruffly, his voice suddenly hard and unfriendly. For just a moment, he'd almost been amicable, sociable, but he seems to remember himself. "You're a bunch of atheists. You don't think we have any purpose or reason for living."

Maybe you *do.*

"I feel sorry for you," he says.

Don't.

"Living without any higher purpose, without some…some higher meaning," he pants as the ground starts to tilt upwards. "Must be pretty sad."

Must be.

"You don't have parents, do you?"

The prisoner huddles as close to the fire as he dares.

He's finally able to stand upright, but walking is still a challenge. He clings to the dissident's neck with one arm, his waist falling heavily on his side, but every step feels like his last.

The dissident has to carry him again eventually.

If he cared at all about the dissident's convenience, he might feel guilty.

Might feel like a burden.

But he still wishes to be left alone out here in the wilderness.

He's been thinking about it rather obsessively as the dissident treks through the undergrowth and up and down inclines.

He would like to die lying on the grass, staring up at the stars, numerous and brilliant, even through red haze, overhead. Although it cannot compare to the sight of millions of stars, bright and untainted, twinkling cold and aloof, overhead and down below, reflected double on a still green and grey spotted ocean, it will do.

But that had been an anomaly. A once in a life time view.

In his plane, often all he could see were clouds.

Flashes of light, gunfire, explosions.

The only stars he'd seen up there most nights had been the twinkling glow of downed planes, their engines on fire, their wings tilted as they fell.

He won't die like them. With honor. And purpose.

He'll die here.

And he would like to die on his back, looking up at the place that had been his home for twelve years, but had never truly felt like home until he'd become earthbound. And only able to *look*.

"I guess everyone has parents. Unless your people do that cloning thing," the dissident chuckles. "But you didn't talk to them, right? They didn't raise you. Your government separates you at birth and raises you in clusters, doesn't it?"

He remembers his cluster.

He doesn't remember their names, but he does remember their faces.

He remembers a boy with red hair, a girl with brown braids, and a weak, sickly boy with marks on his wrists.

They had sat quietly together on a bench in a bright white room.

He can't remember anything before this room.

As far as he knows, he'd been born in it.

When they are let out, it's only to go to another white room, to lie on a table, be poked and prodded, and sometimes put to sleep. When they wake up, it's back in the room.

He doesn't remember any fondness for his companions, just simple gratitude.

They are here, and he is not alone.

They say nothing to him, to each other, but at least he is not alone.

"I'm right, aren't I? They don't teach that in schools, it's something only the resistance knows. From our informants. I hear your parents don't ever see you again. That's messed up, you know. Parents love their children. Or at least, they should," the dissident continues.

"Not true," the prisoner croaks.

The dissident's mouth falls open, clearly shocked that he'd actually replied.

He hadn't said a word to him since he'd woken up in his possession, since his first tired, apathetic "Why?"

"What?"

"I saw her. Once," he forces out, unable to speak louder than a whisper.

"Once?" the dissident snorts. "That's so sad. That's *so* sad."

He shakes his head, his eyes incredulous and dispassionate.

The prisoner says nothing.

I wouldn't know.

"My mother was a singer," the dissident says.

They're sitting by a creek, and he's washing blood out of their clothing.

The prisoner huddles under a blanket, completely naked underneath it and finding it very unpleasant.

"She had the most beautiful voice in town. She could've sung in the capital," he goes on, twisting and turning water out of his shirt. The prisoner had realized that the clothing he'd been wearing, so large on him that he could comfortably pull his knees up under his shirt without stretching it, is actually the dissident's. "Dad didn't want her to go, though. He would've missed her."

There's pride in his voice.

"What about you? Did your parents even know each other?" he asks, voice cold again.

The prisoner notices that whenever he talks about his home, he's full of warmth and eagerness.

He speaks dreamily, languidly, as though paradise exists on his tongue.

But when he asks about the prisoner's home, that same voice becomes hard and unfeeling, heaven lost, his teeth a cold reality, his speech biting at his ears.

Well, that's alright.

The prisoner doesn't expect him to understand.

He doesn't have to defend himself or his people.

"…births are regulated," he murmurs. His voice still surprises him with its revolting monotone, its dull, empty rasp. Ever since hearing this man's voice, full of vitality and humor, he's begun to hate hearing himself talk, despise his own mouth for daring to echo his hollow thoughts. "My parents were unusual. They believed in genetic diversity. Didn't think we could keep using the same designated mothers to produce children. Were worried about the gene pool."

"What?" the dissident spits disbelievingly. He lays his wet clothing out on a rock and hunkers down next to it. "Is that how you reproduce? That's vile."

"Unwanted children are born here every day, aren't they?" the prisoner asks quietly. "You euthanize them, don't you?"

"What does that have to do with anything?" the dissident sputters.

"I am merely curious," the prisoner says evenly.

But he isn't, really.

"Because if they're unwanted, then they're simply here too early. Sometimes resources are too low or the parents just aren't ready for it yet, so they send their baby back to wait until the time is right. When a couple does want a child, God will send their baby's soul back to them, in another body. Nothing wrong with it. But you're telling me that there are designated mothers whose only function is to be inseminated and give birth to offspring?"

As disgusted as he sounds, he seems intrigued.

His eyes are directly on him for a change, rather than disdainfully away, and he seems eager for a response.

"…some women volunteer to spend three to ten years of their lives pregnant, and on leave," the prisoner murmurs. "And yes, the method is artificial insemination. Physical… relations of the marital type do occur, but they do not occur with non-sterilized females."

"Non-sterilized- how sterilized?" the dissident exclaims. The prisoner isn't affected by his outrage. He merely waits for him to settle down before continuing.

"My father was a Commander. She was a Lieutenant Commander. They thought their genes could produce genetically superior offspring. They thought they could produce a more…capable child. They petitioned, I believe, to be allowed to do so."

"They petitioned? To have kids?" the dissident says.

"…my mother did not want to be a designated mother. She preferred her duties as a Lieutenant Commander to the labors of pregnancy. But she did want to combine her own genetic material with my father's. A petition is required for a surrogate to accept an embryo produced by two other volunteers," the prisoner says.

The dissident stares at him.

"…that…is…"

"We don't waste our children like you do," the prisoner interrupts. Although he recognizes the statement as hostile, he himself feels no malice. "There are no unwanted children because they are produced at a stable, regulated rate. Your method of euthanasia is inefficient, it is unpredictable and does not properly address your problems of overpopul-"

"But you don't love your children. I hear you send them off to camps as soon as they can walk, right?" the dissident interrupts, almost morbidly eager. He's in front of him now, his face a little red, his chest heaving as though overexerted.

You believe a lot of what you hear for someone who has so many questions, the prisoner thinks. But he supposes they hear tidbits from spies. Perhaps twisted propaganda and wild speculations based on slim truths.

"They're not unwanted," the prisoner insists. "They are needed."

"But you don't care about them?"

"They are needed. They are cared for."

"But not because God gave them to you. Not because you love them, but because they are *necessary.* That's so many levels of fucked up," the dissident snorts. He crouches down, getting on his eye level. "Were your parents married?"

"No. We don't practice that."

"What about affection? Love? Do you even know what the words mean?"

"Yes," the prisoner says. "But they seem irrelevant to the discussion."

"Pfft. Right. You don't believe in God. Of course you don't believe in love."

"…if my people 'loved' as yours do," the prisoner says tiredly, suddenly feeling a little sick, a little uneasy with this conversation, "-they would have children they did not plan for."

"Sure."

"But we *need* children, and not just children, but capable, viable citizens who can only be produced in a controlled setting. But your people reproduce indiscriminately. You are careless and do not account for your limited living space. This seems wasteful to me," the prisoner sniffs, his limbs feeling frozen to the ground. "Do you 'love' these unwanted children too?"

"Of course we do," the dissident insists. "God just sent them too early. When they're ready, he'll send them back and they'll be loved then."

"And what if they choose never to have children?"

"He'll send them to someone else."

Then they do not love their child enough to raise it, the prisoner thinks. They merely pass it off to the next person.

But he keeps it to himself.

This conversation is giving him a headache. And even though he'd only been talking, he can feel an ache deep in his bones, an exhaustion tugging at his entire body.

He commits himself to saying nothing more.

He doesn't like thinking about home.

He's not sure how he feels about it, as he's never really *thought* about how he feels about it, and having this stranger decry it as "fucked up" unsettles him. He doesn't like the sound of the dissident's lifestyle, this unregulated, carefree world where people can do whatever they like without consequence (for themselves, at least).

He's not sure what the dissident's definition of love is, doesn't understand it outside of its context within the Empire, but he knows the value of children.

These people, he knows, do not.

They throw them away.

He does not like this.

But he says nothing more.

The dissident didn't ask, so he doesn't answer.

As unsettled as the dissident had been after their first real conversation, he seems rather keen on grilling him for information. The prisoner doesn't like it.

He doesn't like talking. He would rather remain silent.

But as his strength returns, as he begins to slowly walk, still aided by his living crutch but improving, he finds that he can't. The dissident likes to talk.

And he seems fascinated by him, in a repulsed sort of way.

"You've never dreamt of having kids?"

"No."

"You don't think you have the genes for it?"

"…my parents were mistaken," he says slowly. "I am nothing special."

The dissident looks at him with a strange emotion in his eyes. The prisoner doesn't care for it, so looks away.

It's been getting colder, but it thankfully hasn't snowed yet. The rivers and streams aren't frozen yet either, which must be a relief to the dissident. He seems to quite enjoy fishing.

"You think you need to be special to be worthy of having kids?" the dissident asks.

"There would be no…point otherwise."

"Ah," the man smiles. "No point. No point in having someone to spend every day with and love with all of your heart. No point in having someone who makes you happy, who makes you smile. No point in having someone to care for, or someone to care of you. What point is there, for your people, in living, exactly?"

But the prisoner has no response.

He merely shakes his head.

"No point," the dissident says, a hint of triumph in his voice.

A response does come to him later.

"What purpose do you have for living?" the prisoner asks.

The dissident, tying his backpack to his chest, looks quickly at him.

"Huh?"

"What point is there, in spending every day with the same person?" he asks. "What point is there in being happy, in caring for another person, and having that care reciprocated, when we all die eventually? One day there will be no tangible evidence that the two of you or even your offspring existed. At some point, your time will run out and your names will be forgotten. So what is *your* purpose for living?"

To love is to love the Empire.

He knows no other use of the word.

"…I can't explain it," the dissident says with annoyance. "It's…it's something you feel, that's it, you just know, in your heart, that…that people are worth living for, not…whatever it is you live for. If you don't feel it, then…you don't feel it."

Can't miss something I've never known.

He merely puts his arm around his waist and leans heavily into him as they begin moving again.

There's no one to mourn your death.
No one, not your family, not your friends, nor even your Empire.
You will die here.
And the world will go on without a sigh.
I wonder though.
Has your time here taught you anything?
Any individuality?
Any sense of being...alone?
I know the Empire raises you with a hive mindset.
You are no better or worse than anyone else. Every part of you belongs to them, not to yourself, not to another individual. That means you are, essentially, immortal, so long as they exist. Because to be a part of them is to live as long as the institution, as the concept, exists.
They don't allow you to have families, do they? No girlfriend, I take it? Maybe a whore here or there to keep you complacent, but no children, absolutely not. I'm surprised that your testicles are intact, actually, I thought they castrated males. I know they sterilize undesirable women.
Did you ever dream of finding someone who would keep you in their memories after you died?
Or does this kind of thing not even occur to someone like you?
There's not a single original thought in that head of yours, is there?
You're made up of air.
Breaking you down has been fun.
Because no matter how deeply I burrow inside you, no matter how many pieces I break you into, there's nothing.
You're a broken cog.
No longer functioning.
And of no use alone, separated from the rest, from the machine.
But that's ok.
We're still only just getting to know one another.
As time goes on, pain will teach you.
Pain will separate you from them, change you, transform you into an individual.
Remember that you're going through this alone, my dear boy.
You're painfully, excruciatingly aware, aren't you, of how alone you are, in your suffering? That is the nature of personhood.
Being alone.
And understanding your place in the world.
And your place, in this particular part of the world, is in pain.
Individualizing, very personal, very intimate, and very solitary agony.
You are no longer a part of their world. You've been chipped off from the collective and made a broken individual, but an individual nonetheless.

And thus you are mortal.

A human. A person.

Very, very capable of dying.

"I never felt so small," the dissident says. "The skyscrapers are truly something else. I couldn't believe it when my father first took me inside one. You could see so much from the top."

I've scraped the sky. It's a long way down.

They'd been huddled inside this cave for much too long. A rainstorm had battered their camp for almost three days now.

The water had risen high, far too high to remain on the ground anymore. They'd switched directions, trying to find shelter that they could hunker down in. The prisoner's eyes used to be sharp, but after his detention period, they'd become blurry and useless, spotted with red and blue that merged into black if he focused too hard. It was the dissident who'd spotted the ledge, the small hollow inside of it.

"I always loved climbing, but I climbed more than ever after that. I just couldn't get the image out of my mind, all the houses and people, looking so small. I would find the largest tree I could and get as high as I could and imagine ants were cars and sticks were roads or something. I actually climbed too high one time. I broke my arm."

If you can recite our Constitution backwards, I'll break your arm quickly. But if you can't, well, I guess the clamp is just going to have to work its slow magic, huh, one spin, two spin-

"I'd broken my arm before. It hurts a lot. Some injuries don't hurt until afterwards, but a broken bone hurts immediately."

Go on. The maze isn't designed for you. But go on through it anyway. Keep that tracking device on your leg or we won't be able to find you. You know, if you were a weaker man, I wouldn't be doing this.

A weaker man would pass out from the pain, immediately get taken back inside, and have his foot fixed up, no permanent damage, but you...you're going to get just far enough to mangle that foot of yours, aren't you?

"...it's raining a lot," the dissident sighs, watching the slippery wet ledge outside of their little hollow. It begins to thunder.

The prisoner might be imagining it, drifting off to sleep, but it sounds an awful lot like there's someone screaming out there.

I am giving you your personhood.
I've wrenched you away from the hive and made a man out of you.
But insects aren't meant to be men, now are they?
You don't know what to do.

I could open this door right now and you wouldn't run. No orders to follow, no commanders to report to, no mission to carry out, no purpose or meaning without them. I could let you go and you'd starve to death waiting for someone to tell you what to do. To allow you to eat.

To allow you to live.

"Yes." The prisoner nods.

"What?" the dissident frowns.

He's rebinding one of the prisoner's many wounds, this one a laceration on his stomach. It is in close proximity to a knife wound on his hip, an older but still occasionally seeping injury. Lacerations are slightly better than stab wounds, the dissident often says, since he can at least see the full extent of the damage, and it tends to be mostly surface level.

The prisoner's back is covered in lacerations.

The bruised, swollen skin and the congealed blood make the dissident's eyes cloud with disgust.

The prisoner is indifferent.

He has no shame for his own body.

It's a twisted ugly thing, but why would he care about it, why would he care even about his heart, his brain, his lungs, when as the dissident himself had said, there was *no point* in living?

He had fulfilled what little purpose he had left.

Stare away.

Cringe.

Or better.

Let him go. Let his purposeless body at least find meaning as fertilizer or as sustenance for animals.

"What information did they get out of you?" the dissident asks.

"None."

"Oh don't be proud," he snorts in response. "I know you guys are tough, but everyone cracks. You had to have told them something."

"I had nothing to tell," the prisoner says simply.

"…you didn't?"

"No. And I still don't," the injured man sighs. "Please…"

Just let me die.

"I don't believe you," the dissident says, crushing his hopes entirely. "You're just shy. That's fine. I'm no torturer. *They'll* figure out what to do with you."

They, meaning the resistance.

For a member of something called the "resistance," he seems to love his home and its system a great deal.

In fact, he hasn't said one bad thing about either one yet, despite having a great deal of bad things to say about the prisoner's home.

The prisoner keeps this observation to himself.

"Nothing as bad as what they…I mean, we're the good guys," the dissident says hastily.

The prisoner winces, but not in response to what he'd said.

The dissident isn't much of a medic.

His bandaging is clumsy and his hands are rough and unpracticed, rather painfully clumsy and amateur.

But the prisoner is alive.

Against his will and prerogative.

He is alive.

They raise you like little robots, beep beep boop, but you feel that, don't you? Look at me, oh, you're crying, aren't you, but not out of fear, just pain?

What a shame.

You really are an animal.

Now I'll give you an ultimatum.

Beg me to stop.

Beg me to stop pulling up your skin, give me a real, honest-to-God human feeling.

And I'll kill you.

I'll put you out of your misery.

"Please…"

…

…

Is that really the best you can do?

It's very curious.

Teacher had often referred to him as emotionless.

But he remembers the pain.

And there was an aversion to it, a sense of terror and panic when presented with it.

He had cried out

He remembers that clearly.

These are emotions.

But Teacher had mocked him, saying that he had the emotional depth of a wild animal, barely capable of reactions outside of fear, hunger, and pain.

I'll teach you to be human.

If that's what being human is like, he would rather not be human.

"I really don't wanna have to tell you this, cuz it's kind of awkward, but…" the dissident winces. "You're going to have to bathe now."

The prisoner looks up sharply.

"I won't look," the dissident says.

"It's freezing," the prisoner responds.

"You smell awful. And you're filthy. I've been cleaning up your wounds, but the rest of you is covered in peeling skin and dried up blood and other gunk. Just get in there really quick, ok? Just let it wash off some of the crap. You don't have to stay that long, but you do need to get in there." The dissident approaches him slowly, eyes determined.

He backs up, legs trembling with tension.

"Where are you going to run?" the dissident says.

Where do you have to go?

The prisoner grits his teeth.

You want to die, why do your clothes matter? Naked or not, hurt or not, alone or not, what difference does it make?

Just obey him.

His orders are the Commander's orders, are Teacher's orders, are your father's orders, your mother's, the Empire's.

Just obey him.

"Leave the bandages on, I'll change them afterwards." The dissident raises his hand, palm facing him, as though keeping an animal at bay. "You just have-"

The prisoner doesn't let him continue.

He struggles to pull his jacket off, but freezes, his shoulder and left arm protesting.

The dissident ends up having to help him remove his jacket, shirt, and pants. It's horrible, somehow still horrible despite everything he's been through, because this man, who is younger than him, has to pull his coat off, then slowly, gingerly lift his shirt up and over his head, and kneel down to pull his pants down, all while looking rather embarrassed.

But the prisoner is feeling something other than apathy now.

The numbness, the resignation to his fate, is at the very least shaken up by shame, which he had not known he still possessed.

In self-consciousness, the prisoner looks down.

He hasn't had a good look at himself since…since he left home.

Somehow, he's seen his body without looking at it, without acknowledging it as his own. He views it like he would watch a film. One of their horrors of war films, the gruesome one about how prisoners of war are to be treated, the one he'd felt irrationally scared by when viewing the first time.

Not himself. Not his body.

An image created by someone else.

Projected on the floor.

But now, in sunlight, in the daylight, under the sky and the judging sun, with another man looking at him, he feels acutely aware that it is *his* body.

And he's sickened.

He doesn't want to look at his skin, stretched so thin around his hunched skeleton, the greenish purple bruises, all in varying stages of healing, or the ugly puncture wounds, from needles and knives, crisscrossing his legs and stomach, or worse, worse, the yellow skin, the skin that's peeling and coming off of him in flakes.

Get it over with.

The cold air instantly attacks his chest and back and genitals as soon as they're exposed to the air.

He's never felt so cold in his life, never felt air this biting.

He walks stiffly, quickly, to the water, not even glancing back at the dissident, who's very red in the face despite presumably seeing him naked a few times.

And he steps in.

Immediately the water stabs his thighs with freezing, jabbing fingers, his blood and skin seeming to solidify instantly.

His whole body is rigid as he clutches at his arms, rubbing vigorously, tears pricking his eyes at the pain as cold, unforgiving water tugs at his still-healing wounds.

He cleans vigorously between his legs, wincing but resolvedly wiping off blood and dead skin.

The stream of water is briefly turned brown as he scrubs at himself, splashing his chest and letting it trickle in a line of icy fire down his body.

When he finally can't take it anymore, he scrambles out as quickly as he can, cringing as he stresses his muscles and falls to his knees.

29

Immediately, the dissident has a blanket over him and is patting him gently, trying to return some heat to his body without opening up any wounds.

His teeth are chattering, his lips blue, his face paler than the dissident has ever seen.

"Ok, ok, now you don't have to do that ever again," the dissident says, laughing a little nervously.

As he pulls off his bandages, tossing them carelessly into the grass, the prisoner, chest heaving, thinks that there's nothing he wants more than to be warm again.

To his credit, the dissident is fast.

He wraps up his wounds with more speed than previous attempts (having gotten better since his first clumsy attempt at binding his wounds) and helps him redress.

The moment his jacket is on, the dissident throws the blanket around him for good measure.

The prisoner feels a burst of almost hysterical laughter in his throat.

It escapes in a brief grunt, a little huff of amusement.

The dissident's brow furrows.

But he doesn't comment.

The feeling dies and the prisoner is left with nothing once more as he stumbles behind him, still only barely able to walk.

But the memory of the feeling comes back to him when they settle down several kilometers later.

He curls on his side by the fire, as close as physically possible.

It's such a relief to be warm.

The dissident settles down next to him, as he often does.

The prisoner does not resist as he takes a hold of the blanket and pulls it over himself as well.

It's not his place.

And besides.

After the initial cold of the blanket being pulled off of him, the dissident's heat more than makes up for it by beginning to fill up the closed space.

The prisoner closes his eyes, focusing on the warmth of the fire on his face and the heat of a healthy human body behind him.

If there exists a greater feeling than warmth, he has yet to find it.

"What are you writing?" Teacher asks.

His bandaged hand trembles.

To be human is to be alone.

"You're learning," Teacher smiles. He grips his hand gently, and the prisoner flinches. "You're beginning to understand."

"…you ok, guy?"

The prisoner blinks.

"Did you…space out?" the dissident frowns, letting go of his hand.

The prisoner looks at it. It's wrapped in fresh bandages.

Because he'd cut himself. With a fishing hook.

"Don't worry about it," the dissident says.

The prisoner stands up slowly and gestures to the nearby trees.

"…I don't know, you'll get lost," the dissident frowns.

The prisoner shakes his head.

"I don't think you're going to try and run off. You can barely walk. I just think, uh, that it's easy to get lost. I'll come with you later, ok? Just wait."

The prisoner licks his chapped lips.

He eases back into a sitting position, careful not to bend his legs too quickly.

"Have you always…walked like that?" the dissident asks.

The prisoner shakes his head.

His right ankle hadn't healed properly.

Neither had his foot.

He walks with a perpetual limp.

If you allow me to break it again, I could set it right.

The prisoner traces the scars on his ankle.

"…my dad was a doctor. He told me how to do…a lot of stuff. But I wasn't as…attentive as I should've been. There're a lot of…wounds that I didn't patch up as well as I should have," the dissident says, scratching his head. The prisoner shakes his head.

"I mean… I think I hurt you *more*, on occasion…" the dissident admits. "Caused you more pain than was necessary…"

The prisoner blinks slowly at him, his eyes blank.

"What?" the dissident's brow furrows at his captive.

The prisoner pulls his pant leg up.

The flesh of his leg is lined with crisscrossing scars, a few shallow, uneven depressions, and seemingly random slashes to his outer and inner thigh. He traces one or two, trying to remember what they were from. One had been from a broken bone, sickeningly clean and white as it poked out of his skin.

He remembers that one painfully well.

The guard had been scared.

Teacher had been displeased.

The prisoner needs his legs, he said, for the experiment.

"Is pain necessary?" the prisoner asks.

The dissident stares, fascinated, at the mutilated skin.

He's seen them before, of course.

He's seen his entire body, every mark, every crevasse. Touched most of it, trying to keep it from falling apart at the seams.

But he still acts surprised, every time, as though he's forgotten.

"Sometimes…to fix people…you have to hurt them a little," the dissident admits.

"Am I fixed?"

The dissident looks shocked.

"No one from my cluster looks like this. No one from my cluster shares these memories, these experiences with me, and they never will. I am apart from them. Isn't that how you, and your people, live? Independent of one another, as individuals, as people who do as they please and do not regard others as one and the same as themselves?"

"Well…" the dissident seems to be distracted by his leg now. "Uh, pull that down."

The prisoner obeys.

"Is that what being human is?"

"I…I don't-"

"I was changed. And now I can never go back."

The dissident doesn't seem to have an answer for him.

He just looks confused.

"I don't know anything," the prisoner says slowly. "You…have nothing to gain, bringing me with you. You could just tell them you killed me. Or that I died of my injuries. There's nothing I can tell your government, and mine would be pleased-"

"This isn't about your government," the dissident interrupts. "It's about the resistance. I need to show them that I… am dedicated to the cause. And that I could not only retrieve you but…keep you alive."

The prisoner closes his eyes.

"…I'm sorry that life is so meaningless to you people that it's a burden," he says, his voice morose, subdued, but with a hint of cruelty. The prisoner won't look at him. He knows what expression the dissident's wearing, and he'd rather not see it.

"What meaning do your lives have, then?" the prisoner asks tightly.

The dissident is silent for a moment or two. The prisoner doesn't think he'll answer. He hadn't last time. Not properly.

But this time he seems to be thinking harder, collecting his thoughts.

His words are slower, more measured, than defensive and unsure.

"We are alone, but being alone is nice. Being…a person who's separate and different from other people is nice. It makes finding people who're… like you, who *like* you, despite your differences, your 'separation,' and wish to be with you, day after day…even more incredible. I've never really…thought of it that way, but…yeah. Yeah." He smiles, seemingly satisfied with himself and his reasoning.

The prisoner merely lowers his eyes and pulls his jacket up over his neck as he huddles against a strong wind.

"There's no one like me," the prisoner says unexpectedly.

The dissident drops his backpack in surprise.

He'd thought the prisoner would never speak again after days and days of complete and utter silence.

"I'm not one of them. I'm not one of you."

"No?" the dissident offers.

The prisoner ignores his response, having only said it aloud to clarify his thoughts, not run them by his companion.

Teacher had promised to kill him after he was done.

Teacher had made more sense than this man.

He was sadistic and emotional, just like they had told him these people were.

But he was logical too.

He had promised to put the prisoner out of his misery when he was done with him.

I wouldn't leave you in misery.

He was honest.

His pleasure in his suffering…it made sense.

The prisoner is the "other."

He is a foreigner and an enemy and an outsider.

Teacher's sadism is limited only to him, an acceptable target. He would not treat a member of his own species that way.

He is simple.

But this dissident…is more complex.

I love the expression you make.

When you cry out.

I love when you cry out too.

Love.

Love was the corrupting force.

Not the love for the Empire-

No, of course not.

That was pure, selfless love.

This was selfish love, the enjoyment of one's self.

At the expense of others.

Not love, for the wellbeing of others.

"Your parents loved each other?" the prisoner asks.

"Unf-" the dissident lets out a sigh and looks longingly at the tree line. "Yes."

"Did you love them?"

"Of course!" the dissident huffs. "Lemme guess, that's weird to you?"

The prisoner is winded.

He doesn't respond.

All he can do is think.

He hates this man.

Hates him for being a steady, reliable crutch for his arm to wrap around, for giving him clothes, for stopping the bleeding and cleaning out his wounds.

He wants the prisoner to stay alive.

He wants to hand him over to his resistance.

He is alive only because this man's selfish needs supersede his own need, the need to leave a world he never wanted to become a part of.

Damn him.

Damn him.

Love is selfish.

He just wants peace.

Love will not give him any.

"Your parents fed you?"

"Yes."

"They clothed you. Bathed you. Taught you."

"Yes, yes, yes."

"Why?"

"They cared about me."

"…what if they saw themselves in you?"

"…pardon?"

"What if they saw themselves in you, and wished to preserve this? What if they wanted offspring just like them to live on after they died? What if their desire to take care of you was a biological imperative?"

"Oh, oh, that's where you're going, trying to compare your mindless breeding to our system of mutual love and affection."

"What if parents…just see themselves in their children…? What if they mold them to be copies of themselves at every step? What if they…only love their children because…they see their own reflections there?"

"Nonsense."

"…do you adopt? Do your people ever…take care of children other than their own?"

"…it's prohibited, but…"

"Children aren't raised by their blood relatives in my home. They are raised by everyone. They are raised by…their caretakers…then their officers. No one cares about blood. We accept all children, regardless of their origin. We even accept the children of prisoners of war. But tell me…do you?"

"…"

"… you also don't *take* prisoners of war. You torture the few that you do not immediately eliminate."

"We don't have the space or resources to take care of them-"

"Or for children who are not yours, children who are not a reflection of yourse-"

"Shut up. You shut the hell up. What would you know? There's no one on earth who would care if I slit your throat right now. No one at all. It'll be like you never existed."

"…I am a part of the Empire. Even if I die, it will live on. Forever. I am a part of something that does not rely on the individual to survive. So please, do kill me. I'm no use to my Empire now. I don't belong in this world anymore. Slit my throat. Strangle me. Or let me kill myself. You won't need the extra mouth to feed anyway, when that stream freezes-"

"Shut up. Stop talking. You're so pathetic I can't stand hearing you talk."

"Once you cross the border, your cluster will attempt to penetrate this latitude and longitude..."

"Understood."

"You are to avoid destruction as long as possible."

"Understood."

"But destruction is inevitable."

"Understood."

"The Empire is eternal."

"Yes."

"Do your duty. Your cluster will do theirs."

"Yes."

"...you made a mistake."

"Yes."

"And they don't want it to happen ever again. You understand that, don't you?"

"Yes."

"It's not because they hate you. It's not because they take any joy from your death. They simply understand that you are flawed. Do you understand that you are flawed?"

"Yes."

"Then you will do your duty to the Empire."

"Yes."

"Good, my dear boy."

He hasn't said a word to him for a few days now.

It wouldn't bother him if it weren't so quiet.

The stream has finally frozen, on the surface at least.

The prisoner touches it gently, seeing that there's still a moving current, and bubbles below the ice.

He'd idly considered how easy it would be to drown himself in it, but had concluded that it wouldn't be easy at all.

It's not deep enough and he has nothing to anchor himself to, nothing that could force him to stay under for long enough.

With the birds gone, the stream silent, and his companion as mute as a child, the prisoner finds himself consumed with an almost irrepressible desire to break the silence somehow.

He is no stranger to silence.

His people do not believe in idle conversation.

He cannot recall any conversations from his youth or adulthood that did not have to do with work or immediate concerns involving work.

But this silence does not feel cordial.

It feels unnatural.

And.

He shakes his head, but the thought infiltrates his mind anyway.

I want his rambling stories.

Now that it's there, a rush of other unbidden thoughts pour in through the tiny crack, the little slip in defenses.

The town you live in.

You tell me they live in separate settlements.

That mother and father and children live together, without others.

You enclose your property with metal and farm vegetables and flowers in the space.

There are many flowers I did not know.

You know the names and faces of these flowers because your mother had some fondness for them.

Why?

What good were they?

What purpose did they serve, they drained unnecessary resources from the earth and provided nothing in return, just wasted space, wasted materials, they were born, they lived, and they died, and in such a short time, without contributing, they wasted space-

Your mother was a singer.

Was that her purpose?

To sing?

What use is that to anyone?

To be a mother?

Mothers are unnecessary in terms of childcare, anyone could take care of a child, surely that couldn't be it.

The dissident had a father. Siblings.

They could've, and did, take care of him.

Her role was fulfilled by others.

So what was her true purpose?

Was it possible not to have-

"Stay away from that," the dissident snaps, his first words to him in days. "If you fall in, I'll have to jump in after you, and then we'll *both* be cold and unhappy. And wishing we were dead."

"You could let me-"

"I just told you, if you end up in there, whether you jumped or not, we'll *both* be unhappy," the dissident interrupts. "I'm not gonna let you drown."

The prisoner pulls his hand back and clutches it to his chest.

"Have you ever drowned?" he asks.

"Drowned? You mean almost drowned?" the dissident snorts. "Well…yeah. I went sailing with my father out on the lake one summer. I took a turn too sharply and he fell over the side. I jumped overboard without thinking to get him. But when I tried to pull him up, he was too heavy, and we both sank like stones. We were lucky, our neighbors from across the lake were out on the water too. They saw our boat idling and thought something might be wrong. They found us quickly and brought us to their place. It wasn't fun, ok, it was terrifying, and I still remember how it felt, blacking out and feeling water in my lungs…"

"They don't teach you how to swim?"

"No."

"Why not?"

The dissident shrugs.

"Why would we need to know?"

"…for that exact reason?" The prisoner grimaces.

The dissident looks at him intently for almost thirty seconds and the prisoner, hating to meet anyone's eyes for longer than one, turns away.

He thinks perhaps he's angered his companion, but then he hears a snort.

"So you do have a sense of humor."

The prisoner feels something like relief warm his chest.

The dissident is less distant after that.

An hour later, he's chattering about types of birds he saw out in the forest and all of the birdhouses he'd constructed out of scrap wood for them.

The prisoner makes no visible or verbal indication that he appreciates it.

He's just relieved that the silence is a little less stifling.

He'd spent his entire life around people, silent, but numerous people, all with the same thoughts, plans, and intentions as him.

The abrupt lack of people had been unsettling him.

He might despise this man, and be nothing like him, but at least when he's talking, the prisoner is not alone with his own thoughts.

He only has to bear the unbearable silence when the dissident is asleep.

"That's not the type of drowning I meant."

The dissident jumps.

"What the-? You're awake?" he says. He has a dead fox in his hand, his fingers clenched around its neck.

"When I asked if you had ever drowned...I meant... a child. Have you ever drowned...a child?"

"Um..." the dissident frowns, crouching by the fire the prisoner had diligently been keeping ever since he'd left to check his snares. "Two, actually. Little sister, she was just hours old, and little brother, who was...maybe a week old? My parents usually dealt with that stuff."

The prisoner nods.

"Lemme guess, you guys never do that kind of thing?" the dissident asks.

"No."

"Of course not."

"Wouldn't that disturb you?" The prisoner watches him slowly, carefully begin skinning the fox. He's a poor medic, but a decent hunter and meat preparer. He does it quickly, neatly, cutting a perfect line from tail to throat.

The prisoner looks away, however.

As skillful as the dissident is, he doesn't like watching him butcher animal corpses.

"Would what disturb me?"

"You know we do not believe in God. Or an afterlife. So if we ended our children's lives believing that there was no afterlife, that there was nothing, and this is the only life we have, then wouldn't that make us more despicable to you? For someone with our beliefs, it's less cruel to preserve our children at whatever cost and never allow harm to come to them, since they have no other life, isn't it?"

The dissident pauses, his hands pulling at the animal's hide.

"...I never thought of that," he says contemplatively. "I guess that's...better."

The prisoner scoots away.

He hadn't been looking but he knows the dissident is beginning to pull out organs now.

The first time he'd done it-

This is a human heart, you know?

Its owner died from heart disease, that's why it's all shriveled up and repulsive.

It reminds me of you.

Hold it.

I said hold it.

There.

You see?

Just like you.

Oh do stop with that face, you expect me to believe you're all vegetarians?

This is a lung.

Hold it now, there's a good boy.

It's black because its old owner was a smoker.

I wonder what your organs will look like, when I pull them out?

You lead healthy lives, don't you?

They need their little toy soldiers in perfect working condition, don't they? I imagine you can't smoke, drink, eat anything too fatty or otherwise bad for your cholesterol, correct?

Perhaps I'll donate your organs to a medical facility. No use in letting perfectly good organs go to waste, right?

Of course, that would be giving you a purpose.

That would be giving you to an unsuspecting person, a very, very sick person who doesn't deserve to have animal parts inside of them.

Maybe I'll just dissect you for fun and keep your organs in a jar on my desk, how about that?

Oh, if I go that route, I don't even have to put you under.

What would I take first?

The bladder, perhaps.

Then the liver.

The kidneys.

I think I would try for the lungs, if I could, but at that point, you may be dying or dead.

Maybe I should start with the heart.

Just so you can get the full effect.

The dissident is done.

He glances at the prisoner.

"Um…you ok, guy?"

The prisoner knows he doesn't mean it. He just said it because he was polite, because it was second nature, because it was natural to speak to a human shaped creature as though it were the real thing.

He nods.

The dissident knows he's lying, but shrugs. None of his business.

He has also seen his father.
Not met, but seen.
On the airstrip.
Walking slowly with a Lieutenant, clearly talking to her, eyes focused only on her.
Childishly, pointlessly, he imagines for a moment that she is his mother.
And they are talking about him.

But the thought goes away in just a moment, slipping away as quickly and irretrievably as a stone sinking into the open ocean. He looks away and only remembers the incident when he is an adult, when Teacher forces him to.

"I've never seen the ocean. What's it like?"

The dissident is a little disgruntled tonight.

The prisoner imagines he's trying to distract himself from the hunger. They'd found very little to eat, even with the prisoner able to walk on his own and offer an extra eye and hand. What little berries they found, the dissident had insisted the prisoner eat.

Now he seems desperate for a distraction.

The prisoner feels uncomfortable, but he's not sure what exactly is making him feel that way. It seems to increase as he watches the dissident push his fists into his stomach.

"It's big," the prisoner says.

The dissident laughs.

"I guess that must seem odd to you, the thought that I've never seen the ocean. Or any body of water larger than a lake."

"…No one's ever asked me that before," the prisoner says, eyes dropping to the curve of his companion's neck, where there's a small pink scar.

"I imagine not."

"It's…like the sky, but below instead of above. And it's rough, always…vibrating. Moving. Like every part of it…moves kind of like blades of grass in a field. But…less…grounded, I guess. Ah." The prisoner covers his eyes with his hand.

There's a different type of discomfort in his gut now.

It's squirmy… warm…and it fills his body with the desire to curl inward.

"It…churns."

"A churning blue field, huh? Sounds ugly." The dissident rolls onto his stomach, knuckles pressed into it.

"Green," the prisoner corrects him. "Brown, sometimes. Patches of…plastic. And oil. And other waste."

"Even better," the man groans.

"…it's…so vast," the prisoner says. "When the garbage clears, near the borderline, there's a place, a place where the ocean…where it meets the sky, on clear, cloudless nights, with the moon above, and it became almost…another place. Another…another…"

"World?" the dissident grumbles.

"...another world," the prisoner echoes. The thought of other worlds had never occurred to him. The phrase feels strangely...satisfying on his tongue. He marvels at the implications of it, the weight of its significance, and feels a chill in his gut. "When the sun went down, it looked as though the light was swallowed by the horizon. The place where the sky touched the sea swallowed it whole. The first time I saw it, it...scared me."

"Scared you? You were flying a plane and *that* scared you?" the dissident asks with a little laugh.

"...I'd never seen the sky so close. I'd never seen the ocean before either," the prisoner says. At the time, he had only felt fear. Before that, the enormity of his first step into the sky had been consumed by regulations and careful, precise steps. He had performed all checks and operations with a detached, clinical efficiency.

And take off had felt the same.

It was only that moment, as he saw the sun, a permanent, immortal fixture of his universe, drift into the sea and drown in darkness, that he felt terror well up within him. A juvenile, innocent terror, the likes of which only plagued children fearful of the unknown.

"Well the ocean is full of water, and the sky has nowhere to land, so I suppose that's scary," the dissident breaks his solemn musing. "Did you like being a pilot?"

Did he like being a pilot? The prisoner tilts his head back against the rock.

"Let me guess. No one's ever asked you that before."

Why would they?

The question disturbs his own mostly empty stomach.

The dissident sighs, gnawing on a knuckle.

"Well...I was a manager for the town's inventory. Not nearly as exciting. It got boring."

"...but food storage is important," the prisoner replies.

"Still boring. I always felt like getting away. Going sailing. Going out to the inn to meet pretty girls, travelers, all types of people. But after a while, you meet them all. They're all from this country, after all. I guess you're the only...type of person I haven't met." The dissident seems stunned to hear himself say it.

"...There are other countries besides mine," the prisoner says quietly. "You haven't met any of them either."

The dissident's eyes go wide.

"No. I haven't. Have you?"

"No."

"But you're a pilot..."

"The only time I ever interacted with people of countries besides my own was during times of war. I did not 'meet' people of other countries before...coming here." The prisoner rubs his fingers. He then shirks away in surprise as the dissident scoots surprisingly, disturbingly close to him.

He's even more unnerved when the dissident's hand comes down on his shoulder, close to his neck, his fingers cold on his collarbone.

"The chip is still in there, isn't it?" he asks conversationally.

The prisoner nods.

"When do they put them in for you? Ten? Eleven?"

"Six."

"Wow," the dissident whistles, his thumb moving back and forth over his shoulder.

It makes him uncomfortable.

But he cannot explain why.

The dissident tilts his finger and presses lightly into the skin.

"They had to modify yours so you could fly abroad, right?"

"Specific coordinates can be inputted to deactivate the chip when necessary," the prisoner confirms.

"So you didn't get shocked or anything when they brought you over the border?" the dissident asks, still touching him. The prisoner struggles to control the irrational unease building up in his stomach.

"No. It was deactivated for this sector. But they…did tap into it during interrogation."

"Ah. I've never been shocked. I've never even left my hometown. Tell me, does it hurt a lot?"

"It…" the prisoner rolls his shoulder, but it doesn't dislodge him.

He's inspecting the scars now, not just the small one, where the chip had been inserted, the device all children had implanted after the age of six in his country, but the others, down his shirt, on his chest, the ones that overlap, the calculated ones, the unplanned ones, the sharp and clinical ones, the blunt and brutal, strangely personal ones. They cross his shoulders and chest and stomach. Against his better judgment, he pulls away from the dissident, away from his grip.

But to his astonishment, the dissident doesn't seem angry.

He doesn't even look shocked, just puts his hand on his leg and starts hitting it lightly.

"It does hurt. The chip. When it's activated. They induced shock sometimes, in training, to teach us what it felt like. It's not meant to kill, just incapacitate, but it feels like it might kill you."

"You can induce shock?" the dissident asks interestedly.

He's chewing on a stick.

The prisoner stares at him, the image of a Commander's dog gnawing on a branch appearing in his mind's eye. There's that warm feeling…

"Yes."

"That's cool." The dissident grins. "I gotta try it sometime."

The prisoner frowns.

"But it hurts."

"Yeah!"

"Why would you do it then?"

"For the thrill, I guess."

The prisoner recalls the nights he spent, huddled and alone, breathless with terror, at the thought of being found by the wild animals roaming the maze, some looking for him, others not.

He recalls the hours and hours he spent on his back, Teacher's needles pricking his skin, the endless days and nights with the light blinding him as he just waited there for something to happen, and hating the instant, terror-filled moment it did.

He recalls Teacher pulling his head back, laying a cloth over him, and pouring water over his face, over and over and over, the overwhelming panic, his body thrashing so hard his wrists bled, the fright and desperation clouding all rational thought as he felt the sensation of drowning.

The dissident snaps his fingers.

The prisoner is brought abruptly back to the present.

"I guess someone like you has had enough thrill to last a lifetime, huh?" he says.

His voice is…kind?
The prisoner chances a glance at him.
The dissident looks…
Well.
The prisoner doesn't know what that look means.
It's not one he's seen before.
He turns away, not liking it one bit.
Even though it makes him feel warm.

Hold your eyes open, hold your eyes open- oh, child...
What are you so scared of?
I'm not going to jab your eyes out.
Not right now, at least.
...
Oh my.
Oh my, are you crying?
There, there.
I'm impressed.
I'm impressed by the emotion you've shown.
You're truly growing up fast, aren't you?
You poor children always come here so emotionally stunted. And then you die, confused and hurt but unable to deal with it because you weren't taught how.
I pity you.

Neither of them have eaten for a while.

The dissident is getting tired.

The prisoner is still injured, and twice as tired, but it's not in his nature or training to complain or stop simply because of that.

He turns over rocks and finds bugs and worms to eat.

The prisoner's eaten bugs before. They do not bother him.

The dissident doesn't refuse to eat them, but he seems to hate doing so, nonetheless.

"They're just…so squirmy. And gross," the dissident complains as he watches the prisoner open his small bag of bugs and reach in for one.

"Have you never eaten one before?" the prisoner asks.

"On a dare. It was nasty, kicking and squirming all the way down." The dissident recoils violently as the prisoner throws a beetle in his mouth. "Ugh…"

The dissident crushes his bugs' heads before he eats them, and then puts their limp bodies in his mouth slowly, his eyes tightly shut, looking as though he has a knife at his throat.

The prisoner doesn't understand.

He is…

Amused.

That's the word he's been trying to find, the one which would describe the emotion he feels every time he watches the dissident, a hardy, earnest young man who skinned and disemboweled animals without blinking, swallow a spider as though it were a hot coal.

"Why do you squash them before you eat them?" the prisoner asks.

"I don't like eating things *alive.*" The dissident looks away, much like the prisoner had when he skinned animals, as he pulls out a longer bug, this one possessing many, many legs.

But he turns back at the last second, morbidly interested, as the prisoner bites into it without a second thought.

"Do you eat bugs in your country?"

"If we must. If crops fail or livestock dies, they're small, but enough of them make a decent meal," the prisoner says.

"Well… I guess if I was desperate…and right now I am!" the dissident snickers. "Then I'd do that too."

"There will be more animals once we cross this…" The prisoner doesn't have a word for this wide, open gap between mountainous valleys. He gestures weakly at their surroundings. "Area."

"And I look forward to it," the dissident groans. "No more grub soup."

"You find eating bugs distasteful?"

"Obviously," the dissident snorts.

"Do you find me distasteful for eating them?" the prisoner asks without a hitch in his voice.

The dissident, having eaten as many bugs as he could typically stand, looks up sharply.

"No. I mean, it sort of grosses me out, but I get it. You have to. And it's important that you get nutrients and stay strong, so…"

The prisoner nods.

His bag is empty now.

Eating bugs feels as natural to him as eating plants and the meat of animals, but his companion clearly feels differently. It's hardly their greatest difference, but the thought stays in his mind as they walk. He can walk without the other man's support now, but he has a long, narrow stick for when his knees shake.

"You look like my grandpa," the dissident had said thoughtfully when he'd seen what the prisoner had picked up in the forest on a foraging trip. "I mean, if my grandpa was your skin color."

"Is that bad?"

"For a man your age, yeah. But… it's not your fault."

There's a look of disdain on his face when he says it.

But the prisoner hesitates in using that word, because although it is a form of condescension, there's something kinder about it, less cruel and imperious than the gazes of his commanding officers as they strutted between trainees.

He thinks he's seen that look before.

When he was punished in his second training camp, he must've been eleven, the on-site medic had had a look like his.

His old eyes had disturbed him.

They were sharp and penetrating, roaming his face for thoughts and feelings and finding none but bemused unease.

They seemed to pierce his mind and body as he cleaned the blood off his back, and radiate disappointment, for some reason.

The prisoner never knew why.

He still doesn't know why the medic had been disappointed in him.

Because he had been punished?

Because he had not met the standards of the Empire and thus could not be trusted to defend it?

Because a traitor who exchanges secrets is no better or worse than a traitor whose body and mind are inadequate?

He hadn't been able to finish his laps.

He hadn't finished his breakfast in the time allotted.

His eyes had teared up when he'd broken his leg after a peer pushed him off the gardening hut's roof.

The prisoner, thinking idly about all of these events from his training period, wonders if he should've expected to die in a foreign land, either in the water or in one of their torture laboratories.

He has always been a disgrace. And a traitor.

If not a traitor in mind, a traitor of information, then a traitor in body, in capacity, who could not serve the Empire as he should.

The dissident's disdain is justified, but something about it gives him pause.

The prisoner remembers Teacher's disdain.

He too wore disdain with a smile.

But it had not looked quite like…this.

Perhaps this is an emotion he's not familiar with.

There must be a word for it, but disdainful compassion is the only phrase he can construct to fit its parameters.

And it will do.

Stop squirming, stop squirming, stay down, stay down or I'll put you down there again for the next three days, do you hear me?

That's it, that's it, breathe, breathe…

Why are you so scared, my dear boy?

You weren't being whipped or beaten or prodded or cut up.

You weren't being burned or drowned or shot.

None of your bones are broken.

Your heartbeat is going so fast.

Oh there, there, don't hug me quite so tightly, dear, I am the enemy after all.

Perhaps you forgot.

You must've, because if I was one of your people, I would've shot you for such an emotional, needy display.

But luckily for you, I'm a compassionate man.

That is our people's way.

As soon as you've had your fill of this embrace though, as soon as they pry your skinny little emaciated arms off of me, you're going back into the box, do you understand?

Do you understand?

Do you-

"Get-off-"

Something hard and fast hits him in the face.

It's not the hardest hit he's ever received, nor the first hit he's received while only partly conscious, but it's enough to force him into the present.

The prisoner's straddling the dissident, legs on either side of his waist.

His hands on his throat.

He lets go quickly, but not before the dissident lurches up, throwing him off and into the wall. He almost lands in the fire, but rolls a safe distance away from it.

The dissident lunges at him as he's trying to orient himself, and punches him in the face again.

He takes it without protest, and says and does nothing as the dissident yanks both arms out and ties them together with some of the ropes he used for snares.

He merely leans back, heart racing, as the dissident finishes knotting the ropes binding his wrists together, looking angry and upset.

"Goddamnit, why did I think I could trust you?" he murmurs crossly. "You were just too weak and delirious before. All that talk about wanting to die, that was just trying to make me feel bad for you, well, I'm not an idiot-"

The prisoner's brain is a little too dazed from being hit in the face twice and being knocked against the cave's wall.

He just lets the dissident move on to his feet, angrily mumbling to himself as he binds them together too.

Even though he can't move, not very easily at least, he's ok as long as he can see the fire. As long as he can see the mouth of the cave, and his companion, rolling over and falling back asleep, he knows he isn't in the box. He isn't in the box. It's alright.

The ropes aren't so uncomfortable anyway.

He pushes himself onto his side and curls into his usual sleeping position with no problem or discomfort at all.

He falls asleep facing the fire-

The next thing he knows, someone's beating him, and he's burning, his clothes are burning, his hair is on fire, and someone's trying to smother him.

He thrashes wildly, still tied up, and feels his attacker still beating him…

Beating the flames off of him…

He's covered in dirt when he sits up, his jacket burnt and coming apart, but his other clothes thankfully unharmed.

The dissident, looking less angry and more concerned now than before, pulls the still smoldering jacket off of him.

It comes off easily without much resistance.

"What the hell is the matter with you?" he asks, but he says it bemusedly, more exasperated than pissed.

The prisoner blinks.

"I don't know what happened."

"Maybe you were…having nightmares," the dissident suggests. "Is that why you attacked me earlier? You were asleep?"

The prisoner hesitantly looks through a curtain of hair at him.

He seems more rested now, less hostile.

"I…I don't believe I consciously attacked you," the prisoner says slowly.

"…well. Ok. But you're going to have to sleep tied up or something from now on because I don't want to be strangled in my sleep," the dissident snorts.

The prisoner doesn't protest.

"What were you dreaming about?"

The prisoner turns to the mouth of their cave.

It's begun to drizzle.

"I was buried in a box. Five feet under. For a few days, with oxygen being pumped in every now and then. I was just…dreaming of that experience…I guess I attacked you thinking you were…Teacher."

"Teacher?" the dissident frowns. "Who is that?"

"The…man overseeing…my interrogation."

"Oh. Was he the head of the interrogation facility?"

"Yes. That was what he told me."

The prisoner shies away from the image that creeps up on him, the firm, virtuous hand, coming down hard on his shoulder, the wispy brown hair, and kindly, experienced eyes that looked down on him with interest. And savage glee.

He doesn't want to dream so vividly about him anymore. And the thought of actually coming face to face with him again…well, dreaming about him had felt real enough, he doesn't know what he would do, what he could do-

"I killed him."

The prisoner's fingers clutch at his sleeves.

"You…killed him."

"You were there," the dissident says. "Didn't you hear him die? You must've been so relieved…"

…

No, he can't remember it…

And he wouldn't have been relieved, he's fairly certain.

"Why are you making that face? You know, you still haven't thanked me for getting you out of there. Even if you're really eager to die, would you rather die in there, humiliated and so wracked with pain that you could hardly move, or out here, on the run with me? At least here it's up to you."

The prisoner's head is feeling rather woozy.

And it angers him, as does the thought of feeling grateful to this man.

"If it truly was, I would've been dead ages ago, you're the one keeping me alive. You seem to love life and all of its carnal, sensory pleasures, but you don't understand those who appreciate it for its greater, larger purpose. I…lived for that purpose. But it's gone now. And I cannot simply abandon the way I was brought up just because you tell me it's meaningless. It has meaning to me. It still does. It's all I have left."

The dissident says nothing at first, his face incredulous.

But after a while, there's a tepid, hesitant response in his eyes, and then in his mouth, as he begins to speak.

"Ok. Ok. Maybe you wanted, want, to die for country. But…you're not a masochist. You didn't enjoy that pain? You just had a nightmare about it, tried to kill me, and almost burned yourself alive. Surely you can at least…thank me for…ending all of that?"

The prisoner exhales slowly, the fire going out of him.

"For…shallow…human reasons… I can thank you for…stopping my suffering. Yes. An animal's response to pain is to stop it, and I…as you have seen…I could not bear it."

"Shallow human reasons?" the dissident chuckles, dissipating some of the tension. "We *are* shallow humans, bud."

The prisoner holds his hand outside, collecting water droplets on his fingers and licking them rapidly.

The dissident looks away hastily.

"Yes," the prisoner whispers. "I suppose that is what I am now."

"What's wrong with carnal, sensory pleasures anyway? What do you people have against fun?" the dissident says.

"…It can lead to pain," the prisoner whispers.

The dissident has no retort for that.

Had the prisoner been looking, he would've seen the dissident grimacing, nodding and conceding to his point.

But he isn't.

He's looking to the rain.

Wondering if someone like him could adjust to being nothing but a mortal, shallow human.

"Ok this is not working!" the dissident says exasperatedly. "Jesus…"

His prisoner hesitantly touches a cold wet rag to his cheek.

The dissident looks surprised, since the prisoner's never voluntarily touched him, but stands still.

"Sorry."

Now he *really* looks surprised.

His prisoner's sleeping fits seem to have gotten worse.

Even if he's restrained, he still manages to wiggle loose and hurt either himself or his companion, who's often awoken by feet or fists flailing wildly at his face, stomach, or chest.

It's actually rather terrifying for him, but he won't admit it.

He can't.

Even though his prisoner's lofty, callous voice and backwards, heartless words about life and death and how society "should" be piss the dissident off, he still makes a pitiful figure after he wakes up and realizes what he's done. He backs up quickly and hunches over his knees, his stomach heaving with labored breathing, his body shuddering.

His eyes are always rather distant, but in these moments, they're clouded and hazy with fear as they dart from him to the fire to the outside (or to the sky depending on if they've found cover or not) as if for reassurance.

The dissident winces.

The rag is nice and cool on his burning face, but it's still rough, still scrapes his skin.

"Uh… I'll take it," he says with a quick smile.

His prisoner doesn't return it, merely letting go and giving him space.

The dissident holds onto the rag now, watching him thoughtfully.

On the journey to the facility, he'd left supplies in several hiding places, intending to replenish the ones he was sure would be out coming back.

If they could just get to them, he could stop worrying about who was going to eat who first.

But at least his prisoner is walking now, he thinks.

The dissident touches his arm.

The prisoner's eyes shoot open.

It scares both of them.

He stumbles back, looking flustered.

"Er…sorry."

The prisoner doesn't shake him off.

Which disturbs him.

The man never expresses any discomfort. He keeps walking even though he looks like he's in pain, he never complains or resists when the dissident touches him, so the dissident never knows if he's hurting him, and he has a bad habit of always obeying an order, even if he knows better.

For example, he'd idly told him to go look for sticks suitable for firewood, sharpening sticks, and snares. He hadn't even thought to ask him if he was up to it.

When the man came back hours later, he had an armful of sticks and blood seeping through his shirt.

The dissident had felt both furious and depressed just looking at him.

Aside from protesting briefly when he'd told him to strip and bathe in the river, the prisoner, for the most part obeys any orders he gives him.

It freaks him out.

It's damn unhealthy, just following orders with a complete disregard for your own health.

He also wonders darkly from that moment on what kind of atrocities this man has committed, "following" orders.

"Do we…need to talk about…it?" he asks awkwardly, throat scratchy from sleep.

The prisoner immediately shakes his head.

"…I know it's not…easy to talk about…nightmares. And fears. It makes you feel…I dunno, vulnerable. But I'm really tired of getting into death matches with you every time we go to sleep, so unless you're actually just trying to kill me and only pretending to be sleep-walking, or sleep-strangling that is, then we need to resolve whatever this is. What do you keep dreaming about?"

The prisoner, although clearly listening, doesn't answer.

He seems frozen, actually, his back to him, staring up at the sky as though the answers were up there.

The dissident guiltily has an idea.

"Tell me right now," he says sharply, authoritatively.

His companion stiffens at his words.

He opens his mouth mechanically, automatically, speaking as though compelled by an inner force he could not resist.

"I've been dreaming about Teacher."

"I see…"

The dissident had seen first-hand what this so-called "Teacher" had done to him.

He hadn't had time to read anything in his file on it, but judging from the condition his body had been in when he'd rescued him, they hadn't been intending on keeping him alive for much longer.

In fact, one of the saddest things he's ever seen in his life had been in that facility.

He'd been running through the hall with a bloody knife in his hand.

Turning and expecting to find a locked door.

But instead, finding a door not only unlocked, but wide open.

And a huddled, purple and red mess of flesh quaking on the ground.

His legs so cut up and his body so broken that the door didn't need to be locked. Or even closed.

He wasn't moving at all. Just lying there.

He would've continued lying there until they decided to kill him, the dissident imagines, if he hadn't scooped him up.

He'd expected a hiss or a grunt, some kind of noise to indicate pain, but the man makes no sound, no movement, has no reaction whatsoever to being picked up.

He might've been breathing, but he was a corpse.

"…I keep seeing him. Keep reliving…his lessons." The prisoner closes his eyes.

"Are you afraid of him? He's dead," the dissident says. "I killed him."

"I know. He is no longer a threat," the prisoner says softly.

"You know that, logically, don't you?" the dissident asks.

"I believe you."

"He's dead. You know he's dead."

"I don't believe I would be here if he was not." The prisoner rubs his eyes tiredly. The dissident imagines he's not getting an adequate rest thrashing about every night.

"Yet you're still afraid."

The prisoner slowly opens his eyes, blinking rather owlishly.

"I am still…unsettled," he says.

"Afraid."

The prisoner doesn't argue with him, but he's resisting the word, his companion knows it.

"They're not afraid of anything!" his brother insists.

"They don't feel fear! Or anger! Or sadness! Or anything!" His sister charges him with her wooden sword. "They're-they're sock puppets!"

Their little dog yelps as the little girl accidentally tramples its tail in her mad scramble to get closer to her brother.

Their swords clash, or rather, thud lightly.

"My teacher said they stick pins in their children when they're young so they stop feeling pain before they're adults!"

"Well my teacher said they're genetically *modified to not feel pain!"*

"That's dumb, you need to feel pain or else you'll get hurt and not know it!"

"That's what she said!"

"You're both wrong," he insists. "They feel pain. They feel everything we do. They just don't show *it."*

"You can admit you're afraid of him. I would be too, he was a dick," the dissident says.

"He was…your fellow countryman," the prisoner says with confusion. "Why would you refer to him like that?"

"Just because we're from the same country doesn't mean we agree on everything," the dissident says. "It upsets my stomach, what he did to you."

"Why?"

The dissident looks up, but the prisoner's eyes have fluttered closed again.

He's slumped over, probably exhausted.

After a moment, he lets himself fall onto his back.

The dissident inches over to him, carefully skirting around their fire and coming onto his other side.

He lies down next to him.

They stare up at the sky.

The prisoner must like stars, the dissident thinks, with all the sky-watching he does.

He likes them too.

"…it just looked so ugly," the dissident snorts. "Great big dreadful bruises, size of my fist. All that scar tissue. Anyone who'd make a mess like that has to be horrible."

The prisoner's face twitches.

"Uh…" The dissident winces. Spoke too bluntly. "I… I don't know. Maybe it's because I had to treat you and take care of you and fix all of the damage he left."

The prisoner nods slightly.

"He inconvenienced you."

The dissident winces again.

"I just meant that…he was…sadistic, is all. Sadistic people are dicks."

"But don't your people value enjoyment over everything else? He was enjoying himself," the prisoner says quietly.

The dissident feels like he should've gotten angry with that statement, like he would've, weeks ago, but he's beginning to see the prisoner has no real malice, no real desire to incite an argument or upset him.

He simply states what he sees, what he believes, and doesn't care how it sounds aloud.

It's grating.

But at least he's just being honest.

"…there's a limit, we're not heathens. We draw the line at hurting people…"

"But he was punishing an outsider. A foreigner. I should not be here. I was not born here. I was spying and intruding. Why would my wounds disturb you? They are rightfully earned, shouldn't they have satisfied you?"

"I mean, from a logical standpoint, I guess it shouldn't have bothered me. But it did." The dissident crosses his arms behind his head. "I suppose you think we're just a bunch of hedonists who do whatever we want, moral or not, to feel good? Well, compassion for one's fellow man feels good too. Being a good person feels good."

As he's talking, he's watching the prisoner out of the corner of his eye.

He's not sure why he argues with him.

Maybe it's because the prisoner intrigues him, and he likes hearing about his lifestyle.

Or perhaps he just has a morbid fascination with the fucked up.

In either case.

The prisoner doesn't seem too keen on speaking right now.

He just blinks and stares pensively into the fire like he always does.

The dissident wonders what he sees in it.

If he sees anything at all or if he's just appreciating its warmth.

"Did you have friends? Back home?"

The dissident pants noisily, then looks back.

Or rather, down.

The prisoner, breathing much harder than him, is on his knees, clutching painfully at a large rock.

The dissident starts to skid down to lend him a hand, but the prisoner waves him away. He merely sits, his head in his arms as he leans on the rock, focused entirely on inhaling and exhaling.

He'd been having a rough go of it ever since they started climbing the next mountain.

His legs seemed weak, trembling with each step, every movement draining him as they climb higher.

The dissident had offered to carry him, but the prisoner had curtly claimed it was illogical and had stoically began the hike without entertaining the notion.

"Listen, man, we can rest here-" the dissident begins to offer.

"I'm fine," the prisoner gasps.

"Fine with killing yourself, yeah, we've established that. Stay there. That's an order," the dissident adds like an afterthought as he begins to scrabble down, rocks tumbling out of place as his feet brush against them.

The prisoner flinches, covering his face as pebbles tumble down.

He flinches again as the dissident crouches by his side, coming down too fast and knocking against his elbow.

"Sorry."

The prisoner just clutches his rock tighter, his forehead resting on its cool surface.

They sit there for a while; for how long exactly, the dissident isn't sure.

They might've sat there all day if the prisoner hadn't suddenly spoke.

"Are you going to move?"

"Um…" The dissident frowns, confused. That couldn't be irritation, right? "Only if you do."

"Why are you waiting on me?" the prisoner says, his voice strained.

"Um…because you're…tired?" the dissident asks, not sure what answer he's looking for.

"No. I mean…I'm slowing you down. I'm weak. My body is impaired." The prisoner won't look up. He's shivering.

He doesn't have a jacket anymore, not since he'd accidentally burned his previous one.

The dissident had used a clip to tie a blanket around him like a cloak.

Not by his request, however.

The prisoner never asks him for anything.

Not even a rest when he clearly needs one.

"I mean…I can't do anything about that. Other than carry you, but you won't let me. Which is kind of dumb." The dissident scratches his head. "Logically, it doesn't make sense, and you're a pretty logical guy…in fact, this is rather…emotional of you, wouldn't you say?"

The prisoner tenses.

His head turns and he stares off to the side, facing away from him, looking down the mountain and at the trees below.

"You don't need to carry me," he says, the tension gone from his voice.

The prisoner makes to get up, pushing against the rock for support with both hands. His heel skids.

The dissident seizes his hand so he won't fall.

The prisoner's hand squeezes his so tightly that he hears a crack.

"Humiliation isn't logical," the dissident says, looking him in the eye.

Or at least, trying to.

The prisoner refuses to meet his gaze, his mouth almost *pouting*, his face downcast.

"You don't need to carry me," he says, his voice slipping.

The dissident pulls his hand gently, dragging him onto firmer ground.

"Ok. We'll go slowly. Make camp at the top and wait till morning to descend, ok?"

The prisoner nods, eyes tightly closed.

The dissident doesn't let go of his hand.

He doesn't mean to pull him, just guide him up the rocks, but he ends up doing just that because the prisoner is much slower than him.

He's eventually forced to let go, as one pull is a little too much and the prisoner wheezes and falls to his knees again, finally letting out the gasp for air that he'd been hiding the whole time.

The dissident, a little tired himself and woozy from the thinner air, sits down.

"Would you look at that?" he puffs, withdrawing his canteen and taking a swig.

He offers it to the prisoner, who takes it with shaky fingers and tries to line it up with his mouth.

Water sloshes from his lips and down his chin as he fails to do so.

The dissident pretends he didn't notice.

"Gorgeous view, isn't it?" he says conversationally.

The prisoner doesn't respond.

"I love mountains. Even if they don't look like the ones at home, they're still breathtaking, aren't they? You get a sense of…awe. They're so huge and immovable, they make you feel small, no matter who you are. Even if you climb to the very top, you still haven't conquered the mountain. It'll be there long after we're all dead and gone."

The dissident pulls his pack off his back and rifles through it.

He pushes aside meat wrapped in plastic, tangled fishing lines, snare ropes, and boxes of bandages.

He begins to organize it, neither of them speaking as he does so, as the sun begins to sink, as the sky grows darker, and the air gets even cooler.

"We need to get…over this mountain, don't we?" the prisoner asks after some time.

"Eventually. No rush though," the dissident says casually. Cursing quietly as he pricks himself with his fishing hook.

Neither of them speak as the sun gets lower and lower. It winks out of existence behind the mountain opposite theirs and its dying golden glow wraps a halo around its peak.

"…If you couldn't perform in the army, they sent you home," the prisoner says quietly.

The dissident nods casually, acting as though he's only barely listening, but he's actually listening very intently. His heart is pounding for some reason.

"They didn't punish you. Not for being inferior. But they were disappointed in you. Ashamed that you gave up. That you weren't good enough. They made you…a teacher. Or a cleaner. Or a miner. Some kind of pointless laborer. They knew you could be more, but you proved them wrong."

The dissident hopes he can't hear his heartbeat, thudding erratically in his chest.

The prisoner's never spoken to him like this.

His voice is always soft, calm, unaffected.

It's a different kind of soft now.

The dissident isn't sure why he's so excited by it.

"I…almost failed my physicals. I barely weighed enough, I couldn't run fast enough, I wasn't strong enough. I thought I couldn't be what they assigned me to be, and would be forced to become something…less. I thought I might fail my parents. They…they had created me so that I might be something better than the two of them. But I would fail them, not only by being average, unremarkable, a waste of a petition, but something less than average. I was…"

The prisoner closes his canteen and sits, or rather, falls. He hits the ground unnaturally, uncomfortably, his ankles twisting a little as he does.

"Humiliated."

The dissident takes his canteen from him.

He pushes a small bundle of sticks together, wraps them together with a small strand of broken rope that had previously been a snare, and searches for his matchbox.

"You're injured," he says simply. "You're not weak. Just hurt."

"That *is* weakness."

"Not a weakness of character."

"There's no difference."

"Between being weak physically and weak mentally? There's a big difference."

"No."

The dissident laughs.

The prisoner stiffens.

"Why?"

"I think that's the first time you've outright said no to me," the dissident chortles. "And told me I was wrong."

"I did not tell you that you were wrong," the prisoner says, miffed.

"You did."

"I did not."

"Not with words. But with your mouth. Your face. Your tone."

"You are conjecturing," the prisoner says flatly.

"And you're…stubborn." The dissident grins. "But I kind of like it. I didn't know you had it in you."

But that's not true, the dissident thinks. He'd known. Even though his passive companion obeyed his orders, went wherever he asked him to, did whatever he asked, and never offered advice or tried to make any decisions on his own, there was a hardness to his obedience.

57

A certain steadfast dedication to obedience that just slipped out, that showed itself a little more palpably today.

The same dedication that drove him to climb a mountain while in serious pain, that would not let him stop until the dissident stopped. That would not allow his body to die.

When his will had been failing, when his mind wished for death, his empty, compassionless heart ready to stop beating freezing blood into cold limbs, the same fire, small but resilient, had burned.

The dissident laughs again.

He is the enemy.

He is not to be trusted.

But he's not quite so like his own people anymore.

He'd been stripped down to the bone, down to the lungs, the heart, the brain, with no mental or physical defenses, no delusions of higher purpose, no socially constructed barricades to get him through the night, no defense mechanisms with which to defend his mind, soul, or body. But his state should have been temporary. He should have died.

Instead, he'd been clumsily rebuilt, the layers of defense hastily pulled back up, but destined to never be the same again, never be as strong or as immovable as they once were.

At his core, once hidden where he had refused to acknowledge it, but now exposed, is something more like the dissident than them.

And he's scared of it.

The dissident shrugs his jacket off.

The prisoner looks up in surprise, then lets out a startled grunt as the dissident's jacket falls over him.

"I guess I can respect stubborn." He smiles.

32

"You didn't answer me, by the way."

The prisoner looks up, the dissident's jacket clutched around his shoulders, his blanket in his lap.

"I asked you if you had friends back home. Anyone who would miss you," the dissident elaborates. "Who misses you right now, thinks you're dead, maybe."

The prisoner shakes his head before he's done speaking.

"No family, no friends, huh?"

He does not know the man's name.

But he calls him Ink in his head, because he always has remnants of black ink on his hands.

They sit in the barracks while the others exercise, look for sterilized women, go to the movies to catch the latest documentary or extended training tape.

Ink is strange.

While he sits in his bunk, playing with his fingers, pulling them until they crack, flexing and stretching every muscle necessary for optimum performance, Ink writes.

He writes in a small, ugly, tattered brown book, sometimes furiously, chaotically, his pen flying across the page, sometimes calmly, deliberately, his pen the slow, rocking sail of a ship.

They never speak to one another.

He just knows that these moments between training, between being reprimanded and criticized, between exhausting work outs and drills, are peaceful. He feels at peace, holding his fingers, looking up at the bunk above his, just barely aware of the man sitting three or four beds away, writing in his book.

When the man doesn't come back one day, they redistribute his belongings to the other soldiers of his unit.

No one gets the book.

The book is thrown away.

"What did he write?" the prisoner murmurs.

"Huh?" The dissident grimaces. He hates how roots taste, but they were all he'd found the other day. Stiff, frozen roots buried in cold, frozen ground.

"What do people write about?" the prisoner asks, ignoring his question and asking his own.

The dissident scratches his head.

"Their thoughts?"

"What could he be thinking about?" the prisoner says, talking more to himself than his companion, who bites into a root. And scowls.

"Uh…his day, maybe. The thoughts he had during the day. The…I dunno, nightmares he had the previous night. Speaking of nightmares, please do your best not to kick me off the side of a mountain, ok?"

The prisoner tries to see his face in his mind, but he can't quite manage it. He can see his quick fingers, rapidly scrawling something in his small book, his back as he sat outside in the sunlight during a break, grass stains on his trousers. He can see his curly hair, his broad shoulders, hunched over, his legs crossed neatly, his head bowed reverently. But all he can really see in his mind's eye are his inky fingers, black and messy and surely smudging his pages with stains as he writes frantically, almost desperately.

"A friend?" the dissident asks. "Is that who you're thinking about?"

The prisoner blinks the pen away.

"I suppose."

The dissident snorts.

Of course he does.

The prisoner feels a lurch of something unpleasant in his gut.

"Well…my friend Reina has curly black hair and skin darker than mine and clear blue eyes and she plays the cello. My friend Leonardo is tall and skinny but fast, and good at football. My brother Rafi looks a lot like me, but more like our father, broader and taller and with bushier hair. I had a lot more friends, but they went to other districts and I haven't heard from them in a while. Some friends keep in touch, others don't."

The prisoner rubs his frozen hands together under the blanket in his lap.

The wind is strong.

The temperature is low.

The fire can't survive, weakened by thin air and constant, pulverizing wind.

The prisoner stares longingly at the smoldering sticks where the fire had been before its untimely death.

He flinches as the dissident's arm comes around his shoulder, the man's knee banging against his. He tenses, but doesn't resist as the man pulls at the blanket, covering the both of them and tugging the corners up underneath their bodies. The dissident, now under the blanket with him and pressed uncomfortably close, grins and claps his shoulder.

The prisoner, feeling trapped in his arm, jammed between his grip and his body, squirms slightly, wanting to get away but begrudgingly noting the increase in warmth.

"Oh come on, don't be shy," the dissident sighs into his ear. "We need to preserve some body heat. Create a little space where warmth can't escape so easily. You don't mind, do you?"

The prisoner minds, but says nothing.

As the dissident had expected.

The dissident falls back with a sigh, his arm falling away from his unwilling victim's shoulder. The prisoner hesitantly lies back as well.

"Look how close the stars are," the dissident says.

The prisoner does.

"My friends and I, and my brother and sister, liked looking at the stars. We liked camping. And chasing grasshoppers. And sharpening sticks into spears and using rocks for hammers and axes. It was fun, see? Did they never let you do any of that stuff, as a kid?"

"Why would you want to do any of that?" the prisoner ask, closing his eyes tightly, but still seeing stars, burning white in his mind. "It sounds exhausting and pointless."

"It was fun," the dissident insists. "We played lots of games. Had lots of great stories to tell.'"

"It was fun," the prisoner repeats.

"Yes. Fun. Did you ever do anything for fun? Climb a tree? Run through a mud puddle? Take a nice, quiet walk through the woods? Come on, don't tell me you just sat on your bed, staring at the wall when you had time off?"

"We climbed trees and ropes for practical training," the prisoner says. "We ran outside, regardless of whether it was raining or not, and it was often muddy. Training was too intense, we could not spare the energy to take meaningless walks through the woods. Not unless we were attempting to forage for extra food when rations were cut back or-"

"Oh my god, your childhood sounds sad," the dissident groans. "You probably never even hit a wasp's nest with a bat and ran screaming for the nearest body of water."

"That sounds horrible," the prisoner states, a jolt of electricity racing up his arm when the dissident's arm shifts and brushes against it.

"It was," the dissident admits. "Those things are persistent, you can only hold your breath for so long and they know how to follow you home."

"Why would you do it, then?"

"'Cuz I was a stupid kid and I was dared to do it. It was really satisfying for the first few seconds though," the dissident chuckles.

"How so?"

"Well…I don't know how to explain it, it was just….satisfying. Felt fulfilling."

The prisoner says nothing.

He doesn't understand the point of any of the dissident's described activities, especially the last one, which seemed only harmful to him.

"It was fun…they made it fun," the dissident correctly interprets his silence. "Friends pass the time when there's nothing else to do. Friends are always around, whether you need them or not, but especially when you need them. They take care of you. They make the worst moments of your life feel just a little better. Have you never had a friend?"

The prisoner hand touches a warm, living wrist.

He doesn't pull away for a moment, distracted by the heavens, and how small they are, how alone, how meaningless, lying beneath the vast, infinite emptiness of space.

A hollowness filled, crowded, bursting to the brim, with the innumerable, incorporeal stars.

They are corporeal, of course, but to mere mortals, they're as real, as palpable, as spirits, as the very light they expel.

"Your description…is inadequate," the prisoner whispers.

"Inadequate?" the dissident almost laughs out loud. "Why do you say that?"

"Because by those parameters, by that poor definition of friends you just gave me," the prisoner says. "You and *I* are friends."

He says it lightly, his voice as close to humorous and flippant as it can be, which isn't close but is decent for him, and he expects the dissident to snort in amusement, or make some other noise, perhaps derisive, but the dissident does nothing of the sort.

"You really think so?" the dissident asks.

Almost as though he's…pleasantly surprised.

The prisoner turns over, pulling his limbs closely to his body and curling inwards.

He does not dignify the question with a respond, because the dissident has misunderstood him, or misinterpreted what he meant.

"So that means…" the dissident doesn't finish the thought, but his voice is oddly…

The prisoner clutches his stomach.

"Well. It's not such a bad description then, is it?" the dissident asks cheerfully.

The prisoner doesn't dignify that with a response either.

He merely blinks, no longer gazing at the sky but the ground, and the path that lay behind them, and tries to quell the uncomfortable feeling inside.

When he wakes up, he's in the exact same position he'd been in when he'd fallen asleep.

"No nightmares, huh?" the dissident yawns.

33

He still has nightmares.

But as long as he keeps them to himself and the dissident thinks that his lack of nocturnal movement is evidence of their disappearance, then he sees no reason to inform him of this.

The problem is eliminated.

"Man, it seemed a lot easier getting here than going back."

The prisoner frowns, not sure if he's making a joke or being critical of their slow pace.

He's doing his best, but to his immense frustration, he's still not able to keep up with his companion. Even at the dissident's slowest pace, he still struggles to move without his lungs burning, flares of pain erupting in his calves, his thighs, a sliver of agony splitting his side. His knife wounds still ache, his back still screams out silently every time he tries to straighten it, and he still limps like a three-legged dog.

He has to relieve himself embarrassingly often, though not as often as he used to.

That, he thinks with distaste and a touch of mortification, at least seems to be improving quicker than anything else.

Just leave me just leave just leave me.

His private mantra, however, has become a little less bleak, and a little more frustrated.

The desire to die seems to have abated into a mere frustration with being alive.

He is weak and dependent, but no longer suffering.

It's not his place to say so, but in the furthest corner of his mind, he recognizes this as an improvement.

The dissident seems to have an endless patience.

He's a strange one, the prisoner thinks, hobbling after him downhill, struggling not to lose his footing.

The man seems to have no problem with carrying him around, feeding him, acting as his crutch, or dealing with his slow pace. Not a sliver of irritation or impatience flashes across his face as he waits for the prisoner to catch up. Whenever they get too far apart, he turns and seems completely unaffected by the prisoner's distance from him.

And yet, he is quick to anger at night.

When they argue.

"Why do you care if children are used for experimentation?"

"It's wrong. It's absolutely wrong, it's-"

"To ensure the survival of future children, some sacrifices are made in the name of research, in the name of bettering the lives of future children-"

"Is there no level you people won't stoop to?"

You people.

The prisoner is learning to recognize that phrase as an insult.

And he tries to recognize that the dissident's personal opinions mean nothing.

His earnest, fervent adulation for his perfect society, his better, superior culture should mean next to nothing to him.

The prisoner has no function anymore.

His opinion, and the opinion of the man ranting to him every other night, are utterly irrelevant in the grand scheme of things.

And yet, despite its lack of functionality, he feels…discontent.

He does not like the phrase you people now. It had been a simple phrase, an innocuous term in his vocabulary before, but it had become something ugly in their time together.

He does not like when the dissident refers to him as though he were…a concept. A state of mind, a group of people, an interactive philosophy.

And not someone lying next to him, speaking to him, sharing a blanket with him.

"Guess not," the dissident says. "Well, that's good. I can stop worrying you're going to roll me down the hill in a huge snowball."

The prisoner rolls his eyes.

"You did it again," the dissident says indignantly, pointing accusingly. "You rolled your eyes!"

It's an annoying little habit he can't seem to shake.

He never used to do it before.

He'd seen people do it, of course.

Watched old men do it when they spoke to children, Commanders when they spoke to cadets, and children as they sat through lessons (during his brief compulsory work as a training camp supervisor).

But he'd never been the type to make such a foolish social gesture.

Now when the dissident says something silly or just boisterous, he can't help but do it.

It feels…disrespectful.

Childishly…satisfying.

Guiltily, he rather likes it, the feeling of doing it.

The dissident freezes.

"Oh my god," he says.

The prisoner frowns.

"Is something wrong?"

"I think you might've smiled," the dissident gasps. "Something horrible's gonna happen today."

The prisoner grimaces, but has come to accept his odd quips as normal, unremarkable occurrences.

Teacher wasn't like that.

Teacher was what you expected these people to be like.

But he's…

The dissident huffs.

"Would you look at that?" He makes a sweeping gesture with his right arm, smiling broadly.

The prisoner does.

The lake is so lovely, so blue, so clear he can see the clouds slowly sailing across it, the surface as perfect and smooth as if the water were a solid mirror.

"See those trees?" the dissident crows. "Animals live in those forests. We'll finally get some real meat! No more skin and bones and insect legs! And that lake is full of delicious, scrumptious, mouth-watering fish."

The prisoner hears him speaking, but is too mesmerized by the view to listen.

He's never seen something so untouched by man.

The ocean...churning and wild, angry and brown in daylight, soiled by oil and pollution, swirling with trash, plastic, polymer conglomerates, hadn't look as untouched as this.

He almost doesn't want to approach it.

Doesn't want the tempting images his companion offers, the promises of good, plentiful food, a more consistent source of water, and shelter in the trees.

Would rather sit here, staring at its wild, unscathed majesty.

More majestic, even, more magnificent and breath-taking than-

"Shit," the dissident curses.

The prisoner looks up.

Something cold pricks his nose.

It has begun to snow.

34

When the prisoner awakes, he is blinded by whiteness and he's so cold that his blood feels frozen, protesting his every move.

He struggles against a suffocating, overwhelming presence, a thick, ineffable weight that seems to bear down on him like Teacher, pressing against his back and legs as though trying to compress his skin and bones into puddles of organic matter.

He can see nothing but white, even though his eyes are wide open, stinging as freezing water and crunchy snow scrape against them.

He closes them, clawing viciously, flailing as fiercely as he can.

As he breaks free of the snow, he lets out a yell.

He wiggles and squirms with his entire body, fighting to break free from the layer of snow that must've fallen on top of the him the night before, when he and the dissident-

He yells out.

He calls to him.

He says, "I'm here. I'm here. Where are you?"

But the dissident does not respond.

The prisoner, fingers freezing, clutching snow, grunts as he pulls his legs free.

He's bleeding.

He disregards it for a moment, looking blearily around.

The night before…

The wind was so loud. It stung his eyes, bit at his hands, clawed at his face; he held onto the dissident's hand, but it slipped away, and he heard him yell.

But he can't see him, can't hear him, through the howling, maddened tempest raging around their struggling forms. When he falls, when he's dragged down the mountainside by gravity, the prisoner knows he's lost him the moment it happens, but can do nothing to stop it.

All he could do was stop moving.

Get on his knees, curl into a tight ball, pull his jacket over his face, and hope the storm dies down.

Hope the dissident is ok.

Because he doesn't know what to do.

He can't see. Can't hear. Can barely move, so hampered by the blizzard.

And he's alone.

If you have no orders, no commanding officer nearby, and nowhere to report to, wait for further instruction.

The first sentence they taught him how to write.

It pops into his mind, genteel and reassuring, and urges him to wait.

So he does.

And now, here he is.

In the same predicament he'd been in before.

The prisoner looks around again.

The canteen.

It lies on its side several feet away from him.

He stumbles over to it.

He gathers up snow inside of it and caps it.

He feels a sharp sting in his bladder, a painful ache that needs to be alleviated.

He grits his teeth.

Please.

Be headed for the lake.

Go to the lake.

So strongly does he feel this, does he think this, that it doesn't even occur to him how miserable he is, trying to force his maltreated body through snow and ice, or how much he would've rather died peacefully, in a room or in the grass somewhere, staring up at the sky.

He has a single-minded, ardent determination that forces him to move. Forces him to fixate on one goal. To go one way.

Towards the lake.

Hopefully, to the dissident, waiting in the place he seemed so enthralled with.

He pictures it in his mind, the dissident's face, his enthusiastic, warm eyes, waiting somewhere on the shore. And he moves forward because he has nothing else to move towards.

Death, oddly, does not occur to him.

Neither does stopping.

35

Say…why don't I give you a treat today?

It's nice and warm, isn't it?

Do you like warm weather?

I imagine you don't get much of it, where you're from.

Ah, you look like you're enjoying it.

Amazing what a little sunlight can do, isn't it?

You look younger.

Now.

I'll leave you out here for two minutes.

You have that much time before…oh, you know what? I'm feeling generous. We're done with the box for now.

But today is bath day.

So…enjoy the warmth.

Enjoy it while you can.

This feels colder than anything he's ever felt, but he knows this sentiment to be false.

He'd been held down in a bathtub full of ice cubes and just a little water until he passed out.

This should feel like nothing.

He's walking, so his blood is pumping.

He's wearing a jacket.

He's not naked.

And this is not freezing water, just freezing air.

And he is not drowning.

He can breathe.

There's only air in his lungs, not frigid ice water.

And yet, he feels colder than he's ever felt in his life.

And his body screams out for him to stop. But his mind forces him not to.

He has no food.

Just snow, which is really only water, and he gets the feeling it's polluted by the toxins excreted by this nation's climate control.

Their environmental alterations upset the natural balance of the atmosphere.

His people do not use environmental control, not unless it is absolutely necessary.

Oh come on now, I know the temperature is usually below zero, where you come from.

Below negative seventeen, by your temperature scale, I suppose.

It's cold at home too.

He'd spent countless days and nights on patrol, standing outside while it was raining, snowing, hailing.

He knows cold very well, having been accustomed to the temperature of the laboratory since birth, the youth training center, the army barracks, purposefully kept cold to weed out those of weak body and immune system.

But a man never gets used to food poisoning, no matter how many times he gets it, and knowing cold, living most of his life in cold, doesn't make it feel any less harsh.

And all of these prior times, he'd been perfectly healthy.

Well equipped, well-dressed.

And with the knowledge that if he collapsed, someone would drag him somewhere warm eventually.

Out here, alone, there is no one to help him.

No one to save him.

No one at all, not the Empire, not the Republic, not the faceless, countless others out there, the world full of humans divided by borders and ideologies.

He is alone.

Truly alone, now, without the dissident.

The prisoner could barely walk before.

Now, encumbered by snow, he can walk even less.

It's tempting to lie down.

But he can't.

The lake.

Get to the lake.

Maybe he's there.

He's already there, of course he is.

Waiting.

36

But maybe he isn't.

The thought occurs to him as he continues, his legs wobbling, his bladder burning once more. He ignores it, however, not wanting to stop and expose himself to the cold air any more than absolutely necessary.

Maybe he'll heed your request.

Finally let you die.

He's moved on.

Decided to keep going.

What does he need you for?

You only slow him down.

In order to survive, he was going to need to abandon you at some point anyway.

Maybe he just kept you around in case he needed a backup food supply.

Are these people cannibals, perhaps?

No matter.

He doesn't need you.

No one needs you.

You no longer have purpose.

You are no longer a working cog of the Empire.

You aren't even useful to this man, or his resistance, whatever pitiful organization that may be.

Why are you moving?

Struggling to breathe?

Just stop.

It'll be painful at first, but then it'll be like falling into a deep sleep.

Why are you still-?

His hands are bleeding from clawing at ice.

His legs are soaked, cold cloth bound to his flesh like a second skin.

He pulls the dissident's jacket close, at the very least keeping his chest warm, but he wonders what will happen if he gets frostbite.

If his toes and feet fall off.

Broken and useless.

Your body was already broken and useless, mangled beyond repair.

You already foresaw a future of nothing but misery, of limping, of pissing yourself, of losing vision in both eyes, just a helpless, cobbled animal waiting to be put out of its misery by a predator. Your spine, how does it feel?

It aches, doesn't it, feels like a lightning rod, bends inside and out, twists like a chain, no backbone anymore, and that ankle of yours, warped beyond help.

Even if you wanted to find another purpose, you couldn't.

Teacher has broken you, and broken things must be thrown away.

No one's watching you.

The Empire would not be ashamed.

The Republic would be pleased.
The dissident will go on, has gone on, without you.
Who are you afraid of hurting?
Just stop.
It's so easy to stop.
So easy to give up.
So blissful, so peaceful, the cessation of effort.
So why, why on earth are you still-?

"I'm here! I'm here!" the prisoner yells, louder than he's ever yelled. "I'm here!"

He must drown out that sultry, soothing voice.

It makes snow seem like a comfortable bed, a perfect coffin, the sky a fitting tombstone, the trees below, the lake, perfect monuments, keepers of his existence. No one will know he was ever here, but they will know.

They will last forever, and because they know his existence, he will last forever as well-

The prisoner slaps his cheeks as harshly as he can.

Is this delirium?

What utter nonsense.

He sniffs, bites his lip, and keeps pushing forward.

What utter nonsense.

Nothing is immortal, not trees, not this lake, and not even these mountains.

The world is always changing.

His life is insignificant and will not be remembered by anyone.

But he must move forward anyway.

He must keep going.

To the lake.

Where the dissident is waiting.

Even if he isn't.

37

"My mother took me fishing more times than I can remember."

"Of course, we ended up not fishing and just talking, just sitting there with bait-less hooks."

"She really listened to you when she talked, you know? I could see why my father loved her so much. She could really make you feel like the most important person in the world."

"When she retired, it was the saddest day of my life."

"My old man retired first, and that was sad, but at least she was there. When she retired, I didn't have her anymore. I didn't have anyone."

His own parents would never know what happened to him.

They could search his name, find missing in action or killed in action, but they would never know exactly what happened.

And he doubts they would even search his name.

He was a disappointment after all.

He's bleeding again.

All he can do is bunch up his shirt and try to quell the blood loss because he can't afford to tear his clothing up. He needs every article intact in order to fight the temperature, but he's feeling a little light-headed, and the ground is beginning to tilt unpleasantly.

But the trees.

At least he can die looking up at the trees.

He walks among them, tripping over rocks and roots, kicking up snow and dirt the further down he gets.

As his vision wavers, blackness threatening to swallow him whole, he walks directly into a pine tree, right into its branches.

"I didn't have anyone."

"But I went out. I traveled. I went around, made new friends. I realized there were others. There were other people who could fill the loneliness the two people I loved most had left behind. I just needed to find them. And my parents didn't need to be remembered with sorrow anymore."

Sorrow.

Grief.

Hurt.

These are things that tug at the soul, at the heart, when something vital is missing.

He is not vital.

Not to anyone.

No one will grieve.

He staggers, knees sinking into the snow, canteen flying from his hand and tumbling somewhere out of view.

"My friend Natasha thinks camping is boring and too much hard work. Yoon doesn't like bugs. Carlos hates the sun. We play cards. Watch movies. Go to plays. Stuff that they like, you know. Well. I like those things too. I didn't at first, but...sometimes you do

something you don't necessarily love for your friends. You compromise. They sometimes go horseback riding with me, sailing, you know, outdoorsy stuff, and I sometimes play poker with them."

Keep moving.

Keep moving.

The lake is ahead.

He can see it.

He's on the same level as the lake now.

Keep moving.

"People. People make life worth living."

Purpose made life worth living.

Purpose.

But perhaps.

Other people had different purposes.

The dissident…

Perhaps his purpose lay with his friends.

Perhaps his purpose was…

Ridding himself and others of this wretched feeling.

This wretched feeling.

Of being alone.

Completely alone.

No one here but him, a contemptible jumble of mangled skin and organs.

Lying face down in the snow.

His chest heaving, his face bleeding, scraped up by the tree and the ice, raw from the wind.

Entire body aching, tired, hurting so much he can't breathe, and yet simultaneously, he feels every breath, as sharp as a blade between his ribs.

"I miss them every day. I was devastated when they retired. I guess you wouldn't understand…"

No.

No family.

No friends.

No…

…?

The prisoner turns his head to the left.

A blurry brown shape.

Not a tree.

Square and perfect, but not in a natural way.

In a human…constructed way.

A cabin.

It's a cabin.

He's sure of it.

He can make it.

There won't be anyone there.

But he has to make it.

If he can just make it to the cabin, maybe his corpse will be found by someone, eventually.

Even though every muscle is pulled taut, every limb on fire, his blood roasting him alive, he finds himself moving as fast as he can. He moves quickly, because if he doesn't, then he'll never move again.

The cabin grows larger with each painful limp. It is much larger than he thought.

It wavers teasingly before his eyes like a mirage.

He reaches his hand out.

Just relax when I put you under.

Just relax and let your lungs fill with water.

The pebbles of the lake's shore are coated by a thin layer of ice, which crunches beneath his feet as he stumbles. He slides a little, unbalanced by the irregular grouping of the rocks.

But he keeps going.

Just like in training.

There's a stitch in his side begging him to stop and his lungs seem utterly devoid of air, his head full of dizzying emptiness, but he keeps going. He has to. He will not fall. He cannot fail, not here.

He cannot fall.

Not here.

His commanding officer is impressed.

He'd never expected such a scrawny little rat to push through physical training.

It's getting larger.

It's no simple cabin.

Clearly whoever owned it intended to stay there for a long time, and in comfort.

There appears to be more than a single floor, and there's a porch with a railing. A chimney.

Keep moving.

His eyes are stinging, but he merely closes them and keeps going.

Frost on his eyelashes and nostrils.

"You're tougher than you look."

The greatest compliment he'd ever received.

And from someone who despised him, who found him inadequate, and tried to have him displaced. Put in the position of a laborer, a contributor to the maintenance of the Empire, but not the preservation, or the integrity.

He could not fail. Could not allow himself to stop.

And the situation feels the same now, just as urgent, just as desperate.

The prisoner gasps and slams his hand on the railing.

Just as hard as he'd slammed his hands on the ground, bent over on all fours, ragged and wretched, but triumphant nonetheless, at the end of physical training.

Here.

He is here.

The cabin seems well-taken care-of, if vacated at the moment.

He lurches up the railing and prays to god it isn't locked.

He pushes at the door, and it won't budge.

He's almost completely overwhelmed by panic and hopelessness, so strong he could puke (although maybe that has to do with his dizziness), until he tries pulling.

It opens easily, swinging open and blasting him with a gush of hot air so welcoming and unexpected that for a moment, he wonders if he'd died in the snow and found his way to heaven.

Heaven.

The prisoner begins to laugh, blood frozen on his face, his lips.

He doesn't believe in heaven.

No one in the Empire does.

And yet, here he is…

Well.

If this is heaven, he's grateful to have found it.

And if it isn't, well, he's still grateful to have found its closest approximation on earth.

As much as the prisoner would like to, he can't simply collapse and fall into a deep sleep.

He might just die if he does that.

Instead, he has to scramble through the house looking for bandages, food, and other necessities.

There are cans of fruit, vegetables, and meat, to his surprise and joy.

He's starving, wants desperately to eat, but there's a more pressing matter on his mind.

Since the thought of crawling up the stairs is more daunting to him than bleeding out on the floor, he is relieved to find a first-aid kit and other medical supplies on the bottom floor.

He strips off his bloody clothes, tossing them into the sink. There are disinfectant wipes in the first-aid kid, but he barely feels their sting, isn't even aware of it as he rubs vigorously at the crusted blood and the new blood all over his body. He's bleeding all over the floor, but can't be concerned with it at the moment.

As he clumsily, rather poorly, binds his wounds back up, his bladder, ignored in his life-or-death crawl through the forest, suddenly comes back to the forefront of his mind.

He hurries to the bathroom.

Shockingly, the water is running.

He washes his hands for the first time in over a year and then stumbles back to the living room couch.

And he finally allows himself to fall unconscious.

He might've longed to die the entire journey here.

He might still long to die, in his heart, in his soul.

But his body had not let him.

Nor had his mind.

He had made it here through sheer willpower.

Tougher than he looks.

Stronger than he looks.

He might fall into a sleep like death, but for the first time in over a year, he knows he will wake up.

And he does not dread it. Dread being awake.

And alive.

He wakes up thirty hours later, so hungry he can hardly move.

The prisoner rolls off the couch, falling painfully hard on hardwood floor, and crawls over to the cans of fruit, meat, and vegetables he'd left on the ground when he'd first gone rummaging through the cabinets.

He pries the flimsy metal tabs up and practically gulps the canned food down in the first thirty seconds, not even chewing once as he frantically fills his empty stomach.

He slows down eventually, realizing that he might choke or throw it back up if he keeps going at this pace. The taste doesn't faze him, sweet or sour, scrumptious or vile. He's not even sure what he's eating at first, just eating out of whichever cans he gets a hold of first, scooping out nutrients indiscriminately.

When he's done, he drops his last can, his fingers trembling, still so exhausted his muscles feel like liquid fire as he sprawls out on the cold floor.

He's still lying on the kitchen floor, waiting for his energy to return so he can get back to the couch, when he hears a thumping sound.

As fatigued as he is, he still fumbles in a nearby drawer for a knife, finds one, and crawls over to the edge of the kitchen. He glances at the door.

Then darts back as it swings open.

Anxiety and dread bubble up in his chest, tightening an iron band of fear around his lungs and heart.

He can scarcely breathe as he hears cumbersome, uncaring footsteps stomp through the hallway, pausing at the living room, clearly distracted by something.

They move forward for a moment, but then stop, and he has a sickening realization.

There's blood.

His blood.

When he'd been tending to his wounds, he'd bled in that very hallway, in the spot where the intruder is clearly pausing.

He knows someone's here, and he knows they're injured.

He grips the knife tightly in his hand and forces his body upright.

He's not a close combat expert.

He'd been taught basic hand-to-hand training, but it mostly involved maneuvering out of someone's grip or wrestling a knife or gun away from an assailant.

He doesn't know how to incapacitate this person, who may or may not have a weapon, and in his present state, he doubts he would be able to, even if he knew how.

All he can do is defend himself as best he can with the dull kitchen knife.

The intruder turns into the kitchen.

The prisoner lunges at him, knife poised to strike at his stomach.

The man yells out.

But as startled as he is, he's still quick on the uptake.

The prisoner finds his wrist caught in a powerful grip a split second before there's a hand on his throat, and he's pinned up against the wall, his feet no longer touching the ground.

He drops the knife.

"Oh-oh my god!" the man exclaims.

The prisoner is let down almost instantly.

His legs crumple as soon as he's allowed to stand on his own, and the man, quick on the uptake once more, catches him by the waist, letting him fall to the ground more slowly, more gracefully, his own body following suit.

They fall to the floor together and end up kneeling, face-to-face. And they get a proper look at one another.

"How did you-?" the man gasps, his face filled with excitement and pure joy.

The prisoner gapes at him.

It's the dissident.

40

"I thought you were dead," the dissident babbles excitedly, circling him like an overenthusiastic dog. The prisoner sits on the couch, nursing the bruise on the back of his head from being slammed into the cabinets.

The dissident paces wildly, seemingly full of energy as he keenly watches the prisoner. He hits the heavy table several times in his delight, but doesn't seem to notice, merely rubbing his knees absentmindedly when he does.

"I was out looking for you, I thought if I retraced my steps, but it snowed and it covered your tracks and I thought I found blood, but it was from a dead raccoon and I thought I would never find you and you'd freeze to death or lose too much blood or starve to death and I didn't know what to do, but I found this cabin and I thought that if you were alive you'd probably head towards the lake and then you'd hopefully see this cabin and head here, but I was still scared you might die out in the snow, so I went out to look but you found your way here all on your own and god, I knew you were tough, I knew you were strong, I was just worried because you're always talking about wanting to die, but I knew you could get here, and now you're here-"

"Please stop," the prisoner begs. "I have a headache."

"Sorry!"

Then the dissident scares him.

He pivots sharply and walks over to him so quickly the prisoner barely has time to register their newfound close proximity before he's being grabbed tightly and ferociously by the much larger, and much stronger, man.

He gasps out in pain, but the dissident doesn't seem to notice.

His arms are so long he could probably grab his own elbows and still hold the prisoner in his grip.

The thought terrifies him for some reason, as does the feeling of being held so tightly.

No one has ever grabbed him like this.

The pressure is overwhelming, and frankly quite frightening.

Panic bubbles to the surface and he pushes as hard as he can against the dissident's stomach. The other man gets the point.

"Sorry," he repeats. "I'm really sorry, I just… I'm a little hungry, I haven't eaten anything since last night, and I thought you were dead. It made me all soft for a moment there."

The prisoner nods uneasily.

"Are you ok? How are your injuries? Let me check," the dissident says, reaching for his shirt.

"Later, please," the prisoner flinches, slapping his hand away.

"Boundaries," the dissident says. "Right. Sorry. Sorry. I just saw all the blood and thought…I dunno. I didn't want to get my hopes up, but I couldn't think of who or what else could get in here and drag its bleeding body all over the place. I guess I'll have to clean that up before whoever owns this place gets home…"

"Do you know anything about them?" the prisoner asks.

"When I came here, the power was off. So was the water and heater. Luckily, the guy left a list of instructions in his basement. I got the place running before I went out looking for you. I broke the lock getting in, I figured it was ok for the time being, since there's nobody out here, but I'll have to fix it before we leave. Don't want anyone to know we stayed here, right?" The dissident hits the table again. He curses and pushes it out of his way.

"What if they come back?" the prisoner asks.

"Um… I don't know, it's been snowing a lot," the dissident says. "This seems like a winter cabin, so if they're not here now, then maybe they skipped this season."

"We can't count on that," the prisoner says. "We should leave."

"When you can," the dissident insists. "You look like hell. Um. No offense."

"…I feel like hell," the prisoner says. The dissident's face lights up.

"I mean, you went through hell," he grins. The prisoner is struck by how much younger his already youthful face looks at this moment.

It causes a peculiar, conflicted jolt in his stomach, part warm feeling, part apprehension.

"Well….as soon as you're ready, we'll leave here immediately. We'll…look for a tent and other stuff while here. We can't bring a lot of food with us, because it'll attract animals and be too heavy to carry, plus cans make a convenient litter trail for anyone who might be following us, but I'm sure the guy has a fishing rod or extra rope in here. Oh man," the dissident sighs. "This is the part where the journey finally gets a little easier."

"I feel like I've heard that before," the prisoner says dryly, laying his dirty, matted hair on the couch as he leans his head back.

The dissident laughs long and hard at that.

The prisoner falls asleep almost instantly and the dissident does his best to be quiet as he stomps away. But as soon as he's out of earshot, the dissident grins ear to ear, hits the wall lightly with his clenched fist, and stomps his foot like a child. He can't help it.

The prisoner is alive. He's alive.

Once again, he's surprised him.

41

The dissident squeezes his hands tightly between his palms.

The prisoner winces.

"Your hands are freezing," the dissident groans. He rubs more vigorously, trying to return some heat to his fingers. "And you really mangled them, look at this…"

The prisoner, feeling unreasonably self-conscious, pulls his hands away and stuffs them in the warm hollow between his crossed legs.

The dissident throws a fluffy, luxurious blanket around his shoulders.

"They're from clawing at ice, huh? I have the same, look, my skin split from strain!" He shows him his palm and the back of his hand.

"Do you have eczema?"

"I do now," the dissident laughs. "I'm lucky I still have all ten toes. Oh wait a second, do you? Need a warm bucket of water?"

The prisoner opens his mouth, but before he can answer, the dissident kneels and inspects his feet.

"Oh man."

The prisoner curls away from him, once again, irrationally self-conscious.

"These are some bad blisters. And that's some ugly chafing, did you know you were bleeding?"

"I had…more pressing concerns."

"Hm. Well. This seems infected, so-"

"I'll handle them."

"You can hardly walk, don't be stupid-"

"I said I'll handle it," the prisoner says sharply.

The dissident looks taken aback.

"Um…ok."

The prisoner pulls his legs up underneath him, hiding his swollen feet from him.

"Well… I'll at the very least make dinner, if you have no objections?"

The prisoner shakes his head.

"Great! This guy's microwave is state of the art. I wonder if he's middle class or upper class."

"This doesn't seem upper class," the prisoner murmurs.

The dissident squints, looking very carefully around the cabin.

"You're right," he says. "Upper class houses might be rustic, but they're high-tech. They'd definitely have some kind of alarm system in place. Plus I checked the bed. It's a regular bed, not a water bed or a hover bed or a massager. It's just a bed. That screams either middle class or upper class weirdo that likes to rough it. But then I saw there were no TVs or moving screens or voice-automated interface systems. Which definitely confirms middle class. It's very twentieth or twenty first century rustic. I kind of like it. At the very least, it's good for us, since this guy will have a harder time detecting us."

The prisoner gives him a look.

"You cleaned my blood off the floor?" the prisoner asks lightly.

"Yup. That seemed like the most suspicious thing. It had to go," the dissident says promptly.

The prisoner makes a sound.

The dissident blinks.

He makes it again.

"Was that…"

He playfully pokes his shoulder, but his teasing scrutiny is unnecessary.

The prisoner looks directly at him, making no attempt at all to hide the fact that he's laughing.

He's grinning broadly like someone who's not in pain, who's not hysterical, who's not on the brink of crying. Someone who's smiling because there's something to smile about. He's making funny little gurgling noises, choking sounds, as though good humor is literally taking his breath away.

If he couldn't see the smile on the prisoner's face, he might've mistaken the sounds for sobbing. For sorrow.

But the dissident's smiling back and then he's laughing back.

It wasn't even meant to be a joke, but he laughs anyway.

"First sign of something wrong: door lock broken. Second: lights on. Third: pools of blood in the kitchen."

The prisoner's shaking, his entire body wracked with giggles. His laughter is infectious. The dissident's chest is filled with a balloon-like relief, which continues to swell until it feels like it'll burst. They laugh.

And continue laughing until the balloon finally loses air and sags, limp and content, to the bottom of his stomach. The prisoner is out of breath, still letting out hard gusts of air, almost like he's hyperventilating. For an alarming moment, the dissident thinks he might be, but when he approaches him worriedly, the prisoner waves him off, his face red, but not pained.

"I'm-I'm going to go heat up some food," the dissident says, happiness still coloring his voice.

The prisoner nods. But the dissident just stares at him stupidly, awkwardly, for a few minutes, unable to stop himself.

He's alive.

And not just alive as in breathing, heart beating, lungs pumping air into his system, but laughing. Alive in the most meaningful sense.

He can't help but feel accomplished.

Giddy, really.

He's so ecstatic that he actually forgets for a split second that this is the man who'd strangled him in his sleep and begged for him to just let him die.

That this is the man from beyond the border, from another continent, his enemy, and an enemy to his way of life.

For a split second, it ceases to matter.

42

"No."

The dissident scowls.

"Did you just say no to me?"

"Yes."

The dissident feels a flicker of both irritation and pride.

"Well... you don't have a choice."

The prisoner opens his mouth to protest, but only coughs weakly as the dissident scoops him up in his arms bridal style and begins to walk up the stairs.

"Stop!" the prisoner growls.

"It's not a big deal, just take the bed," the dissident says. "Hey, stop struggling, this isn't safe!"

"I don't want it!"

"I'm serious, I could drop you!"

The prisoner wriggles, trying to free himself, but the dissident holds tight, merely pulling him closer and bending his knees to accommodate for his bizarre bodily contortions.

"I-don't-want-to-sleep-there," the prisoner forces out.

"Why not?" the dissident grunts. "It's more comfortable!"

He growls out a garbled, incomprehensible threat as the prisoner's elbow hits him in the stomach.

But he still doesn't let go.

"I...don't want... to be up there!" the prisoner insists.

Still fighting.

But they're both exhausted, so at some point, the dissident sinks to the ground, the prisoner in his arms, then his lap as they cease their efforts almost simultaneously.

He expects the prisoner to squirm out of his grip, to get as far from him as possible, but the man seems tired.

All of the fight seems to have gone out of him, his head lolling back and hitting his chest as he pants.

"What is the problem?" the dissident sighs. "Just tell me. What are you afraid of? Embarrassing yourself? We're passed that now. Besides, I got the impression when I first, er, *met* you, that you really didn't care what I thought."

"We're passed *that* now," the prisoner says, exhaling slowly through his teeth.

The dissident raises an eyebrow.

"Ok. Alright."

Since the prisoner doesn't seem to be uncomfortable, he decides not to budge, only shifting slightly to put the prisoner in a less bent position on his lap.

"I don't want to be upstairs," the prisoner says after some time, his matted, messy hair tickling his nose slightly as he moves his head.

The dissident doesn't know it, but the sound of his heartbeat, sure and strong within his chest, like the beating of the Empire's drums, had given the prisoner the desire to explain himself.

"The…the fireplace is down here. I…"

And suddenly it comes to the dissident.

All those nights he curled up next to the fire, wanting to be as close to it as possible, even though his night terrors might toss him right into it, how stupid it seemed, how odd.

"Are you scared of the dark?"

Now the prisoner jerks out of his hands.

Since he caught the dissident by surprise, he can do nothing as the prisoner scrambles out of his hands and sits promptly on the couch.

"No," he says stiffly. "I just…prefer to sleep on the ground floor. I'm cold."

"And you want me to start a fire?" the dissident asks skeptically.

"If you could. Please."

"Well because you asked so nicely," the dissident says, rubbing where the prisoner had hit him in his struggle to get away. "Sure. You're cold and just like sleeping on the ground floor, ok."

He goes rummaging through drawers, knowing that he'd seen a matchbox in one of them when he'd first arrived.

The prisoner shuffles behind him, gathering blankets.

When he turns back, the prisoner's almost completely cocooned himself within what must be at least four blankets.

The dissident stifles a laugh, since he gets the feeling this time the prisoner might not share in his humor.

There's a single log in the pit, but judging by the pile of logs in the corner, they have enough to spare, at least for now.

"Well alright. I'll sleep upstairs. Call me if you need me, ok? Or even if you just want something," the dissident murmurs as he gets a fire going in the fireplace. Once that's finished, he turns back and gives the prisoner a sharp look. "Ok?"

"Ok," the prisoner murmurs in response.

But one look at his face and the dissident gets the feeling he wouldn't call for help even if a bear was eating him alive.

"Oh, man…" the dissident sighs.

The prisoner's eyes narrow as he glares at him, daring him to continue speaking.

But how can the dissident be intimidated or cowed by a man wrapped head to toe in blankets glowering at him like an angry kitten?

He stifles another laugh.

"I thought we were passed this," the dissident says, voice mock-tragic.

The prisoner finally turns his back to him, but the image of him glaring is too much for the dissident to bear now.

He bids him goodnight, trots up the stairs, darts into what is now his room, slams the door shut, puts his hand over his mouth, and laughs harder than he'd laughed before.

43

The prisoner scares the living daylights out of the dissident when he rolls off the couch late at night and slams his hand through the glass table.

In hindsight, the dissident realizes he's an idiot for not realizing how hazardous a table with a glass top would be to a sleep-walker/thrasher.

As he's picking glass out of the prisoner's knuckles, his patient wincing, he begins to mentally calculate all of the potential dangers in the room. Oil lantern, could cause a fire, logs in the corner, could trip and hurt himself, get a splinter, fire poker, could impale himself somehow-

"I'm sorry," the prisoner says as the dissident begins to wrap his hand in tight bandages. He presses lightly on his fingers, his knuckles, his palm, making sure the tape is sticking, and inexplicably runs his fingers briefly down his wrist.

The prisoner doesn't seem to notice, or care, as he slowly pulls his hand back to his chest, nursing it with the other hand, running his own fingers along his wrist contemplatively.

The dissident looks away hastily, not sure why he'd done that, but quite glad the prisoner hadn't noticed.

That wrist had been dislocated when he'd found him.

It's still marked with scars, carefully arranged as though by a skilled hand and a precision instrument.

The dissident scratches his head tiredly.

At first he insists on having the prisoner sleep upstairs with him, but the prisoner refuses.

Then he insists on sleeping downstairs with him…in the chair.

But after sitting in it once, he brings a mattress down and makes a nest of blankets and pillows next to the fireplace.

Now he sits on this mattress as he watches the prisoner unconsciously rub the scars of his wrist, looking distant.

He seems reluctant to speak.

That brief moment of levity seems like a trick of the light, a glimmer of sunlight in the eye of a storm.

He had never talked much, but now he doesn't even make eye contact or any attempt to communicate with him.

It's very unsettling and rather disappointing.

"Um…"

The prisoner doesn't look up, but his head tilts to indicate he's listening.

"Are you sure you don't want to sleep upstairs with me? It's a lot less dangerous-"

"There's nothing to fall on now," the prisoner interrupts him, glancing at the table, which the dissident had pushed far away from the couch.

The dissident frowns.

"The floor."

"It won't kill me."

"It'll hurt. You can't keep falling, you'll just hurt yourself more."

The prisoner's face is in his arms.

The dissident huffs.

"You know, you're filthy."

The prisoner looks up with an almost affronted look on his face.

"I am too," the dissident says hastily. "Why don't you take a shower? The water should be nice and hot."

"..."

"You can go first."

The prisoner looks like he wants to say something, but he doesn't. He merely nods tightly.

The dissident isn't so easily fooled, however.

He has a vague feeling, a nagging suspicion that he confirms when he walks back into the living room a few minutes later to find the prisoner on the floor, on his side, his back bent in pain.

"You idiot," the dissident growls. "If you need help, can you please just admit it and stop making this so damn hard? First you can't admit you need a fire to be lit, then you can't admit your sleep thrashing is really harmful, and now you can't even tell me you don't feel able to stand. I mean, what the hell, are you a masochist? Or can you really just not accept help? How did they drill that into you? How can I pull it back out?"

The prisoner shoves his probing hands away from him, his body shaking as he forces himself upright.

"Don't touch me," he hisses.

The dissident, angry and exasperated, obeys his demand, but stays close, watching him with frustration.

"I'm not going to hurt you. I'm not going to *humiliate* you. I just want to help you-"

"No, you don't," the prisoner says through gritted teeth, on his knees, his back heaving. The dissident stares at it for a moment, remembering the scars there, the bandages he'd wrapped. "No. You don't. You're just like him, you're just like Teacher, you're the same, the two of you, from the same place, from the same womb, full of the same blood. You just want to make me like you before you kill me, you just want to-to change me from what I was, you want to cut *it* out of me, but it's what I am, it makes me who I am, I'm not like you, I'm not, don't touch me anymore, I don't want to be touched by-by *you people.*"

The dissident recoils.

You people.

What an ugly-sounding phrase.

The prisoner grips the cushions of the couch in his hands.

"You've done this to me," he whispers so low the dissident almost can't hear him. "The things he made me feel...I hated them, I hated him, I hated being alive for his amusement, and now I'm alive for yours-"

"That's not true," the dissident can't help but shout.

"Why else would you stay? Why else wouldn't you move on?" the prisoner says frantically. "Why else would you be here? Why else would you...ask me questions about-about how I'm doing or how you can make me comfortable or-or anything? Why else would you-would you give me...offer me anything I want?"

"Because-"

"Because you're just a different kind of Teacher," the prisoner whispers. "You just want something *else*. Just like the rest of the Republic. The Empire used me, but it never lied. I wanted to be used. I wanted to be useful. I wanted to…serve. And be immortal…and perfect. Just as the Empire is. But you've broken me, just like him. He made my body useless and you've made my-my mind useless. Your-your goal all along was-was -"

His eyes roll back.

His head falls limply onto the couch, his entire body sagging lifelessly as he loses consciousness.

The dissident catches him as he falls back, laying him down gently on the rug.

He's sweating and trembling and radiating a familiar heat.

"Oh hell," the dissident whispers to him.

44

"Can you recite your times tables?" Teacher asks sweetly.

He bows his head, feeling scared and ashamed.

There are eyes on him.

So many eyes.

All watching him.

He wishes he were wearing clothing.

"Pity. You're not unintelligent," Teacher sighs.

He quakes, wishing he could sit down.

Or leave.

Anything but the unbearable feeling of being different, distant from the rest, apart from their easy, comfortable sameness. They all look at him from separate eyes, yet appear to him as one.

He longs to be one of them, but something marks him as different and he's afraid that whatever it is will never leave him.

"Don't be afraid of that difference," Teacher says kindly. "We'll fix you."

He nods, feeling tears welling up in his eyes.

Tears?

"That's not who you are."

A different teacher, but the same Teacher.

The classroom is not his old classroom, but the facility.

White walls.

Windowless underground room full of innocent, immaculate instruments of torture, the scalpel, the pliers, the dreaded clamp.

"You don't cry. You don't feel things like that, and you never have. You've changed since I last saw you. What changed, my dear boy? Who's been speaking to you?" Teacher snaps his gloves against his skin.

He shakes his head.

"Still not talkative, huh? That's alright. Even *we* aren't so talkative all the time. The lesson here is that you're learning to be more like us. That's a good thing, you'll find. Or perhaps not."

He closes his eyes, but the room remains.

"Would you betray us more?"

His stomach clenches.

He feels like he could vomit.

But he still turns in his seat, his six year old body sweaty and nervous.

His mother stares down at him, a blurry, shadowy, barely distinguishable mess of colors.

The distortion seems to frown at him.

"I'm sorry."

"What are you doing? Why haven't you died yet? Your last duty to the motherland was to die. You could not perform?" the distortion asks.

"I'm sorry."

"Such a disappointment," she sighs. "If you'd simply become a teacher, I could've at least forgotten about you. But here I am."

She's jabbing at a holo-interface, her hands trembling with anger as she rearranges flight plans, pulling up little arrows representing planes and moving them around a tactical map.

"What are you doing now? Helping them?"

"No," he rasps.

"Becoming one of them?"

"No, no-" he wants to explain, but finds he can't.

"This man is one of them," she says sharply, waving her hand.

Pulling up a familiar face.

"Y-yes-"

"You went to him. Waited. *Slept* with him," she says disdainfully.

"I…I wasn't ordered to-to kill anyone-"

"Irrelevant," she snaps. "You already disobeyed orders. You've failed three times now. You were meant to die as a distraction, as a ploy to draw their forces away, but you were captured. You were meant to die at their hands, but you were re-captured. You should've died in your new captor's hands, but instead you-"

"I couldn't stop him," he protests, fear making every word come out slurred and distraught. "I-It wasn't my decision-"

"Irrelevant," she snaps again.

He's sitting in the barracks.

The man with ink on his hands pauses.

"You do not make decisions," he sighs.

He sounds suspiciously like Teacher.

"That is the privilege only of the Empire. It's a blessing, isn't it? Who wants to make decisions? People who want to take responsibility for their actions. Or people who refuse to take responsibility for their actions. Do you truly want to be one of them?"

Cluster base.

His Cluster.

The sickly boy with marks on his wrists sits beside him on the bench today.

The others have been moved out.

It is just the two of them.

"They would drown me," the boy says solemnly. "I'm not wanted. Here, I'm wanted. I'm needed."

"I know."

"Doesn't it sicken you? The thought of drowning children because their parents don't want them, not at that time? Taking care of offspring only when it's convenient?" the sickly boy coughs. "Do you hate me? Have they taught you to hate me?"

"No!" he gasps.

His skin's on fire, he's burning alive, no, no, he's underwater, he's boiling alive, his skin is bubbling.

He thrashes, his lungs full of burning liquid.

Teacher taps on the glass window of his plane.

Somehow, he can still hear him clearly through the water and the screaming in his own head, coming out of his mouth in desperate bubbles.

"You chose not to die out there. To keep walking. To find that place. To find him. You are no longer one of us, one *with* us. What a shame. But that's the worst part of making decisions, my boy. Sometimes you make the *wrong* one."

The box.

He has to get out of the box.

He would rather bleed out on a lab table with his organs held aloft before his eyes than stay another second in this empty, suffocating darkness.

"You'll never be one of us ever again," the sickly boy says, black ink dripping from his hands like blood. "And you'll never be one of them. That is the decision you've made. Goodbye."

No, no, no, please-

Everything is spinning, lurching, catapulting from side to side until he feels so nauseous he could throw up.

Something beats against the inside of his skull.

It feels like the dissident, sticks in hand, gleefully dragging his weapons along his brain, hitting anything he can reach with childish delight, making as much sadistic noise as possible.

There are other pains, other aches, but this is the worst, this earsplitting racket, this cacophonous hellish beat.

Tears are streaming down his cheeks, and just knowing that he's crying seals his fate.

He knows he is doomed, and just like that, he finally succumbs.

He returns to the hollow, vacuous blackness.

45

The dissident is glad the prisoner's too delirious to understand anything he's seeing, because he doesn't want to explain why he's crying.

The prisoner, who's probably never cried in his whole sad life, wouldn't understand that he's crying out of frustration and exhaustion, not sadness.

The prisoner's been wracked with a fever for three days now, almost constantly thrashing and shouting out in delirium.

The dissident's been awake with him, putting cool rags on his head, forcing water down his struggling throat, forcing him not to move around and hurt himself.

He's exhausted, deep bags around his eyes, sweat constantly on his brow, his hands twitchy from lack of sleep, but he keeps at it.

Although he's completely drained, he's more afraid of the moments when the prisoner is calm, his body motionless, than the moments when he's fitful, tossing and turning like he's being jabbed with a cattle prod. At least when he's moving, he's showing signs of life. There are times when he doesn't budge an inch and the dissident has to use a handheld mirror to make sure he's still breathing.

That split second where it seems like there won't be a little cloud of breath on the mirror is always terrifying.

Then when it comes, he's inevitably left with the frightening possibility of the moment when it *doesn't* come.

After all this time, after all this work, this *effort,* planning on getting to the facility, getting into the facility, and getting him *out* of the facility, he can't go home empty-handed.

He just can't.

The prisoner hadn't even been his objective to begin with.

The fact that he failed to complete his original mission could only be offset by a different conquest, by a retrieval of equal value.

If the prisoner dies, he'll have nothing.

So the dissident, his arms and face clawed to hell after a particularly fierce fever dream, stays vigilant.

Even though the prisoner is weak and scrawny, he stills packs a nasty hit.

The dissident isn't surprised though.

He can't be, not anymore, not after everything he's seen the prisoner survive.

He takes every blow without complaint and keeps giving him water. Trying to cool him down. Trying to feed him. Making sure he doesn't hurt himself during one of his nightmare-fueled convulsions late at night.

As the prisoner's fever begins to abate, slowly but surely, and he starts sleeping longer, and less fitfully, the dissident's fears abate with it.

No, the prisoner will not die.

Not to this.

And when it finally breaks, when he's sleeping soundly, his head no longer feeling like a furnace, he can't help but silently scream out in victory and pump his fist.

When the prisoner wakes up, his eyes finally clear and not clouded with fear and a delirious, zealous light, finally able to properly see the world around him, the dissident is asleep at his side, too tired to stay awake any longer.

The prisoner looks down on him with morose, worn-out eyes.

Even though he's just woken up, his headache gone, the invasive, tingling, frenzied heat finally gone, and his temperature back to normal, he still feels more tired than he's ever been in his life.

He thinks briefly about getting something to eat and then he's out like a light again, falling back onto the carpet, the dissident snoring beside him, the two of them next to the empty, fireless fireplace.

The prisoner has no nightmares that night, or at least, not any he can remember.

46

"Get off of me, get off of me, you're killing me, you're killing me!"

"I didn't want this! I wanted to die, I wanted to die, why would you take that from me, get away from me, get away-"

"Who are you, who are you, I don't know you, I don't-"

"Just kill me like you killed your family! Kill me like you killed your sister."

The dissident bangs his head on the underside of the couch.

"Son of a-" he groans as he gingerly moves his head away from it, his mouth tasting foul.

He looks over and sees the prisoner is sitting on the hearth, head in his hands.

"You're killing me."

His words echo in the dissident's head.

Even though the prisoner had said them while not in his right mind, the dissident can't help but wonder if he really means everything he said, deep down, perhaps unconsciously.

He knows, after all, that even in the beginning, when the prisoner had most definitely wanted to be put out of his misery, his body would always resist its mind's beliefs, no matter what.

Maybe his resilience and the fact that he made it to the lake, that he didn't just allow himself to sit in the snow until he froze to death, was just a biological impulse, and not a choice at all.

More importantly, the dissident thinks with startling clarity.

Why does it matter so much to him that the prisoner want to live?

"Hey," the dissident says automatically.

The prisoner doesn't look up or move in any way.

"I'm glad you're feeling better," he continues. "I imagine you're hungry-"

"I ate."

"Oh. Good."

The dissident scratches his head awkwardly.

"Well...I haven't, so... I'll go...do that."

The prisoner still doesn't move as he gets up.

The day is charged with uncomfortable silence and a peculiar, unidentifiable tension emanating from both men.

The prisoner doesn't seem to want to talk about it, and the dissident doesn't know how to talk about it.

Instead, he just aims a polite, quick smile at the prisoner, jabs his head in an approximation of a friendly nod whenever he passes, and then continues on with his business.

But he remembers something he needs to do.

"Uh…"

The prisoner, who'd merely shifted from the hearth to the couch, looks up now.

His reddened eyes, as rimmed with bags and weariness as the dissident imagines his own eyes are, blink sluggishly at him.

"You need to…bathe. Or shower," the dissident says. "I…can help you-"

"No-" the prisoner starts to say something else, but the dissident cuts him off.

"You just got over a fever, and just before that, you exacerbated wounds you already had by staggering through miles of snow. Your bandages need to be changed. Also, the bathtub slash shower is upstairs, and I don't want you trying to tackle stairs out of some misplaced sense of pride. We're over this, I'm officially calling it, ok? We've…We've seen each other at our worst-"

"You've seen *me* at my worst," the prisoner interrupts mulishly. "I am your captive. There is a power imbalance here, don't try to deny it."

The dissident blinks, stunned by both the keenness in his voice and the truth of his statements.

"You're right," he says, chuckling a little. "But…I'm just…trying to help."

He knows immediately what the prisoner is thinking as soon as he says it.

Trying to help yourself. Not me.

But the prisoner seems to know he's thinking it too, so he doesn't bother saying it aloud.

Instead he merely sighs and leans back.

The dissident takes this as permission.

He bends over and puts one hand on his back, and another under his legs.

With one tremendous effort, he pulls the prisoner into his arms, bridal style again. He's always surprised by how light he is, how he's just short enough to fit mostly comfortably in his arms, on his back. It's a good thing, really, because if he'd been too tall, it might've made the journey even worse.

The prisoner doesn't move or struggle, but he's as stiff as a brick, his body radiating tension.

"I'm not going to drop you," the dissident says.

"That's not what I'm-" the prisoner shuts his mouth abruptly, cutting off whatever he'd been about to say mid-sentence.

"You've gained some weight, but it's nothing I can't handle," the dissident says jovially. Then, a moment later, "Did you roll your eyes?"

The prisoner doesn't respond, but he's much more relaxed now, gripping his neck a little less tightly.

The dissident grins as he begins climbing the stairs.

As he reaches the top, however, the man begins to squirm.

"I can stand."

"I'm sure you can, but I need to check your injuries, and I don't think they're ready for running water yet-" the dissident frowns. "Open the door, would you?"

The prisoner reaches for it and pushes the handle down.

The dissident pushes the door open.

He brushes passed the sink and turns sideways, carefully putting the prisoner on the toilet.

"Now," the dissident says sternly, pulling off his shirt to take a look at his bandages. "Oh Jesus…"

"This was you, not me," the prisoner says.

"You were thrashing around a lot! Opening up old wounds and making it hard to wrap you back up properly," the dissident winces as he peels off the rather loose, clumsily wrapped bandages. "Ah crap, you bled through them quicker because I couldn't wrap them tightly enough..."

He quickly checks on the prisoner's progress as he slowly peels off some of the soiled wrapping.

If they hadn't constantly been on the move, his wounds would've definitely healed by now, the dissident thinks as he surveys their progress. For the most part, none of them are fatal anymore, not unless they're infected, but thankfully none of them seem to be. He's probably in some pain, but that was to be expected, since he had crossed a great distance without much or any rest, and had not eaten anything the whole time. His fever had also aggravated some of his injuries, since he'd been moving quite a bit, and there was of course his hand, which he'd broken on the table...

"You know, you're a real glutton for punishment..." the dissident murmurs.

"Why are you so obsessed with bathing?" the prisoner asks unexpectedly. He doesn't sound angry or defiant, but he does seem a little frustrated. "It's just you and me. Can't you...put up with odor until I heal properly?"

The dissident feels guilty for a split second, but he isn't sure why.

"Do you not bathe in the Empire?"

The prisoner blinks.

"We do."

"So why are you so-?"

"You forced me to get into a cold stream to wash myself even though I was very, very hurt. It wasn't necessary."

Although his words are accusing, his tone is rather mild.

It eases some of the dissident's discomfort.

A discomfort he doesn't understand, which seems to correlate with his brief flash of guilt.

"You smelled."

"I could've gotten infected from that water."

"But you didn't."

"It was too cold. I could've gotten hypothermia."

"You weren't in there that long. Besides, it's much colder where you're from."

"I didn't need to shower."

"It didn't do any harm."

"And I don't need to shower *now*," the prisoner says persistently. "I can't even stand on my feet, or use my hand."

"I'll help you."

"Why are you so...intent on having me bathe?"

"Why are you so resistant? I would think you'd want to be clean. Do you not want to be clean?" the dissident asks, a little defensive now.

"I can't stand on my own," the prisoner says slowly. "I can't bathe or shower, I'll probably just start bleeding. I can't move my right hand or fingers very much. The abrasions on my body are not fully healed. And they were in far worse condition when you first made me wash. Why are you so adamant on this?"

"You...you smelled like...like piss, ok? It was stinking up the caves. I could smell you from three feet away. And-and now you're leaving...stains and things. On the furniture. You're-you're leaving evidence-"

95

"Maybe those are some of the reasons. But certainly not the main reasons," the prisoner interrupts. "Tell me why you need me to bathe."

The dissident doesn't have to.

Pettily, childishly, he thinks that the prisoner doesn't have a choice.

He might've been able to walk on his own before his little solitary trek, but he can't now, not properly. It would be easy just dumping him in the tub and washing the prisoner with or without his consent.

But he doesn't really want to do that.

They should be passed that.

And they should be passed him using his commanding voice to force the prisoner into instinctively obeying his "orders."

"I just haven't showered in ages. I feel disgusting, ok? I haven't showered since I first headed out here. *I* really want to shower, but I also really want *you* to because… sweat and-and human odor is just wrong. It's disgusting. It's vile."

The prisoner lets out a huff of confusion.

"That's just how the human body works-"

"I only made you do it once! Twice now, I guess," the dissident exclaims, trying to derail him before he can go down that path.

"But-"

"It bothers the hell out of me. Your body was-ok, it was gross, but that wasn't your fault. I could handle it being ugly and bruised. Underneath that, I could see that when you healed, it would be acceptable. Healthy, whole, functional. You'll always walk like-like *that*, I guess, and your back is ruined forever, as is most of your body, but for the most part, you're just a normal human being. But you stunk. You stunk so badly, I couldn't even look your way without being revolted. And right now…it bothers me. I can't stand the smell. I just can't."

The prisoner, confused by his tirade, looks at his bowed head, just as matted and ruffled as his.

"And you don't know why."

"I…I hate being grimy and unclean, and I hate when others are grimy and unclean. But what does it matter? You didn't end up worse for the wear after your first bath. I didn't make you do it again. I just…want you to do it now. Please. I'll help you. I won't look, I swear, just…let me help you. I'll give you a sponge bath, you can be clean without opening any wounds."

He tries an encouraging smile, but the prisoner still looks perturbed.

But he doesn't push the matter.

He just closes his eyes, looking ten years older, the scars on his back twisted and harsh in the daylight.

"Slowly."

The dissident lets out a sigh of relief.

"Thank you."

47

"Do you know how periods work?"

The dissident nearly spits out his drink.

"Periods? Periods of what?" he laughs nervously.

"Menstruation. When a female's uterine lining passes through-"

"Stop!" the dissident gags. "I will throw up."

The prisoner, testing a theory, nods in confirmation.

"But you know about sex."

"Of course I know about-about that."

"Say it."

"What?"

"Say the word I just said."

"Oh, don't be such a little kid," the dissident scoffs.

He turns the dial on the stove up a little.

Now that he actually has a pantry and real cooking utensils at his disposal, he's remembering how much he enjoys cooking.

And the prisoner, sitting in the living room, seems to enjoy watching him do it.

Well.

He's not sure if he actually enjoys it.

The man watches him clean, search for supplies, and cook, but doesn't *seem* to prefer one activity over the other.

His face is always blank and he never talks.

Which is why it's such a surprise to hear him talk now, after days without a peep.

And about periods and sex, of all things.

He would never have guessed it.

"Do you know how birth control works?" the prisoner asks.

"Birth control? What is that, promising not to…to do it for a month?" the dissident asks. Flinching just a little as oil in his pan sizzles.

The prisoner doesn't say anything for a while, forcing the dissident to look up.

He's staring right at him, looking disbelieving.

"What?" the dissident asks, self-conscious.

"If I asked you what the female reproductive organ was called and what role the fallopian tubes play in the development of a human fetus, would you be able to ans-"

The dissident turns quickly, looking scandalized.

"What's gotten into you? Do you have a fever again? One second you're as quiet as a library, the next you're babbling about sexual deviance, jeez, did you hit your head while you were walking here?"

"Curious," the prisoner says.

"What?"

"They told us you were sexually active and had many children. But you don't know the biological facts of reproduction?"

The dissident, grimacing, looks back at his pan.

"Can we please stop talking about this?"

"Does it bother you?"

"Well, we're about to eat…"

"Are you a virgin?"

"Ok that's it!" the dissident exclaims. "Not another word out of you or else I'll make you shower again."

The prisoner's eyes narrow, but he puts his head down and acquiesces to his demand.

He thinks he's beginning to understand.

He'd been thinking about it ever since his second forced bath with the dissident, a less physically uncomfortable, but more mentally uncomfortable one.

They loved sex. Love. Copulation. Whatever they chose to call it.

But not reproduction.

They loved the human body, loved to see it, touch it, taste it, but loathed to come in contact with it (paradoxical as that may seem).

The dirty, the unclean, veins, lumpy flesh, unshapely limbs, blood, sweat, vomit, organs, biological waste, excrements, the simple facts of organic processing…these things were detestable in every way to them.

The prisoner thinks about their journey and feels a spark of gratitude.

Given the man's distaste for body odor and bodily imperfection, he's lucky he wasn't left behind.

Lucky?

The prisoner pushes the feelings of disbelief and indignation away.

He's getting better at ignoring the little voice that calls him a traitor for being alive.

He has no need for it at the moment. Has decided to pay it no mind until he knows where to go from here.

But he still needs a distraction from time to time, and the dissident's curious beliefs and behaviors are all he has right now.

Despite the dissident's warning, he can't help but press the subject again, this time after dinner.

The dissident is seated in the chair and he is on the couch.

The dissident had just gotten a fire going and was prepared to fall asleep watching it, but the prisoner, completely out of the blue, questions him.

"Are women allowed to have sex outside of marriage?"

The dissident's shoulders immediately tense, but he does answer.

"Yes, of course, why not? We're not like you people, we don't believe in controlling people's sex lives."

"But she may become pregnant."

"As long as she doesn't keep the baby, it's fine."

The prisoner sniffs.

"What?"

"Nothing."

"Well what about you?" the dissident asks defensively, looking peeved. He crosses his legs, trying to get more comfortable in the chair. "Your people seem like they talk an awful lot about sex for people who don't have it."

"It's a biological process. Nothing more," the prisoner responds. "We're taught about it before we hit puberty and engage in dangerous activity."

"Dangerous? When is sex dangerous?" the dissident snorts.

"You wouldn't know, would you?" the prisoner says smoothly.

For a brief second, he feels a terrible fear clench his heart.

Had he overstepped?

Should he not have said that?

It's very…sharp.

Unappreciative.

The dissident might get mad.

He has no right to anger him or argue with him or accuse him or his people of anything.

The prisoner keeps his head down.

But after a while, he can't resist looking up again.

The dissident is grinning, shaking with silent laughter.

"You're developing quite a bite, kid," the dissident chuckles. "I like it."

The prisoner feels an unpleasant jolt in his stomach.

He doesn't like when the dissident acts unexpectedly.

And he especially doesn't like how he can go from angry and defensive one moment to appreciative and impressed the next.

It reminds him of Teacher, cruel and impatient as he's digging into his hand, but patronizing and sickeningly sweet the minute after, patching it up like a kind old doctor.

It's so upsetting that he turns away from the dissident, curls up, and closes his eyes.

48

"You don't like being naked, is that it?" the dissident asks.

The prisoner shifts uncomfortably.

"Why would I enjoy being cold and exposed for no reason?"

"Ok, your reason is that you're showering," the dissident says. "And if you're showering, it's not cold. It's warm."

"The showers were never warm in the military barracks," the prisoner protests.

"Ok, fine, but you don't have a problem being naked when you're showering, right?" the dissident presses.

The prisoner grimaces.

"No."

"But you don't like being naked when I'm in the room, even if you're showering?" The dissident eyeballs him from across the basement.

The prisoner, sitting on the stairs, touches his neck, thumb subconsciously rubbing the spot where the chip had been inserted.

"No."

"Did you never shower together in the military?"

"Of course we did. It made economic sense."

"So why does it make you uncomfortable having me bathe you? It's...practical, you can't bathe yourself, but when you can, I'll stop. Why so upset at being naked in front of me? Just think of me as...a member of your unit," the dissident says. Cursing as he accidentally knocks over a box of batteries in his haste to get to the other side of the room.

"...it's different with you," the prisoner murmurs.

"How?"

"It just is," he responds.

"Well...I can't think of any reason why other than...well." The dissident looks rather flustered. "But that's not...that's not the reason, right?"

The prisoner's eyebrows furrow. "What reason?"

The dissident is almost glowing, his face is so red.

"Uh. Nothing. Never mind."

But the prisoner doesn't talk again.

So, because it's gnawing away at him inside, preying on his conscience, he has to ask: "Were you...uncomfortable when I undressed you to patch up your injuries?"

"Of course not," the prisoner says. 'That was different."

He says it so calmly, so certainly, and yet the dissident can sense hesitation radiating off of him in waves, waves which only increase in intensity when he plops down beside him on the stairs, a lamp in hand.

"How?"

"...I knew you were looking at me like...a doctor. Or a surgeon."

"But why is it any different now? I'm still only looking at you like that, I promise." The dissident puts the lamp down next to his right foot and claps his hands together, rubbing them vigorously. He doesn't seem to notice or care when the prisoner edges away from him.

"I didn't care what you were doing. I didn't care how you viewed me. Enemy or not, whatever you chose to do to me did not matter."

"But now? Now it matters?" the dissident asks, not sure if he's upset or happy to hear this.

"Now…" The prisoner hesitates. There's conflict in his eye, something tortured, maybe even fearful. "It…does."

"I'm still the enemy?"

"You always will be," the prisoner whispers. "But now…I don't know what to make of you."

The dissident shifts, rocking a little as he contemplates his hands.

"I'm not sure what to make of you either," he says thoughtfully back.

49

"I used to have nightmares about the ocean."

The prisoner, finally able to move away from sponge baths, is lying in somewhat lukewarm water.

The dissident leans against the tub, facing respectfully away from him.

"Why?"

"...oceans are neutral zones," the dissident murmurs. "You're free game if you cross them. I've always preferred being home. Where I know what to expect."

"And where you're welcome." The prisoner closes his eyes. His neck is beginning to hurt from leaning against the tub, but his body aches too much for him to consider changing positions.

"That too." The dissident tilts his head. "Hey...is it true the thermal borders can detect foreign chips from up to three miles away?"

"No. They have to be within a kilometer," the prisoner replies. "Planes they can sense much sooner, though, within three kilometers. As they approach, the aerial mines are tripped and detonated or the system alerts the operators and they send out their own patrol battalion to meet them."

"Doesn't your country use aerial mines?" the dissident asks interestedly.

"We mostly use pilots. It's mostly your continent and the southeastern continent that employ mines and naval detonators."

"Huh....don't they use aerial mines to the south of your continent?"

"No. They use laser-guided missiles. A little archaic, low tech, but efficient. The moment a ship or plane approaches, their own Border system detects its passage and they manually direct missiles towards the coordinates. Low tech or not, they're fairly deadly." The prisoner holds his hand out of the water, watching droplets roll down his wrist. "I attempted to cross that border once."

"Really? What happened?"

"Got shot down, had to eject. They would've blown me out of the water or taken me prisoner if a second fleet hadn't been right behind ours."

"Wow. They picked you up?"

"I swam back to our border. They detected my chip and picked me up eventually. If the second fleet hadn't come and distracted them, I would've been shot or I would've drowned."

"See, that sounds scary. Open ocean. I mean, I've never seen it, but...we have books on it..." The dissident rocks against the tub, as fidgety as a small child.

"Outdated, I'm sure."

"Well, yeah. We're landlocked, our Border is right on the coast. It's not far from the shoreline. We have enough territory to fish, and that's about it."

"You don't trade, correct?"

"No, trade is bad. People are always trying to trick you or scam you out of your money and resources," the dissident says this automatically, as if by reflex more than anything else. He pauses, though, and the prisoner gets the impression that he's actually thinking about what he just said and is confused by it.

"Well...I imagine this country needs resources," the prisoner says.

"Yes. Yes. It does," the dissident agrees slowly, sounding far away.

"Will you war with your southern continent?" the prisoner asks.

"...they don't want to. Our government, I mean. They want to stay isolated. They think we can support ourselves completely autonomously for...well, I guess forever. We are independent, they say. We don't need anyone's assistance, we are strong. We reject help offered to us and offer none."

"But you disagree."

"...I do."

"Is that what your resistance believes in?" the prisoner asks.

He has never heard of this resistance.

But that's not surprising.

If his government had been in contact with them, then it would be limited to the ears of the higher-ups, not even Captains or Admirals, but the General and his inner circle of politicians.

"...we...believe things cannot continue as they are now," the dissident says after a long pause.

And he says nothing else, merely draining the tub, helping him stand, and wrapping a towel around him.

He rubs his hair down with another towel, helps him limp his way downstairs, and begins singing a bizarre, wordless song as he prepares their dinner.

But the prisoner gets the feeling that he's shaken him with his question.

And he doesn't know how to feel about it.

Nor does he know how to feel about this newfound intuition.

He'd never had it back home, nor had it ever felt like he needed it. People simply stated their feelings. Or opinions. They said what they thought and you agreed or disagreed, but either chose to politely agree or say nothing at all.

The dissident, rambunctious and demonstrative, expressive and tactile, scares and intrigues him.

The motions he makes with his hands, the slight twitches of his face, the way he rolls his eyes, or gives him a disbelieving look, eyebrow raised, all interest him.

He's never met such a person (other than Teacher, but he had never been intrigued by such things while under his care, for obvious reasons).

Perhaps because he has nothing else to do, nothing else to watch, or occupy his time with, he studies the dissident.

An endlessly engaging subject, he's beginning to find.

"Why do you send pilots to Borders? What's the point of it? Do you intend to take over the countries you're attacking?"

The prisoner watches the dissident chop wood from the back porch, wrapped tightly in blankets.

Snow has begun to fall. The wind is harsh. He wraps a blanket around his head, and notes with puzzlement the amused, almost charmed look on the dissident's face.

"I don't…know," the prisoner admits.

"How do you not know? Don't they give you orders?"

"I've never thought about it. They tell us where to go and we go. They tell us what our objective is and we carry it out. But we've never landed anywhere. And the Empire has never broken its treaty. It stays within its own Border, as agreed upon in the twenty first century."

The dissident's brow furrows and he stops working, staring at the prisoner from across the yard.

"We rejected that treaty."

"So did most other countries."

"I guess we rejected it before you even wrote it." The dissident smiles apologetically.

"It was because you rejected the rest of us that we wrote it."

The dissident shrugs.

"But why send planes if you're not trying to expand your power or influence?"

The prisoner shrugs in return.

"Maybe a display of power?" the dissident suggests. "Willingness to enforce your borderlines?"

The prisoner doesn't have any answer.

"They say you're the ones using up our resources. That your attacks are what make our nation weak. But I…we don't think so."

He hasn't talked about the resistance in weeks.

The prisoner, able to walk on his own, bathe on his own, and even shower, looks up, his hands trembling as he washes a pan.

"We…think that it's time to…invade. The south, I mean."

"…an invasion," the prisoner murmurs.

"An actual invasion. Using ground troops. We can't go on living in a bubble. We're running out of oil and coal. There's a finite amount, you know," the dissident says.

"…We use solar power."

The dissident shrugs. "We don't."

There have been many Border attacks. But full-scale invasions, well, the prisoner doesn't believe such a thing has been attempted in his lifetime. It goes against their treaty.

But then, that was only the Empire's agreement. The rest of the world had not agreed to it.

Ever since the development of the Border system, no nation or continent had felt the need to invade another, not for glory, religion, or resources. It's mandatory to study the wars of the past, however, and remembering the gruesome lessons, with cerebral link ups to recreated simulations of what it would have been like fighting in one, the prisoner shudders.

"Could there be another…solution?" the prisoner asks.

"No. There's a finite supply," the dissident insists.

"There's no alternative energy source? No way to reduce usage or increase yield? No…avenue for…negotiation?" the prisoner asks. The dissident scowls.

"When was the last time any continent bartered with another?"

The prisoner cedes to his point with a grimace.

"It's the only way," the dissident says.

"…the only way," the prisoner repeats after him.

But he does think, traitorously, as he curls up on the couch, the dissident on his mattress on the floor, that there are other ways. The country simply would not consider them. As is its right. But the sentiment of distaste remains, and it lingers in the back of his throat the next morning, when he sees the dissident hadn't turned the back porch light off.

"Stop turning the lights off on me," the dissident says, irritated.

The prisoner merely frowns.

He notices the dissident never turns lights off, leaves the water running, doesn't turn the stove off.

It makes him feel itchy.

Now that he's regained his own mobility, and only feels a dull, quiet ache when moving, he's taken to following him and turning off everything in his wake.

Sometimes leaving him in darkness before he's ready.

"I thought you were scared of the dark. I guess not," the dissident complains, flicking the light switch back up.

"I didn't tell you I was."

"So your pathological need to be near a fire is probably pyromania. Great." The dissident rolls his eyes.

The prisoner bites his bottom lip, tempted to laugh.

But he's learned not to do it.

Because the dissident gives him such a smug, triumphant look that he wants to leave the room and not look at him for a few hours.

"If the electricity bill is too high, the owner might get suspicious," the prisoner says.

"We'll be long gone."

"Maybe they'll send someone out to check."

"In this weather?" The dissident hands him a broom.

The prisoner holds it in his lap.

"You need to turn off the water."

"Water needs to run or the pipes will burst."

"No, I mean…the sinks. You leave the sinks running. And you take hour long showers."

"Are you timing me?" the dissident snorts.

"I can tell."

"Stop nagging me."

But the prisoner gets the rather bizarre impression that the dissident is enjoying himself.

Even as he's saying dismissive things, he's smiling and he chuckles a little, meeting the prisoner's eye, and pats his shoulder with his rough hand as he passes him.

"It doesn't matter. We should leave next week anyway. You're ready, aren't you?"

The prisoner is a little uncertain, not liking the look of the snow swirling outside, or the ice he broke through this morning, trying to clear the porch, but they can't stay here forever, and they have to leave before the weather gets worse.

Besides.

He's much stronger than he was when he arrived.

He can walk.

Stand.

Stretch.

Stand at the sink, washing dishes, albeit rather gingerly since his hand is still healing.

Make his dinner, although the dissident seems to like making it for the both of them, so he doesn't often.

"Well that's good. Man, that guy's gonna be mad when he comes all the way out here and finds half his food missing. But he should be ok," the dissident hastily adds at the prisoner's concerned look. "He's got hunting equipment and it seems well-used. He probably just had that other food as backup or supplementary."

The prisoner eyes the dissident's backpack, which seems larger than it used to be.

"If you've left him any."

"Hey, I needed to replenish. And I wanted a fishing rod, I'm tired of just using string. Besides."

The dissident points to the hunting rifle leaning against the wall in the foyer.

"The only thing he's really going to miss is that."

The prisoner, looking at the gun, feels a quick jolt of unease.

The dissident notices.

"Let's go to the lake. I want to show you something."

The prisoner walks passed the gun quickly, not wanting to be in close proximity to it for long.

The air is biting, so sharp and abrupt he feels a cold shock like electricity run through his entire body. He pulls his hood up over his head. The owner of the cabin is larger than him, so all of his jackets swamp his body, a fact which made the dissident laugh so hard he couldn't breathe for a few minutes the first time he'd seen him try one on.

The hood keeps falling in his eyes.

He pushes it up impatiently with his gloved hands.

"See that?" The dissident points.

They stand on the edge of the frozen lake, a smooth, perfect, still surface, appearing as though made of glass, or diamond, lightly dusted with shimmering white snow.

The prisoner stares at it, but the dissident impatiently waves his hand in front of his face. "No, I mean this." He points again.

The prisoner looks.

"That there? We need to go that way. If we get separated, we meet on the other side. There's a river there. Just stay near the river. If you must, follow it. It splits off into a delta. I can wait for you there."

The prisoner stares at the peak of the mountain, rather daunted, remembering the last time they got separated.

"We'll do our best not to get separated," the dissident says, almost as though he'd read his mind.

The prisoner nods, feeling rather small.

When they get back, the dissident puts the gun in the basement.

107

53

"You're sure you're ok with carrying this much?" the dissident asks.

The prisoner nods.

"You can't carry everything," he says solemnly. "If you're carrying the tent, cooking gear, and food supplies, then I can carry sleeping bags, clothes, and medical supplies."

The dissident doesn't look convinced.

But the prisoner is determined.

It's too cold to not have a tent with them for the rest of the journey.

Even though the dissident is doubtful, they have no other choice.

Besides, he's a little eager to show the dissident that he's not always been as weak as he was when they first met. And that at almost full strength, he's more than capable of keeping up with him and bearing some of their load.

"If you get too tired or can't handle it, the next time we make camp, I'll rearrange some things and take on more," the dissident says.

The prisoner doesn't argue, but he zips his backpack shut determinedly.

The dissident fingers the hunting rifle.

"You know how to use this?" he asks.

"I know how to use most firearms," the prisoner says. He glances at the weapon and feels his stomach flip just a bit.

"Good," he says. "It's too bad there aren't two."

"Not even a handgun?"

"No. Just this. I imagine it's a spare. It's in decent condition."

The dissident ties it tightly to the side of his pack, where he can grab it quickly.

"How good of a shot are you?" he asks conversationally.

The prisoner raises his hand, still wrapped in bandages and not quite healed.

"Oh," the dissident says, feeling a little foolish. "But...if your hand wasn't broken, how good of a shot are you?"

"I don't know," the prisoner says. "My eyes aren't as good as they used to be."

"You sound like an old man. You're only twenty six," the dissident laughs.

"How old are you?" the prisoner asks. He's been wondering for a while, but hasn't had any opportunity to bring it up.

"Twenty one."

The prisoner stares at him, quite flabbergasted.

"What?"

"You're so young," he says.

The dissident flushes.

"I am not! I'm just five years younger than you."

"Five years is a lot where I come from." The prisoner frowns. He'd thought the dissident seemed young when he'd first laid eyes on him, and now it's confirmed.

"What's your life expectancy?" the dissident asks.

"About fifty."

"Really? Ours is seventy," the dissident exclaims. "Fifty, wow. You're more than halfway through your life. This is like your…middle aged. Wow."

He stares at the prisoner as though looking at a bizarre, new, alien plant.

The prisoner leans away from him, but the dissident follows, putting his hand on his knee and scrutinizing his face.

"No wrinkles yet, old man." He smiles. "You've still got your whole life ahead of you."

"Seventy…" the prisoner murmurs. "The life expectancy in the Far East is one hundred."

The dissident's mouth drops open.

"No way," he gasps. "How is that possible?"

"Their borders are tighter than even yours," the prisoner says. "They're also much stricter when it comes to birth control and population manipulation. It reduces disease and pollution from urban centers. They reduce the amount of metropolitan waste, air contamination, and environmental degradation through their advanced climate control spheres and strict governmental waste surveillance. They've also modified their food supplies to provide the best possible nutrition for their people. In addition, they've made great strides in genetic enhancement. They've developed and altered antibodies to better fight diseases."

"Uh…" The dissident smiles without understanding. "Wow, that's…cool."

"…we'd attempted to make the same changes, but people found the reforms too cumbersome and unnecessary. It was decided that increasing life expectancy would only destabilize our resources, as elderly people are of no use to the Empire," the prisoner says curtly. "They eat, but do not produce food. They require healthcare, but offer no health benefits to anyone else. They take resources away from infants, who are more necessary, and from the young, who provide labor."

"Wow. That seems…cold. Does anyone ever get older than fifty or do you chop off their heads?" the dissident laughs a little nervously.

"They're permitted to reach whatever age they reach," the prisoner says, a little irate. "We do not kill our citizens. It was just decided that prolonging life was not necessary."

"Oh, ok. Fair enough." The dissident shrugs.

"I suppose you do?" the prisoner asks dryly.

"We…I mean, you're right. Old people really don't have much of a purpose." His companion runs his fingers through his hair. "But we keep 'em living as long as possible. We like 'em."

He laughs again.

"Sometimes, you keep people around just 'cuz of how they make you feel, and nothing else. Man, I remember my grandfather-"

The prisoner frowns and holds his non-wounded hand up.

The dissident stutters to a halt, and looks in the direction he's pointing.

"Oh shit," he swears.

54

"We should've left earlier." The dissident, in his agitation, slams his hand on the counter.

The prisoner, sitting in the dining room, flinches at the sudden noise.

"Shit. There's no getting through that. It's too white, too blinding, the snow is building up too fast, the landscape will be completely unrecognizable, much worse than when we first got separated. And if we go out there right now, in that absolute blizzard, we will definitely get separated again!" the dissident shouts.

The prisoner doesn't like his raised voice.

His ears begin to ring and he begins to hear Teacher's voice mingled in with the dissident's, his drill commander's, the General's, a scream he cannot identify, all screeching like air whooshing through his helmet as his plane begins to fall into open ocean.

"This just…this just really sucks," the dissident groans.

"I'm sorry," the prisoner says quietly.

"What? Sorry for what?" The dissident turns on him, looking rather aggressive for his tone, which is more excited than hostile. "What are you sorry for?"

"If I had been ready to leave earlier, we would've been passed this valley," the prisoner says steadily. "I'm sorry. I didn't mean to betray you."

"Betray me?" the dissident questions. "How is that a betrayal?"

"…I wasn't…ready," the prisoner says bemusedly. "My body was not prepared for the stress. It did not heal fast enough."

"That's hardly your fault," the dissident snorts. "Unless you were purposefully banging your hand on every wall you passed or were doing your best to make sure your legs weren't healing, I fail to see any betrayal here."

"Then…who are you angry at?" the prisoner asks.

"No one," the dissident says, now confused, not angry.

"…but…"

"I'm not angry at anyone, I'm just…angry. At luck. Fate. Destiny. Whatever you call it." The dissident pushes off of the counter, arms swinging rather indolently at his sides now.

The prisoner is rather flummoxed. He's never known anyone to be angry at no one or nothing in particular.

"Ok. We'll just have to delay our departure. How much food do we have? Enough to last out this storm? I would loathe to go hunting right about now." The dissident glances out the window. It's completely white out there, not a hint of any other color.

"I'll…go through everything. Write down how much we can eat a day. But…I don't know how long this blizzard will last, so-"

"The blizzard itself can't last an entire winter season, but maybe calculate how much to get through an entire winter season, just to be on the safe side?" the dissident suggests.

"I don't think we have enough to last that long. But I'll…do my best," the prisoner says, easing his way into the kitchen.

He walks by the dissident, opening the first cabinet and carefully pushing things aside, his injured hand at his side.

Thoughtlessly, impulsively, the dissident takes a hold of it.

The prisoner stops immediately.

He seems frozen almost as if in fear as the dissident lifts it up to his eye level, looking at it carefully.

"How long until this heals?" he asks, voice oddly gentle.

"I don't know," the prisoner says. His fingers twitch. The dissident lets his hand fall a little, holding it as his own chest level.

"Does it hurt?"

"Yes."

The dissident runs his fingers gently over his wrist, brushing skin between bandages. It tickles when he comes to the prisoner's palm, his hand sending chills through the prisoner's entire arm. He stops and pats the back of his hand, his calluses, rough but warm, on his knuckles. The prisoner draws away from him, feeling perturbed.

"Your hands are so cold," he comments idly.

He drops his hand and walks away without another glance back.

The prisoner grabs his injured hand and holds it close to his chest, feeling…jittery.

The dissident's hands were so warm.

55

The snow doesn't relent.

It actually gets worse.

Wind howls outside, whistles through the chimney.

The dissident insists that they sleep upstairs, because the draft will give them colds.

The prisoner reluctantly agrees since he knows they can't afford to waste firewood anymore. They need to save it for the really cold nights, or for when the electricity goes off and they need to cook in the fireplace.

So he goes upstairs without a fight.

The dissident takes the bedroom next to his.

Up until that point, the prisoner's nightmares and night movement had been subsiding.

But the night he sleeps upstairs, in the master bedroom, wide and large, its ceiling slanted, a skylight above his bed, letting him look up at the snow as it collects on the roof, they come back in full force.

He dreams of the laboratory and his training camps, his punishments, his lessons, and desperately swimming miles and miles of open ocean, full of adrenaline and fear that he would be shot, that he would be blown into pieces and eaten by sharks. All he can think is that he'd rather drown in his own country's waters, let his body sink to the bottom of the ocean floor, coming to rest among the seaweed and the crabs, than die in foreign waters. The Empire will not remember his name, nor his body, his existence, but his watery grave will at least be *home*.

He wakes up gasping for air.

Sometimes the dissident is there.

He's sitting on the edge of the bed, his head in his hands.

He's not staring at him, just looking off into space.

Sometimes he's out cold, as though he'd been there for hours and simply couldn't stay awake anymore.

At first, it's something of a relief.

It gives him a feeling he's unaccustomed to…one of ease.

The dissident is there to make sure he's not hurting himself.

He's once again forfeiting his own comfort for the prisoner's.

He sleeps slightly easier with the dissident in the room, and when he doesn't, his companion taps him awake. Or he wakes up with the dissident lifting him up and putting him back into bed.

But after a while, as the days begin to drag, and their conversations begin to dry up, the dissident starts to make him uneasy.

He's rather uncharacteristically slow to respond to his surroundings as he moves about the cabin.

He almost walks into the prisoner a few times, so dazed has he been. Each time, he's almost collided into him, stopped, put his hand out, and touched his chest with confusion, as though bewildered to find someone else in the room. Sometimes he trips coming up or down the stairs, he's so out of it. One time, the prisoner even catches him at the bottom of the basement stairs, having clearly fallen, but not bothering to get back up. He stays there until dinner, and the prisoner has to bring his portion down to him. He eats it down there without a word of acknowledgement or thanks.

The prisoner doesn't normally begin conversations, since the dissident normally does, but now he tries to, if only to fill the unbearable silence.

But the dissident is not forthcoming.

He seems contemplative, pensive, staring at the prisoner for much too long, so long the prisoner is forced to go to the bathroom and hide there just to leave his gaze for a little while.

It's deeply unsettling, but he doesn't know how to approach the subject.

Before, there had been a certain…ease between them.

But it seems to have evaporated with the constant close contact. The dissident's interest in his home country had seemed endless before they'd gotten trapped inside. Now he doesn't want to ask him anything, or answer any questions.

It's very hard for the prisoner to start conversations. The dissident is usually the one to initiate and maintain them. The prisoner had fallen into an easy responding role, a position that only required a prompt reply to do his part in an interaction.

The dissident didn't seemed to mind it.

But now he doesn't come to him at all.

When the prisoner had hesitantly asked the dissident what his school system was like, it had been devastating when he had merely shrugged and said it was fine.

Feelings of overwhelming panic and anxiety had clenched his stomach and he'd left the area as quickly as possible.

He starts trying to avoid him, but it's rather difficult in such close quarters. The only place he can be alone is in his room, and he feels like he's going mad up there, just staring at a pure white skylight, in a dark room with a slanted ceiling.

It almost feels like-

No.

Not Teacher's room.

He's not here.

He's dead.

The dissident killed him.

They are not the same.

Teacher had never won a baseball tournament or gone kayaking with his friends over rapids or fallen head first into a bush full of spiders.

He drives thoughts of *him* away with images he's painted of the dissident, images he's constructed from his stories and endless chatter. His animated stories make him who he is, color his personality, shape his identity, and breathe life, a distinct sense of vitality, into the feeble, earlier caricature constructed in the prisoner's head.

He likes the dissident's stories.

He likes them.

The prisoner hadn't meant to admit that, not even to himself.

But the moment he does, he rolls onto his stomach, presses his face into the sheets, and thinks it over and over again.

He likes the dissident's stories.

He doesn't like when he's mad, thinking about the resistance or his government. His face is cold and tight and his eyes are all wrong.

He also doesn't like when the dissident's eerie and quiet and his eyes burn with a curious, almost ravenous light as he watches the prisoner.

And he doesn't like this silence.

The prisoner blinks, eyes watering, staring up at the blinding snowy white blanket overhead, and sighs.

He hasn't seen the stars in what feels like a long time.

He would like to.

He wonders if the dissident would too.

He closes his eyes.

56

Teacher's weight is overwhelmingly immense, smothering and overpowering. He smells like sweat and desperation and he's breathing hard, he's panting in his face, like a dog, like one of the dogs, chasing him, sinking its teeth into his leg and tugging, shaking its head, forcing its canines in even deeper, merciless in its ministrations, and Teacher is the same, he's merciless, his teeth are on his throat-

But Teacher is dead, what is-is he asleep-is this a dream-where is he-what-?

The prisoner blinks, body as stiff as a board, trying to will the nightmarish weight off of him.

But it's staying, it's still here, it's real, it must be real, and it's on him-

It looks up.

The prisoner looks the dissident right in the eyes, blinded for a moment by pure incredulity. He squeezes his eyes shut and opens them again to make sure he isn't dreaming, that the dissident is right there, on his bed, bent over him, breathing hard.

"What-?"

The dissident says nothing.

He merely moves forward, crushing the prisoner once more beneath him, and forcing him back down onto the mattress.

His lips crash against his, and the prisoner lets out a noise that is swallowed by his tongue, eager and probing, licking at the inside of his mouth like-

The prisoner shoves at his chest, trying to force him off, putting as much strength as he can into his hands (his mostly healed hand still twinges in protest), trying to pull his knees up to get some leverage, but the dissident is strong, he's so strong, pushing against him is like pushing against a brick wall.

The dissident doesn't even seem fazed or interested in his resistance. He merely adjusts his weight, pinning him down more effectively by moving back onto his waist, causing him to yelp out in pain.

The dissident ceases touching him for a moment, letting him breathe in tattered gasps, head dizzy from lack of oxygen, but it's hardly a respite as his teeth are once again on his throat, worrying at his flesh like the dogs, the dogs that bit at his legs and dragged him back to their owners like downed game.

"What are you-ow, stop it, please," the prisoner hisses. "What are you *doing?*"

"I thought they taught you everything," the dissident murmurs.

His hand is tugging at the prisoner's shirt, unfastening his buttons and exposing his collarbone to the dissident's restless eyes.

"What are you doing? I don't require medical attention," the prisoner snarls, finally injecting some real venom in his voice. He grabs the dissident by the hair and forces his head back. "What is the meaning of this?"

The dissident, more amused by his fingers in his hair than anything, chuckles a little.

"They teach you everything and nothing, huh?" he sneers. "Maybe you guys think it's meaningless, but here, sex is something special."

The prisoner's blood feels like it freezes in that moment, cut by a wind sharper than the wintery gusts passing over the roof.

He opens his mouth, only intending to say something, to protest, but the dissident takes it as an invitation and lunges forward again, like a predator overtaking its prey in one bound.

Overtaking it and sinking its claws and teeth in.

He lets go of his hair in surprise, and the dissident, unimpeded, takes a hold of *his* and pulls him in for a demanding, horribly sloppy, chaotic kiss, more of a mauling than anything else, his tongue sweeping through his mouth once more, insufferably slippery and invasive.

His first thought is to bite down, but he's struck with a fear of retaliation, with a sense of self-preservation as the dissident's arms fall and squeeze him in an inescapable embrace, hands locking on his waist. He shudders, imagining those hands crushing his spinal cord, those arms squeezing him like a python, compressing his every bone into dust.

But worst of all is the confusion.

This alien feeling, these foreign feelings emanating off of the dissident, so different from the aura he normally projected, the carefree, laidback energy.

All he can feel is hostility, a bizarre aggression that's focused on something he doesn't understand, something that's targeted him as its quarry, its only possible victim, and with a sudden spike of adrenaline, he manages to wiggle his hands between them and shove the dissident off.

The dissident indulgently lets him, wiping his mouth carelessly, suddenly rather relaxed and playful, a glint of humor in his eye. He rolls off of him easily, voluntarily in fact, as though to let him know he's only off of him because he chooses to be. He blinks affably at him.

"It's a little cold in here, isn't it?" he asks pleasantly.

The prisoner stares at him.

"Why are you looking at me like that?" his companion laughs, his voice high-pitched.

"Why are you doing this? Stop it," the prisoner says, afraid of the sudden change in mood. Afraid of the dissident, who hadn't been like this-this creature, not once, this entire journey.

"Sure," the dissident murmurs, leaning forward, his mouth brushing against the skin on his-

The prisoner jerks back against the headboard and attempts to scoot out of bed, but the dissident grabs his hand and pulls him back sharply.

The prisoner lets out a grunt as he's pinned down again, the dissident straddling him, heavy and painful on his lower half, and putting his hands around his neck.

He instantly freezes.

"I'll play along with you," the dissident says, his voice almost childishly eager, a toddler trying to please an officer. "There's something you want, something I want. We can exchange, can't-?"

"There's nothing I want from you!" The prisoner struggles to push him off again, but there's no use.

He's weak.

The dissident is strong.

He's carried him, after all, carried him on his back through mountainous terrain, carried everything it took to keep him alive, bandages, clothing, food supplies, hunted for him, fed him, given him water, carried him through this house, to the bed, to the shower, and outside the one time he'd asked to look at the stars just once before they slept.

The prisoner's hand holds the dissident at bay, fingers curling into his collarbone.

"This doesn't-this doesn't make sense," he hisses. "Stop this right now."

"What doesn't make sense?"

"You and I are not-we are not compatible. I'm not female…it's not possible," the prisoner insists.

The dissident's face crinkles up as he laughs.

"You don't think so, huh? That's funny, you know everything there is to know about sex and the human body, and yet you don't know this? Well that's fine. I'll be your teacher."

The word fills him with a panic he's never known before, a panic worse than drowning, than swimming back to shore with a hostile country shooting at his back, explosions shaking the sky, the water boiling, the line where they meet disrupted by smoke, than demonic dogs dragging him back to their hellish masters, than Teacher lowering his box into the ground.

His hand slips and he finds his hand gripping the dissident's chin, trying to force his head upwards and away.

The dissident merely smiles and leans into his hand as though enjoying the pressure.

"Why are you doing this? I haven't done anything to hurt you." The prisoner's fingers dig into his face, but he finds himself unwilling to claw at his eyes.

"You poor kid. Is that what they told you sex was? That it's just a painful ritual act between two emotionless breeding stock? It's so much more, it's really something beautiful, it's indescribable, it's the greatest feeling on earth, it's-" words seem to fail him for a moment.

"I don't want it," the prisoner snaps.

The dissident doesn't seem to hear him, lost in his own world.

"I wish you had been a girl, this could've been easier, but I don't mind this." The dissident abruptly and carelessly forces his hand up his shirt, simply ripping through the remaining buttons and leaving his chest completely exposed.

The prisoner instinctively curls in, his hand on his heart, which beats hard against his fingertips.

The dissident touches his shoulder.

"Hey, you think tomorrow we can go hunting?" he asks conversationally as he slides the shirt over his shoulder.

He pauses.

The prisoner, so tense that every muscle feels like it could snap at any minute, doesn't move.

"It's ugly, but it'll do," he sighs. "It's not your fault."

His back.

He's talking about the scars on his back.

His back, so much worse than his front, so much more mutilated.

The subject of most of Teacher's ire.

Teacher.

117

"Why are you resisting?" Teacher whispers. "Don't you owe this man your life?"

"So what if he wants something you don't want to give him?"

"Those who are in positions of power have the right to impose their will, their very being, on those who are not."

"This is the way of your Empire too, isn't it?"

"This is the way of all human society. This is what allowed us to evolve."

"And yet. There's something delightfully bestial about this, isn't there?"

"Something wonderfully...simple about baring your throat to the dominant male, isn't there?"

"Oh do relax. It'll hurt more if you resist. This boy has really undone you, hasn't he? You never resisted me this much."

"Where's that winning subservient attitude? Your Empire would be ashamed."

"Think of him as...your Commander."

All the tension leaves his body at once.

Teacher.

Teacher, cruel and imperious as he stands above him.

Kind and knowledgeable and wise as he crouches next to him.

Offering advice and the choice in deciding which hand he breaks tonight.

Power.

Power, my dear boy.

You might lack power, but you are not wanting in wisdom.

He feels his neck droop, his forehead cushioned by soft fabric.

He takes a deep breath and waits.

But nothing happens.

He opens his eyes and looks at the dissident.

The dissident, who's sitting on the other side of the bed, looking appalled.

"What are you doing?"

The prisoner, nonplussed, says nothing.

He still doesn't move, his side bathed in white moonlight streaming in between clouds.

"What the hell are you doing?" the dissident says, his voice angry.

The prisoner almost flinches, but he forces himself to remain calm.

Teacher got angry too.

It's ok.

The pain will just hurt worse for a while.

"You...you're being such a child!" the dissident says, his own voice rather juvenile as he stares at the prisoner. "Why are you doing this? Why are you doing this to me?"

There is wisdom in accepting defeat.

In accepting inferiority.

"Stop it," the dissident spits suddenly. "Why are you acting like that?"

He lunges for the bed again, scrambling across it to the prisoner's side again.

The prisoner, flinching from the unexpected rush towards him, makes his stiff body uncurl, lie limp on its side again.

"Why are you acting like that?" the dissident asks, pushing him on his back and holding him down by the chest.

The prisoner imagines Teacher holding him in a similar manner, feeling his heartbeat, turning his head and putting his ear to his chest, smiling as he listened.

So many teachers.

The dissident kisses the curve of his jaw, stopping close to his ear.

"Is this how you people have sex?" the dissident jeers, his hot breath fanning his skin unpleasantly. "One of you just lies there and lets the other do whatever they want? Have you done this before? No, you can't have, you had no idea two men could have sex, did you? You only have sex to make children, and even then, it's heartless, isn't it? Heartless…stop…stop just *lying* there."

"What do you want me to do?" the prisoner whispers. "Tell me what to do."

The dissident stares at him, watching him without a word for so long that he thinks he might go mad.

But after what seems like an eternity, the dissident exhales.

The prisoner chances a look.

The dissident's staring at him with smoky ire in his eyes.

He's off of the bed, backing up, looking upset.

"You don't want to do this?" he says, his voice…defensive?

The prisoner blinks, mouth perfectly blank, face perfectly empty.

"Do what you want."

That seems to be the last straw for him.

The dissident grits his teeth, spins on his heel, and leaves the room.

Slamming the door shut so hard the wall shakes.

57

The boy moves out of reach.
"Stop it," he hisses. "Don't move."
His friend giggles.
"Knock it off."
He's too fast. He keeps evading his touch, dodging away before he can get him.
He doesn't like this game.
It seems pointless.
And he doesn't win often.

The dissident paces furiously, kicking aside discarded clothing and anything else in his path. Because of their confinement, he's become messy, dropping things whenever and wherever he's done using them, never cleaning up after himself. If it wasn't for the prisoner constantly on his trail, he's sure the place would be ten times worse.

The dissident pauses in his frantic pacing.

The prisoner, standing at the sink, absentmindedly washing dishes, staring off into space.

Pushing clothes into the washing machine in that one-by-one system of his, in that meticulous manner, which takes much longer than it needs to because the prisoner likes to check for wear-and-tear.

Sitting on the couch, bundled up in blankets, staring wordlessly at the empty fireplace as if wishing, or perhaps imagining, there were a fire in it.

But never complaining.

Never asking for anything.

Content to simply…wait.

The dissident isn't sure when he started watching the prisoner while he slept.

At first, it was because he was concerned.

Because he worried that the prisoner would roll out of bed and hurt himself.

Because the prisoner sometimes made *noises,* low and distressed, which sounded like pleas for help to his ears, and how could he ignore them? He came in and waited, watched. If the prisoner awoke, he just nodded. Just sat there and waited for him to fall back asleep.

It was supposed to be for the prisoner's benefit, but the dissident gets a little anxious sometimes, sleeping in the other bedroom. Sleeping in the prisoner's room gives *him* a sense of relief too, at least in the beginning.

But he starts to have nightmares, vivid dreams about the state he found the prisoner in, his back, permanently disfigured, his chest marked with unattractive bruises and entry wounds, and so much blood on the floor. He takes a single step and his foot sinks into it, his entire body falling in soon after, the hot, unpleasant liquid filling his throat as he screams.

The first time he had that nightmare, he immediately lurched to the side and threw up.

So coming into his room makes him feel a little better.

At least he can wake up and know immediately that it was only a dream and in reality, he is not alone.

But as the days drag, as he begins to retreat into his mind, where the frustrated, pent-up rat-in-a-cage feeling is building, he starts to feel…restless.

And when he feels restless, he tends to lash out.

But this feels…different.

As a teenager, he lashed out at his parents. His friends.

They made easy targets because he knew they would forgive him later.

And something about their generous, sympathetic looks made him want to lash out even more.

Something about their serene understanding of his anger made him uneasy, and more upset.

But it's different with the prisoner.

He's still a stranger to him.

He sees him while he's pacing and *doesn't* want to lash out.

But he feels something else.

Still the desire to…vent some of this restlessness.

But a different impulse, one he would never feel for his family or friends.

Perhaps it's the proximity.

Perhaps it's the exotic nature of the situation, trapped and alone with one person, a foreigner, someone he'd met under extreme, unique circumstances.

Someone who in no way wanted-

The dissident's fingers tremble on the back of the couch.

No.

No, he couldn't…

Didn't he feel something too?

Some kind of attraction, an itch?

It was nothing personal.

Just a way to let off some steam, same as…screaming into a pillow or hitting a punching bag a few dozen times.

So why had the prisoner reacted like…like he was being hurt?

Why did he go stiff like that?

The dissident has never seen anyone go stiff like that during-during-

It's the way they are. Why did you expect him to act like one of you? He isn't.

But it was a basic human instinct, wasn't it?

It was biological.

A universal human feeling, no, an experience.

Cultural and societal differences aside, shouldn't he feel something-?

He was upset. He kept telling you to stop.

Why?

He knows why.

The prisoner doesn't-he doesn't like-doesn't want to-

But how could someone not want it?

It was the greatest-

Not to them, perhaps. Didn't you know that?

He had known that on some level.

Logically, it made sense.

He could've logically assumed…

And yet…

He looked so confused…

Almost…betrayed…

But you didn't betray him…

Where was the betrayal…?

The dissident grits his teeth.

He sits on the couch, thrumming with energy, agitatedly jiggling his leg against the fabric.

The prisoner had been sitting on this couch when he'd finally identified the urge.

He'd had it before, of course, he wasn't a virgin, but he wasn't like his friends.

The prisoner acted so afraid of him, but he was lucky he wasn't more like his friends.

They felt the urge much more often.

A day didn't go by when they weren't…

But he's much more patient.

The prisoner didn't have to act like that.

Like he was hurt.

The dissident's anger begins to fade as the hours creep by and light begins to enter the cabin.

It's replaced by consternation.

The prisoner isn't the type of person to play around.

He isn't the type to act coy or hard to get.

Perhaps he…genuinely didn't want to…

The dissident's stomach seems to curl inwards, buckling like the skin of a rotting pear.

Had he really not…but was that possible?

The prisoner hasn't left his room.

It's still early.

He'll wait.

But he doesn't know if he wants to talk about it or if he just wants to see the prisoner, to be reminded that he's not alone in this cabin, slowly losing his mind.

He hears a door squeak.

He looks up.

The prisoner's door opens just a crack.

And then it closes shut with a soft, but final thud.

58

The prisoner wishes he could remain in his room until the snow thaws, but unfortunately, it's starting to drive him mad, only leaving to use the restroom.

He hasn't dared shower for days now, afraid…of what he cannot say.

He'd only been eating the food he'd found sitting outside his door.

He has no idea if it's conciliatory or merely a matter of practicality. After all, the dissident wants him to remain alive.

For multiple reasons, so it would appear.

Try as he might, he can't banish the slimy, degrading grate of that voice, a familiar, mocking speech with all the spite of a tomcat.

The dissident is nowhere to be found when he finally crawls out of his room for something other than the restroom. It's the dead of night.

He couldn't bear the thought of running into him in the daytime, when he hears him pacing. He imagines him walking holes into the rugs, wearing the floor down all the way into the basement.

A rather silly thought, he thinks, as he tries to move down the stairs without making a sound, but he's been in that room for too long. Strange thoughts were bound to crop up, weren't they?

But he can't help but feel, as he takes each step with the care of a man walking on thin ice, that they weren't.

They had never "cropped up" before.

He'd gone much longer in isolation without strange thoughts.

He had spent the majority of his life in isolation, because even when he was surrounded by men and women, by comrades he had known for years and strangers he had just been thrust with, he was still completely and utterly alone.

And he'd been perfectly content to be alone under Teacher's care.

It meant no one was hurting him.

It was only after…after meeting the dissident…

But no, no, he'd begun to…feel things under Teacher's care too.

He had been educated.

By both of them.

Perhaps this is what it means to feel…as they do.

Unpleasant.

Anxious.

Fearful.

Lonely.

Isolated.

The Empire has never felt so far away, has it?

What else is a feeling they never taught you?

A feeling that would never exist back home?
Oh yes.
Violation.
The prisoner shudders.
He grips the banister tighter.
His vision seems to blur, the room spinning rapidly.
Did you like how his mouth felt, on your throat?
You are quite the masochist, aren't you?
It's so easy to end a human life.
Delicate place, the human throat.
He could've bitten right through it.
And you would've let him.
The prisoner stops on the last step, legs shaking.
He sits slowly, using the banister as his support.
His back twinges with pain.
How repulsed he was by your back.
How repulsive your back is now.
It's amazing he finds this part of you useful, this body, that is.
There's nothing appealing about it.
I was the one who made it this way, and even I find it utterly distasteful.
But he was desperate, I suppose.
The prisoner grips his wrist with a hiss of pain.
The dissident had held him here, gently, carefully.
He'd wrapped it himself, his hands were so-
He had his hands on your ribcage.
He could've crushed it.
He's so strong, so much stronger than you.
What a perfect specimen.
Handsome, intelligent, resourceful, and physically powerful.
Why would he touch the likes of you?
Easy answer.
He's bored.
Just a shame his toy wasn't in better condition.
The prisoner cradles his arm like it's his child, staring out the windows at the darkened sky, the moon the only source of light. It casts a pale, eerie shadow on the mountains, the lake. The reflections of clouds sail over the surface of the water, occasionally blotting out the moon like their counterparts.

He watches them.
Is this self-consciousness you're feeling?
Do you serve this man now?
Is that why you wish you weren't so broken?
My, my, I should've been kinder to you.
If I'd known it would pervert your ideology this much, we could've had so much
more fun.
You didn't say much to me.
You begged, you pleaded, sometimes, but deep down, I knew you weren't changed.
You were a machine, with automated responses to pain stimuli.
No charisma.
No...delightful suffering or charming pain.
But now...

Oh, I wish I could go back in time and start all over again.

I might've given you some humanity, but he gave you the full experience, didn't he?

Not pain, but compassion.

Not fear and desperation, which are two integral parts of being human, but sympathy and...dare I say, kindness?

Just so he could take it all away.

Show you that these things are not mutually exclusive.

And that to be human is to exist in duality, contradiction of one's self.

He's a much greater teacher than I ever was.

The prisoner makes to stand up again.

"Can I get you something?"

He freezes, fear locking every muscle, every limb, into place.

Yet, resignedly, he looks to the sound of the voice.

The dissident doesn't move.

He's lying on the couch, virtually invisible in the darkness.

The only reason he knows he's there at all is because he announced himself.

The thought sends a jolt of fear shooting through his gut.

He feels a prickle in his neck, the ghost of a touch, and he swallows.

"...was thirsty," he manages to croak.

"You could've drank out of the bathroom sink. Isn't that what you've been doing?" the dissident asks idly. If he's moving, the prisoner cannot detect it.

He takes a step back.

"Where are you going to run?" the dissident asks softly. "It's just you and me. No one out here. Nothing out here for...miles."

"...I wasn't going to run," the prisoner says.

"Hm. No, I guess not," the dissident says thoughtfully. "Just curl up and wait for it all to be over, is that it?"

His tone is colder than the air outside.

The prisoner takes a small, tentative step forward.

The dissident makes no move to stop him.

Not one he can see, anyway.

The prisoner, keeping an eye on the spot where the dissident's voice seems to be emanating, gives the couch a wide berth.

He walks a little more quickly once he passes it, and shuffles into the kitchen, heart pounding.

Hands shaking, he touches the cabinet handle and pulls at it.

"You know, you're not my first choice," the dissident speaks up. "I didn't have thoughts like this about you since I first met you or anything."

He sounds strange.

Defensive, but also...a little...

"We're going to be here a while and we don't...have anything to do," the dissident says. "I can't knit one more second, and you're bored, aren't you? Just watching the sky the whole damn time, looking at the lake, eating, shitting, and showering, just...just sitting on this couch watching the fire when we have one. God, it's driving me mad. Not...at you, of course. Did you think I was mad? I wasn't. Not until after, I mean, but maybe that was a misunderstanding. I'm just mad at the situation. Hey. Hey, are you listening?"

The prisoner is. Rather intently.

He flips on the light switch.

He can barely see the back of the dissident's head as he lounges on the couch, his arms stretched out lazily on the backboard.

"Well…it's just been hard. I'm not made to be indoors, I like open space and walking and running and hiking-"

"Is that why they picked you?" the prisoner interrupts.

The dissident pauses.

Something in the air shifts.

The prisoner can't explain it, but he can sense it, can almost feel the power imbalance tipping between them for a moment.

"What?"

"Is that why they picked you? To get me?"

The dissident's moving towards him. The prisoner forces himself not to flee.

"They? You mean-"

"Your resistance," the prisoner says, feeling oddly…elated. He wishes he knew why, but all he knows is that there's a squirming eager feeling in his gut, a sensation that swells as he continues pressing him. "Did they send you because you're the most qualified person to take on a mission that involves resourcefulness and peak physical condition? And knowledge of all types of terrain?"

The dissident is…uncomfortable.

The prisoner has never seen him so hesitant.

There's something he's getting at, something the dissident is hiding, that the prisoner has just scratched the surface of.

Unbidden, curiosity stirs within his chest.

The dissident knows everything about him.

There's nothing to know.

But this man…

He has a wealth of strange knowledge he'd never even thought existed before they met.

"What did you know, before going-?"

"That's…irrelevant. Confidential," the dissident adds, looking a little proud of himself. "Right now all that's important is…what you and I are going to do."

The feelings of curiosity and anticipation die immediately.

"What do you want to do?" the prisoner asks quietly.

To his shock, the dissident slams the cabinet door shut before he can take anything out.

He backs up quickly, but the counter hits him in the back, and then the dissident is in front of him, blocking any escape.

"Why do you keep asking me that?" the dissident snaps. "You're always asking what I want."

"I don't understand," the prisoner answers, feeling a little queasy with the dissident staring down at him again.

"I don't understand why you keep asking me what I want!"

"Because I don't understand what you're *doing,*" the prisoner says exasperatedly. "Because I don't…understand what you *want,* so I *have* to ask you.*"

The dissident looks rather taken aback.

He backs off, leaving his immediate space, and puts distance between them, looking like he's thinking so hard he might implode.

The prisoner grimaces.

"…I owe you my life. And I…have no function here. No objective. I'm in a world I don't belong in. One I also do not understand. But I'm willing to try. It's all I can do. I'm…sorry if my questions…seem strange to you, but I've never needed to ask questions before. Just obey orders. I'm not…used to it."

The prisoner lets his hands fall into his pockets, self-consciously rubbing the material of their inner lining with his fingers as he awaits the dissident's response.

But the dissident seems incapable of one.

He looks…

Well, the prisoner isn't sure.

His emotions are so much more complex than he would've ever imagined emotions could be.

Back home, you were content…discontent…excited…bored…

There were variations of the four, of course, but they didn't stray far from their core emotions.

The dissident seems to feel a lot more, with much more variety and intensity.

"You…just don't know?" the dissident asks slowly after a few minutes.

The prisoner shrugs uncertainly.

"I don't."

The dissident's face twitches.

He sluggishly, almost lethargically, walks back to him, retracing his steps, pinning him to the counter once more, his fingers dangerously gripping the prisoner's waist as he does so.

The prisoner feels a jolt of fear again, but he forces it down, recognizing that he doesn't have the right to feel that way.

The dissident seems to notice it, however.

He lets go abruptly, looking…upset.

Guilty is the word you're looking for, love.

"I'm sorry."

The prisoner's eyes widen in surprise.

The dissident strides out of the room before he can formulate a response.

The dissident leaves him alone after that.

The prisoner sneaks downstairs again, only to find that the dissident has left a note simply saying he's gone out.

It's a relief to have the place to himself for a while.

Only on very rare occasions had he lived alone back home, and even then, he still had not lived in a dwelling without other tenants above and around him at all times.

He likes the silence.

And he doesn't mind doing nothing.

He doesn't mind sitting and staring thoughtlessly at the lake for a while.

At home, they had enough leisure time to ensure maximum performance and stave off exhaustion and mental instability.

But here he can sleep as long as he wants, do whatever he feels like doing, which is sleeping, usually, and sit in a warm, comfortable place with a blanket draped over him.

He's never known peace like this.

He still has nightmares, but they feel…contained. They still torture his subconscious, but the moment he wakes up, they fade to the back of his mind where they belong, in unreality. They do not linger in his waking mind anymore.

The voice is quiet.

But as serene as he feels, there's still a sense of…guilt in his gut.

He's not being productive.

He's not making himself useful.

He waits for the dissident to come home, sometimes with an animal, sometimes not, and they eat, neither speaking to one another, and then retreat to their rooms.

He is of no use to the dissident.

He never has been, but now it feels even more poignant, given that the dissident had almost given him a purpose, but he'd forced him, somehow, to take it away again.

Did he do something wrong?

Is that not what the dissident wanted?

Or had he…stopped wanting?

The question puzzles and unsettles him, but he would take it to the grave if the dissident hadn't brought it up again.

But he does, albeit in a roundabout way.

The prisoner is at the sink, his bad wrist trembling from the strain of holding heavy plates, when the dissident comes up from behind, takes a hold of him, and steadies it.

The prisoner, stiffening with surprise and a little discomfort, slowly lowers it.

"I can do that."

"It's the least I can do," the prisoner murmurs.

"You do a lot," the dissident murmurs, backing off.

The prisoner's hand falls out of his as he moves the plate into the drying rack.

"…I don't know what you mean."

The dissident's brow furrows in consternation. "You're always doing laundry, cleaning up after my mess, cleaning dishes, washing the floors, washing the tub and sinks, sweeping the house, shoveling snow off the porches, putting everything in the basement back in careful order. I would never bother with any of that."

"Because it's useless," the prisoner concludes. "All of that. You wouldn't do it, it's unnecessary."

"No." The dissident shakes his head. "I'm just too…lazy. Just because I myself wouldn't do it doesn't make it useless. It's a lot of work, and you do it on your own. I kind of feel bad, actually, I'm constantly trekking mud and blood and snow in here when you've just done the floors."

"…it's not necessary to survival or to any objective," the prisoner says. "So it's not productive."

"…I mean, would it kill us to live in squalor? No, well maybe, but…it's still hard work." The dissident scratches his head.

Then an idea seems to come to him.

It's rather fascinating to watch, the prisoner thinks.

A little half grin forms on his face and his eyes light up as he begins to formulate a thought, and then the grin becomes a full-fledged smile as realization floods his body with energy.

He watches the process occur in real time, and is so focused on it that he almost doesn't catch the dissident's words.

"Productive? You think you need to be productive."

"…I do not feel…comfortable being unproductive."

"But you are productive. You're working a lot."

"It doesn't feel like work. It's housework. It could be done by laborers."

"That doesn't make it *any less* work. Holy. Do you really think you don't contribute at all around here?"

The dissident's making him uncomfortable again.

He makes him feel like he's done something wrong, or like he's under constant surveillance and is regularly being caught committing some act of treason.

And this now…

Even though he isn't being accused of being unproductive, in fact the opposite, he still feels…well. Accused.

"I daydream," the prisoner clarifies softly. "All I do is wait for you to come back."

"Usually at the sink or in the basement sorting through things or picking up my crap."

"I stare off into space doing nothing."

The dissident snorts.

"When? When I'm gone? Every time I see you space out, it's with a broom or mop in your hand."

"You *provide* for both of us. Without you, we would die. Without me, we would go on living. It is apparent who is more important here." The prisoner closes his eyes.

The dissident pokes him in the back and he drops the cup he's holding in pain and shock.

Luckily, it's a thick cup.

It merely clatters in the sink, sturdy enough not to shatter on impact.

"Sorry," the dissident says quickly. "You just seemed so tense. What are you so worried about?"

A lot of things.

None of these things feel like work, so he does not consider them work.

He would be called lazy and a waste of space, if his senior officers were here. Unfit to be a soldier. One was expected to clean up after themselves; not even laborers sunk so low as to clean the messes of others.

These things, these trivial chores, they are merely perfunctory, obligatory, making up for one's own visible presence in a structure.

The dissident…does not do these things because they do not occur to him.

It does not make these things matter simply because he puts his effort into them.

On a practical level, he has no purpose.

So the resulting feeling of uselessness prevails.

The sense of contentment is outweighed by guilt.

Leisure outside of acceptable parameters is to be punished.

Leisure that does not function as a necessary, temporary split from utilitarian concerns, is not to be tolerated.

The words chip at his thoughts like icepicks, prying apart his feelings and emotions and churning his ruminations into unintelligible chunks.

The dissident is saying something else, but he can't hear it, he turns away, fingers fumbling to turn off the faucet.

He says something urgent, concerned, but the prisoner shakes his head.

What does he want?

What do they want from him?

Why is he still here?

What reason could he have for keeping him around?

At least if the dissident had gone through with whatever he'd been intending to go through with that night, in his room, then maybe he would've understood.

And even if he hadn't, he would've understood at least, that his body had purpose.

That some part of him had purpose.

But this…this existence, while mildly pleasant, feels so utterly…

You were meant to die meaninglessly.

No. They needed him to die.

They could've used anyone else. Your Empire uses its drones indiscriminately.

Oh, poor child, did you think that serving the Empire gave you meaning? Did you cling to the hope of immortality, of sentiment, in their image?

There was never any.

Do you see that now?

You've denied yourself…everything that makes the human experience so unique in the hopes of becoming a part of them, a piece of a whole, a perfect unit.

But you never attained that.

You never could, human beings do not complete one another, human beings are whole. They are born whole.

But now you've fractured yourself and become less of one.

And now you're scared because you don't think you can be a whole person, because you never were, because the Empire breaks people into manageable chunks before they truly become people and puts them together into broken but functioning wholes.

Perversions of nature. The human ideal of wholeness, instead of the wholeness nature intended.

Together, you were something.

But take you away from your other broken, perfectly mutilated jigsaw puzzle pieces, and what's left to fill the gap?

Nothing.

Leaving you *nothing but an inoperable fragment of a mad science experiment gone horribly wrong.*

Adrift. Disfigured. Mangled beyond humanness.

"Hey!"

The prisoner blinks.

He's on the floor, hands on his head, knees bent in front of him.

The dissident has a hold of his wrist again.

He pulls it gently away from him.

The prisoner watches, detached, as he takes it into his hand.

His hand runs up his arm gently, leaving an odd tingling sensation trailing behind. It tickles his forearm, comes to his wrist, and interlinks their fingers, the dissident's palm rubbing against his own quite pleasantly.

His fingers feel warm and secure in the dissident's grip.

The prisoner looks dazedly at their held hands.

His fingers fit the spaces between the dissident's fingers. And the dissident's fingers fit the spaces between his. Their hands form a perfect, if distorted and disjointed, whole.

The dissident doesn't let go.

He's not sure why; he looks to him for an answer.

The dissident is much closer than he expected.

He's frightened by his proximity, by how close his eyes seem, peering into his without any barrier, any form of protection.

He feels exposed.

He makes to move away instinctively, but the dissident squeezes his hand again, not allowing him to pull away, so he remains.

The dissident touches the back of the prisoner's hand reassuringly, cupping it with his other warm palm. For a few moments, the prisoner's hand is caught between both of the dissident's hands.

He feels a shiver of something… indistinguishable in his chest.

"You still with me?" the dissident chuckles nervously. "You spaced out on me there."

The prisoner nods, not trusting himself to speak.

The dissident's thumbs, crossing one another, rubs soothing circles into the side of his hand, sending nervous jitters shooting through his entire arm.

It's like…being electrified.

But…more pleasant.

With one last squeeze, he lets go.

The prisoner's hand feels rather cold as he lets it fall into his lap.

"Thank you," the dissident says simply.

The prisoner looks at him as though to ask for what.

"You might not consider it work, and that's fine, but I do. So thank you. I appreciate it."

He smiles.

The prisoner is struck with the odd, inexplicable urge to have his hand held again.

Without another word, the dissident pushes himself back to his feet.

131

He offers him his hand again.

The prisoner takes it almost too eagerly, allowing himself to be pulled up.

He holds on for a little longer than strictly necessary, and the dissident seems to notice, but doesn't comment, merely smiling and letting their hands remain together for a moment or two.

But as he holds on, something comes over him, something less amusing or intriguing as a realization.

Some dark feeling crosses his eyes, and he lets go abruptly.

The prisoner brings his wrist involuntarily to his chest.

Cradling the back of his hand like the head of a newborn child, rubbing soothingly, fearfully at it.

The dissident looks at his posture, at the way he's holding his hand, and seems to stiffen.

"Goodnight," he says curtly.

And then he turns and leaves so abruptly the prisoner blinks and he's just not there anymore.

The prisoner doesn't move an inch, doesn't even think a single thought, until he hears the dissident's bedroom door shut.

And even then, his only thought is:

I do not understand.

60

The dissident had wanted very much to kiss him.

But he can't.

And that is very, very confusing.

The dissident stares out his window.

Not much of a view on this side.

The prisoner has the nicer room, the master bedroom, with the skylight.

All he sees are mountains.

They're beautiful, but they're not like home.

And they feel like the bars of a cage, trapping him in here, with this…this confusing person.

This person who seemed to enjoy holding his hand for a few moments there…but what if he imagined it?

What if he was just projecting his own hunger for intimacy and close human contact on an entirely arbitrary gesture? Maybe the prisoner didn't "understand." Maybe he just liked physical warmth. Maybe he was just curious and intrigued by their contact. And maybe the dissident was just reading too much into it.

He's been raised his entire life in close contact with others.

Being isolated with just the prisoner for company…

It's made him touch-starved, ignited a fire within his chest that he's having a difficult time controlling, and thrown his compassion into overdrive, hyper-charging affection into desire.

Just touching his hand had…

The dissident rolls onto his side, hand crushed between his thighs.

But he hadn't acted on it.

The prisoner doesn't play around.

He's not like him.

He's not like anyone he's ever met.

He doesn't understand these feelings, might not even have them himself…

But the dissident can't help but wonder.

But fantasize.

He indulges for a moment, imagining that the prisoner had actually felt something.

What if he'd leaned in, when they were eye to eye, when their faces were so close, and touched his lips with his, joined their breathing, opened his mouth wider to accept his tongue, let out those little grunts he had the first time, the soft little gushes of air that had left the dissident light-headed, because of how much more spirited the prisoner had been, underneath him, than he'd ever seen him…

Guiltily, he thinks about that night, a soft flush caressing his face.

The prisoner is hardly a looker, not the type of person he would spare a second glance, but he's acceptable. His face is pleasant enough, his skin different enough from his own to be exotic, and his body is stripped entirely of any extraneous fat from near starvation and constant, almost fatal exercise.

The thought is almost funny in a dark way.

Stripped of all fat?

Sounds like a model's dream.

Not even a hundred pounds anymore, all skin and bone, waist couldn't be more than twenty six inches.

He didn't even know guys like that back home.

They were muscular and toned from private work outs, carb calculations, and miracle diets.

Some went for muscle mass, others went for the sinewy, svelte look (although not as "svelte" as the prisoner; even those most obsessed with thinness wouldn't go that far).

Some simply had different ideas of what their bodies should look like; others had significantly different tastes and audiences to appeal to.

That had never been the dissident's thing, not really.

He had friends who were interested in that, were interested in switching, having both, sometimes migrating to one or the other depending on the day, but sex had never been a hobby for him. He didn't experiment or broaden his horizons in the bedroom; it was never an arena he felt like excelling in. He'd stuck to women his whole life.

But he supposes extenuating circumstances…

He's rather desperate here.

The dissident pauses, rather intrigued by his own line of thought.

Would the prisoner be attractive to him if they met on the street?

The prisoner is more like a woman in terms of body shape, in muscle mass than a man. He's thin, small, maybe even delicate in a way, which the dissident has always found attractive in a woman, but he also looks tired and beaten, two things which the dissident has never found in the vibrant young women he's taken home. His body might appear perfect, or at least, perfect for some of the horny old geezers he'd seen in bars, the type to hit on anything with a waist with a circumference less than thirty inches, but underneath his clothing is a horror story no one would touch.

Ribs that had been broken so many times the scars where they'd broken through skin are clearly visible. A flat belly that would've been lovely if there weren't surgery scars, cuts and evidence of poorly healed, infected wounds, and discolored patches of skin.

And the worst part, his back.

The ridge of his spine, his delicately curved vertebrae easily traceable from his neck to his rear, would've been lovely if not for the scars, thick and crisscrossing, so abundant in size and frequency that his back is more ropey, ugly bumps and ridges than unbroken skin.

It's so red.

It's so dark and repulsive that he wanted to puke for a moment that night.

But he was determined.

He was willing to close his eyes and just feel the warmth of another body beneath his, around his, smell his skin, alive and musky, feel his weight, his presence, and know he was not alone in this world, in this hellish boxed-in space.

 Thinking about it now upsets him.

He hadn't realized that the prisoner had…could not…or perhaps would not…feel the same way.

He was used to his partners not being interested at first, but eventually succumbing to the physical and emotional need for…sex.

It was human nature, wasn't it?

They gave in eventually, they always did.

But then the prisoner hadn't been reluctant.

He'd been terrified.

And the dissident is a fool for not realizing how damaging cultural conditioning could be.

The prisoner had been repressed his whole life, hadn't he?

He didn't know strong emotions.

The dissident had never seen someone so stoic, flat, and inhibited, in fact.

So he recognizes what a fool, what an inconsiderate ass he'd made himself out to be.

And he feels guilty now, thinking about how the prisoner felt obligated to…compensate him in some way.

It was sad.

He couldn't just exist to exist, exist to be alive, to be happy, content, but for another's purpose.

Although he feels his nether regions stir at the fantasy, the sexual allure of self-objectification, his mind remains intact.

The prisoner is off limits.

At least, right now.

He can't help but hope…

That maybe he'll come around.

It's not so crazy.

After all, he's changed so much…

He's begun to feel…hasn't he?

He actually…smiles.

Sometimes.

Shyly. Awkwardly.

Sometimes to himself, absentmindedly, his eyes off in some unknown world.

The dissident has a hard time leaving sometimes, thinking about that smile.

If the dissident's thinking at all, and not just staring off thoughtlessly into the void, he's thinking about his companion's smile.

It's rather…

What's the word?

The dissident, looking out at the gloomy sky, the snow swirling by, the frigid winter wasteland outside their stronghold, finds himself longing to see the sun, in all of its…

Ah.

Radiant.

That was the word.

That radiant smile, like the absent sun, shining on a spring day.

He finds himself longing for that smile instead.

61

For the most part, the dissident feels better.

Being able to go outside now might help.

He just didn't feel right, being inside for so long with so little to do.

Going out, even if it's just to look around, build an ironic, ugly, misshapen snowman, eases some of his cabin fever jitters.

The gap between himself and the prisoner has also shrunk noticeably.

Instead of keeping a polite distance from him and cordially avoiding eye contact, the prisoner's deemed a nod and a half-wave to be acceptable greeting.

The dissident, whenever he can, pats him on the shoulder as he passes.

At first the prisoner seems to dislike this.

But then he stops flinching and tensing every time he does it.

He actually tries it himself once.

A swift little pat on his shoulder as he scoots by him into the kitchen.

It takes all of his willpower not to laugh.

The prisoner moves so stiffly, so strangely, like a yard stick is taped to his spine.

The dissident can't help but comment.

"Have you always walked like that?"

The prisoner, startled, stops, looking rather self-consciously at his bad leg.

"No."

"No, I don't mean the limp. You walk so…straight."

The prisoner frowns.

"You're confusing."

The dissident grins a little at that.

He's glad the prisoner's at least verbalizing the sentiment after weeks of keeping it to himself.

"I mean…see how I walk?"

"Inefficiently," the prisoner says.

"Inefficiently?" the dissident chortles. "I guess, but you walk like you're marching somewhere all the time. Like a robot."

"Robots can be programmed to walk any way you want them to walk." The prisoner's brow wrinkles as he makes another one of his cute bemused faces.

"I mean…like a badly programmed…point is, we walk differently. I walk like I'm on a stroll. You walk like someone's taped a gun to your back. Is that how they trained you?"

"No," the prisoner says. "They used a ruler."

The dissident's mouth drops open.

"That's-that's-"

"A joke," the prisoner finishes for him.

The dissident chokes with unexpected laughter, half-shocked, half-impressed.

"You got me!" he says.

"They did use tape, however," the prisoner admits.

The dissident pauses, and the prisoner thinks he might have upset him, but the next second, he's smiling again.

"Explains why you walk around like you have a book on your head. Actually, let's try it, I'm going to get a book."

"A book? Why a book?" the prisoner asks.

"If you can balance a book on your head while you're walking, it's supposed to indicate you're walking with good posture or something," the dissident says. "Guess they never did that to you in training camp."

"It seems excessive."

"The whole Empire seems excessive to *me,*" the dissident sniffs.

"The Republic lives on excess," the prisoner retorts.

This time, he thinks, he's surely crossed the line.

The dissident loves the Republic after all.

If he keeps this up, this pointless back-talking, he might just-

But the dissident is shaking his head with a bitter, regretful smile.

"You're right," he admits.

The prisoner relaxes a little.

He glances over at the frozen lake, his multiple blankets wrapped so tightly around himself that he can neither move easily, nor feel the cold anywhere but his raw, reddened cheeks.

So clean.

So...clear.

The sky is so blue, the snow so blinding, so pure in its untouched whiteness.

Snow at home was dingy and brown, soiled by the ground it touched or the sky itself, coming down like ashes. It came tainted and covered in filth. It did not possess this...immaculate quality. This snow falls perfectly, complementing the landscape, the timeless mountains, the smooth frozen lake, and the straight, tight lines of the trees.

The snow collected so neatly, so rigidly, on every natural feature that he can see.

It's marvelous.

It seems impossible for something so whole, so flawless, to exist without human intervention.

But as the prisoner watches the snow fall slowly, lazily, seemingly chaotic but secretly very ordered, almost as though by some divine plan, he thinks perhaps his mind has been opened to the impossible.

The world he knew...feels so far away now.

In his memories, it is...limited.

Small.

He has seen the ocean, and yet not been enlightened by its depth.

These mountains are nowhere near as tall as the ocean is deep, but...they take his breath away, they steal it as the ocean had tried to, but had never managed.

He has lived among his people for twenty six years, thought of himself as one of them, and he'd never once found reason for doubt in their lifestyles, their way of being.

It lacked conflict.

It lacked chaos.

Structure was good.

He had not been harmed by any of his own people.

He had been given purpose too, a place in their large, overwhelming world, without needing to ask for it.

Without purpose, he would've been lost in time, in space, without stability, without reprieve from unshakeable loneliness.

Even though they do not talk or regularly fraternize, he knows they are there.

A man once collapsed in front of him, wracked with some kind of seizure, and everyone on the street had stopped to make sure he would be alright. They waited for a medical team to come and take him to the hospital. Everyone had been taught what to do in various emergencies, but for some reason, even though it was not necessary, they had all waited with him.

Silently, noiselessly, they had huddled around him, some crouched, others standing nearby, and waited.

The prisoner had waited too.

And after the injured man had been taken away, everyone had remained where they were, frozen, staring at the leaving ambulance in shock.

Then they turned to stare at each other, confused, unsure of why they were still here, still standing together.

But they were unwilling to walk away for a moment or two, bound for just a split second…by an unnameable feeling.

One they could not express.

He could see it in their faces, was affected by it too, deep in his chest, where an ache had built up, one he could not repress.

But the moment had passed, as all must.

And when one person begins to walk away, his footsteps slightly off, as though he were startled out of complacency, the rest quickly followed.

The prisoner is the last person to leave.

He stands there for a while, staring at the spot where the man had fallen.

He had dismissed the incident.

When the feeling was gone, it was gone, and he couldn't miss something that was no longer there.

He couldn't miss something he no longer had.

But it's here.

It's here again.

That hurting feeling.

He thinks about those people and wonders if they ever felt it again.

The dissident shakes the snow off of his blankets, helping him inside.

He feels a sudden longing for his people.

But not for their stability, their calm rationality, which are pleasing concepts in their own way, but…in another way.

A way he struggles to connect to this ache he's feeling now.

They had given him everything he needed to live.

But why does he only now feel *living?*

62

The dissident can't help himself when it happens, when he slips up.

It's a complete accident.

It's no one's fault.

The prisoner is just…

He's trying so hard not to laugh, his hand clutched over his mouth, his sides heaving from the effort of not making a sound as the dissident recalls an incident in which his friend had awoken with a lizard in his sleeping bag and screamed so loud he'd scared away the bear lurking outside of their tent.

His face is flushed, his mouth curved behind his thin fingers, his eyes shining brighter than he's ever seen them, than he would've ever thought those lifeless, dark brown orbs could.

They're also on the same couch.

For once, he'd foregone his chair and huddled next to him, both watching the fire, feeling warmer than usual. The prisoner had thoughtfully extended his blanket to him and he'd gratefully pulled it over himself.

It was just peaceful at first, in the moments following that welcoming laughter.

But then he becomes hyper aware of his own body, of the emotions welling up inside, the longing for home, for his friends, and the laughter they had shared, the budding ache in his heart for the happiness he'd left behind, and it channels itself into affection for the person he's with, an affection that catches him completely off guard.

He's not accountable for his impulses, is he?

The prisoner, who'd been turning to say something to him, a story of his own, perhaps, had been caught completely by surprise.

He does feel a little guilty about that.

The prisoner had finally begun to feel less guarded around him again, and what does he do?

Catch him off guard.

He'd leaned in and kissed him.

And even though the prisoner stiffens, and leans away, he'd kept going, he'd shifted and kept going until the prisoner's head hits the armrest. The dissident's body slides on top of his. His right knee pushes between his legs, his right hand stroking his hair, and all the while, he's kissing him, a pleasurable electricity tingling in his stomach, his entire body, as it connects with another.

He's giddy, ecstatic, that the prisoner doesn't push him away.

The prisoner's rigid at first, but then he relaxes, his right hand coming up and gently touching his neck. He breathes a little less frantically, leaning back and accepting his eager lips on his mouth, his throat, his collarbone.

The dissident knew it, he knew he would come around, cultural barriers be damned, he was going to feel the urge eventually, *he* had just needed to be more patient-

But as he unbuttoned his pants, began to pull them down around his hips, suddenly the prisoner goes stiff again.

And when his fingers snag on the rim of his underwear, pulling at the elastic and partially exposing him, the prisoner shoves him off.

He hits the ground hard, since he wasn't expecting to be pushed off.

"What the hell?" the dissident yells.

The prisoner stares at him, his hair a mess, his lips red and a little puffy from being kissed, his pants undone and the white of his underwear peeping out.

For a moment, the dissident sees Monica in his place, the first girl he ever did it with, who'd pushed him away too, who'd told him to stop, but had started liking it the third or fourth time, and wanted to do it again once she'd gotten used to it.

But then he blinks and all he sees is the prisoner.

Looking hurt and upset and disturbed, his face as fearful as the first time.

Only this time, it isn't masked by darkness, only faintly visible by slivers of moonlight.

It's made clear by the warm, orange glow of firelight.

It's so clear on his face that he doesn't, and will never, want this.

And the dissident feels a hole opening up in his chest, humiliation and frustration and his own confusion pushing at its edges, expanding it into a crater that feels like it's splitting his entire body in half.

The sensation is so alien, the feelings of shame and guilt so heavy, that he makes no move to get up as the prisoner does, as he pulls his blanket to his side and hurries passed him.

Running into the basement and closing the door.

The dissident waits for hours in the same position, waiting for the prisoner to come back out, but as the fire dies, and as night becomes day, then afternoon, his hope that he will come back up on his own dies with it.

The prisoner isn't coming back.

Not as long as he's here.

So the dissident packs his bag with just a little food.

He pulls on his coat.

Ties his boots.

And he goes down into the basement. He doesn't turn the light on, but he can almost sense the prisoner, can almost see him ducking down, lurking somewhere behind the boxes between the stairs and the desk. He opens his mouth, but has nothing to say. And he isn't here to make amends anyway.

He remembers exactly where the rifle is.

He takes it in both hands and begins to ascend the stairs, going towards the gentle light of day streaming in from above.

He hesitates one stair from the top though.

Looks back, into the darkness.

Can almost see the prisoner's shadowy silhouette.

He speaks to it.

"Goodbye."

And then he takes that last step and lets the door swing shut behind him.

63

What does he like, do you think?

What does he have in mind?

Come on.

You know so much about sex, couldn't you have figured out how two men go about it, child?

It's not rocket science, ahaha, my dear pilot.

You're shaking your head.

Why so upset?

She was miserable and bloated and moaning.

She was regretting her decision, he knew, to be a mother.

He is fifteen years old.

All fifteen year olds are required to assist voluntary mothers, take care of their needs, medical or otherwise, and be present at the moment of birth.

He'd been forced to miss a lot of training, clean up her vomit, bring her the foods she wanted, obey and carry out her strange demands, and handle her very particular schedule.

He never complained.

He couldn't be upset; it was his duty, regardless of how unpleasant the experience was.

And…logically, he knew she was miserable too. More miserable, if her bloated stomach, hunched over back, or labored breathing were anything to go by.

Sometimes he stared at her belly hard, stared at the rounded, bulbous, sickeningly distended flesh, and wondered why the creature that she was carrying, nurturing, giving life to, was hurting her so much.

She would often snap at him, however, if he stared too long.

Sometimes throw things at him, then begin crying and moaning that she couldn't bear it for a second longer.

"Some women aren't meant to be mothers," his drill commander had said idly.

He'd been on the floor, recovering from his punishment for missing all of those trainings, lying on his stomach since his back would've screamed in protest if he rolled over.

"She won't terminate, will she?"

"No, sir."

"Fine woman," the drill commander sighs. "They can terminate at any time, you know. It's their decision. From beginning to end, they always have the right to decide whether or not they'll carry a baby to term. But they don't terminate, because they know that their suffering has a purpose. Suffering with a purpose is bearable, isn't it?"

"Y-yes, sir."

"Breathe through your nose."

"Yes, sir. Sorry, sir."

"That woman is stronger than you. She is doing her duty. You, on the other hand…"

Men can't become pregnant.

You know this.

And she didn't have sex, her uterus was fertilized and implanted with an egg fused with the sperm of a genetically synthesized donor.

So why are you so upset?

He thought the day of delivery couldn't come quickly enough.

It wasn't that he disliked her.

He had no feelings of any kind for her, since she was his responsibility and nothing more.

But he would like to stop missing training and be able to sleep on his back again.

One day, a full month before she was due, his drill commander had left a much deeper cut on his back than he'd intended to. It had taken longer than usual to bandage the wound up, so he'd come to the birthing home a little later than usual.

It wasn't a requirement, but most voluntary mothers chose to stay on leave at birthing homes rather than at their own dwellings.

This way if anything happened, they would have health professionals nearby to take care of it. The birthing homes also offered a safe, stable environment with carefully regulated resources, specialists, and fellow, possibly more experienced, mothers.

He enters her room, expecting to find her in bed, desperately in need of a foot rub or someone to help her into a hot bath, but instead hears running water and a strange squeaking noise, like the sound of a dying animal, coming from behind the closed bathroom door.

He announces his presence, but is shocked when she merely screams expletives at him, telling him to leave and never come back.

He goes to the door, but is disturbed to find it locked, and blood pooling underneath the crack at his feet.

He calls for help, only to find that she already has, and they're on their way.

That day is the day he sees something he's never seen before, something he doesn't ever want to see again.

He's seen blood before.

He's seen boys and girls alike hurt in training accidents, with broken legs, arms, and even necks.

He's seen people die in hospitals, medical tents, and surgery centers, seen many things from age ten to fourteen, the years in which medical volunteer work is mandatory.

But he's never seen this.

They force him to leave.

But not before he sees blood gushing from between her legs, staining her gown and lower half, her agonized face, full of panic and pain and disgust, her mouth, terrible in its rage, in its ferocious defensiveness, her back bent over, her legs and shoulders shaking. He's pushed out of the room when they arrive, when she unlocks the door and stumbles out, but he still has to see the look on her face.

Ah.

You'd never seen such emotion.

You'd never seen someone hurting so badly they could barely breathe.

And it wasn't the blood, it wasn't the labor cramps or seeing her collapse that scared you.

It was seeing her pain.

Seeing such raw, splitting emotion, so much feeling, anger, horror, disgust, self-loathing, hatred towards her own body for doing this to her...

To her baby.

Because as much as she loathed being pregnant...

She never hated that child, did she?

Not until it gave up on her.

Not until it failed her.

What an emotionally backwards people you are.

Here we mourn the loss of our children because we've lost something precious.

I suppose across the pond, you only mourn the loss of a laborer and a functioning citizen-

We don't drown our children.

We do our best to make sure every single one is born healthy and remains healthy.

You're right.

I had never seen anyone so primal, so raw and unfettered, in my life.

But we aren't emotionless.

We just...we...

Strive to keep emotions out of your duties.

But your duty, it is your life, is it not?

So where do emotions fit, my dear boy, in those strict, meticulously planned existences of yours?

...I was scared.

And I didn't like feeling that way.

The Empire was right to help us move passed emotions.

I don't like them.

They're harmful.

They're...a hindrance.

How could he do his duty if hampered by sentiment?

It's better not to feel.

Ah.

That's how they do it.

Here I was thinking they beat it out of you or genetically altered you in some way.

But all they had to do was condition the feelings away.

What an effective method of discouraging sex, hm?

They let you watch a woman as she's torn apart by a stillborn baby, as she's covered in blood, sweat, tears, and a crippling sense of punishing inadequacy, and most importantly, the bestial, repulsive, true nature of reproduction, in all of its...boorish mess.

...it's still...better than your people.

Excuse me?

Your people would...be disgusted by the birthing process.

Look away.

Be ashamed of a woman's body doing what is natural.

Blood, sweat, mucus, vaginal discharge, fetal tissue...these things repulse you even though they are simply...natural processes. They are the human body removing what is...unclean.

But you think these things make a person unclean.

How disgusted he is, by me... and how disgusted you were, by my blood...

The fluid and flesh that hold a person together…

Perhaps you're ashamed of it because of what it represents, this…boorish mess of human existence.

But you still want sex anyway, even though you believe the body is unclean.

Even if you truly felt bad for that mother, you'd still have reckless intercourse. You'd still waste human lives with reckless abandon.

You have sex without protection, without thoughts of responsibility or health, without thinking about the consequences of your actions.

You… use the afterlife as a repository for the souls you carelessly toss aside when they are inconvenient.

Oh… I was fooled.

I was fooled, I thought your emotions were…were different than ours.

I thought this contentment, this feeling of freedom…was understandable.

Desirable even.

The only emotions I've ever known were the ones that bring a man to his knees, that force a woman to confront inadequacy, that make a child weep when he should be training, and these things I learned early on to discard.

The ones I've experienced here…

I thought perhaps I understood why your people chose not to lose all emotion.

But now I see.

The good ones do not outweigh the bad ones.

They are small and insignificant.

You're hurting.

You're hurting worse than you ever hurt with me.

I'm so jealous.

He gets you all to himself.

They are…small…and insignificant.

They are worthless, they come and go, they're fickle, unstable, uncertain, they are inferior emotions, the Empire at least, understood, it calculated, it knew the emotions that crippled, that drove a man to madness, were not worth the small, meaningless drivel that so entertains you-you hedonistic-

You felt the heat too, don't lie to me, you felt warm all over, his weight was a little scary at first, but you liked it, felt a little confusing itch when he shoved his knee between your legs, when he tugged at your hair.

If you just let yourself enjoy it, maybe you'd understand these meaningless little emotions of ours, hm?

I don't want to. Not anymore.

It's too late now.

You should've died when you had the chance.

Now you have the worst duty of all, my dear boy, the cruelest of responsibilities.

Now you're responsible for living.

Why did he say goodbye?

For the first few days, the prisoner doesn't feel like eating.

All he can do is sit in the basement with his blanket, staring at nothing, thinking.

After hunger becomes unbearable, he does finally get up. But dinner is quiet and he finds himself eating as fast as possible so that he can go to *sleep* as fast as possible to escape his thoughts.

He hears the wind outside.

The snow falling off of trees and thumping onto the roof.

The creaking of the empty cabin as he lies alone in his room, staring up through the skylight.

It's the little noises that get to him.

It's not the silence, but the little noises that could drive him mad.

In an effort to get away from his thoughts, and distract himself from noise, he organizes.

Makes a mental estimation of how much food he can afford to eat, assuming the dissident is gone for a week. He doesn't believe he will be, but there's no harm in being cautious.

He cleans, moves things around, re-organizes all of the dishes in the house, stacks cups in more efficient formations, does the laundry over and over, makes his bed, fusses over how he arranges the sheets. It's nervous work, the fidgeting of a man waiting for something, someone, but he can't help it.

If his hands are busy, his mind can be controlled.

Kept away from the realities of his past and present.

During the day time, he's mostly successful in hiding from them.

During the night time, not so much.

He hears Teacher whispering to him at night, sees shadows moving in his room, shadows of his mother, the General, the drill commander, the woman who'd miscarried, the man with the ink on his hands, his Cluster. They flit around the borders of his room, watching, observing, but unwilling to participate.

He blinks and they disappear.

Appear somewhere else.

Looking neutral, bored, rather uninterested in him, yet simultaneously unable to stay away from him.

He blinks and sees the dissident coming out of the darkness to grab his ankles, to smash the bones of his feet, to break his kneecaps, to cripple his legs permanently in some form to keep him from escaping. From running away from him.

Him and his cheerful ways, his energetic grins, his passion for the outdoors and human interactions.

His hand.

His fingers, intertwined with his.

They squeeze and squeeze and squeeze until he imagines his fingers snapping.

He closes his eyes and feels the dissident's fingers in his hair.

They pull and pull relentlessly, tauntingly, pleadingly.

The prisoner wraps himself as tightly as he can in blankets and lies in bed for hours and hours on end.

When, unbidden, thoughts of their intimacy come to him, he pulls as many blankets as he has around himself.

They make him feel safe.

Untouchable.

Sex is agreeable.

He had been told this from time to time, in the barracks.

The other men seemed to view it as a hobby, something to do to pass the time.

They ascribed no particular meaning or passion to it; it was simply an activity that had a pleasant build up and enjoyable culmination.

But he hadn't felt anything like that.

He'd felt a prickle of unease when the dissident's skin made contact with his, strange, electrifying prickles when he'd been kissed, but these are not things that make him feel…good.

Sitting on the couch and watching the snow fall feels good.

Watching the stars or the fire feels good.

Being touched…it had been…

Was it really bad?

No.

Not exactly.

Confusing.

It was confusing, *and thus deeply disturbing.*

It made me unhappy.

In the desk in the basement are several writing utensils and both used and unused notepads.

He doesn't write things that makes sense, just what he feels the need to write.

I am unhappy.

I am unhappy.

There is nothing here.

I do not understand.

Where are people?

What do they look like?

What do they look for?

I am writing.

I do not write.

Will he come back?

Is he gone?

Is he safe?

Why did he say goodbye?

On the seventh day, he still believes he will come back.

It's snowing again.

He waits on the porch during the day, and on the couch at night, eyes on the empty fireplace, ears alert, waiting for the sound of crunching boots, approaching footsteps.

But on the tenth day, he begins to wonder.

On the twelfth day, he doubts.

And on the fourteenth day, he wakes up knowing he's gone.

He's left.

And what can he do now?

What should he do?

Leave?

The prisoner frets.

He walks back and forth, wasting valuable energy.

He's never felt such an all-consuming anxiety.

What to do?

Where to go?

He knows no one.

He knows no destination.

He knows no goal. No mission.

He makes small, unrushed, uncoordinated attempts to collect items he might need for a journey.

Gathers them inside the bag he wasn't going to carry, the bag with the tent.

It's heavy, but he takes to carrying it around the cabin to help himself grow accustomed to it.

It's not so bad.

Thanks to the dissident's care and the recuperation time, he's almost as strong as he was before.

His weight has at least recovered some.

He checks himself in the mirror and finds that he's not quite so deathly thin. His skin is no longer pulled taut against his bones, as he's recovered some fat and muscle, and it's regained some color. His eyes are no longer sunken in, merely rimmed with tiredness, and his face is a little less gaunt and starved.

Not to mention a little less beaten to a bloody pulp.

The prisoner touches his chin, his cheeks, running his hand over his face, brushing the bridge of his nose, his forehead.

Then he pushes his hair back, pulling at the strands and feeling the tug on his scalp.

But upon realizing what he's doing, he lets go quickly, and hurries away from the mirror.

Goodbye. Goodbye. Goodbye.

He writes it multiple times.

He scribbles it into his hands in ink sometimes, smudging it, letting it stain his fingers like the man he remembered, the man whose words he never read.

Had he written goodbye too?

Goodbye. Goodbye. Goodbye.

To whom?

The sixteenth day, he is ready to say goodbye to this place as well.

And to the dissident, although he's already left.

The prisoner goes out early in the morning.

He wants to remember where the dissident had said to go, what river he had said to follow, where the delta they were to meet at if they got separated was.

How long ago that felt.

We'll do our best not to get separated.

He follows the path, but goes a little further, wanting to see where the ground begins to incline, where the trees begin to grow more and more spaced out.

He's cold, but determined as he marches forward, careful to mark trees with the kitchen knife he had brought along with him for that purpose.

He'd stumbled through these trees.

Injured and alone and frozen to his core, in every manner possible, soul hollow but eager to find something to fill itself with, he'd staggered his way to the cabin, to the dissident's waiting arms, where he'd found respite. He'd been searching for clarity, not comfort, but had allowed himself to be distracted.

Now he will look for clarity again.

He will keep searching.

But as he walks, as he tries to dismiss the dissident from his mind, and fails, he thinks that he had found something.

For a moment, he had definitely found something in his companion.

But it was an illusion or only temporary.

He hadn't found the right thing.

But…

The prisoner smiles to himself.

He thanks the dissident anyway.

Illusion, temporary, artificial, selfish, no matter.

The dissident had still given him something…

He'd given him the opportunity to ask this question.

The knowledge that he *is* searching.

And something to search for.

He is grateful.

He is very grateful to the dissident.

But he can't help but wish the dissident had stayed long enough for him to express it.

In his musings, he begins to pay increasingly less attention to his surroundings. And he stumbles, his foot tripping over something long and hard. He catches himself just before he falls, his knife dropping out of his hand reflexively so he can catch himself. He fumbles for it as he straightens, trying to see what he'd tripped on.

It only takes him a moment.

A long black line in the snow.

That's what it looks like.

But when he bends down to touch it, running his fingers over its smooth, freezing metal exterior, his heart seems to tighten, and his breath catches in his throat.

It's the dissident's rifle.

65

The dissident's skin feels raw, gnawed on and scratched by the wind and chill of the air.

He feels a stiff movement somewhere on his face.

The ghost of a smile, perhaps. His muscles imitating a social gesture. A natural twitch, a flex, with a culturally assigned meaning.

He smiles.

Not at you, though.

He appreciates his discomfort.

The squeezing, coiled feeling of coldness creeping up his neck, between his fingers.

He rubs the latter together, then touches the former absentmindedly.

He hasn't eaten in a couple days, but that's alright.

He ran out of food a week ago, but had been hunting for raccoons, squirrels, anything he could find, to keep himself going.

He'd gotten lucky a few times.

Killed a bobcat.

A lynx.

Nothing large enough to bother taking home, though.

You mean the cabin.

The cabin.

He can't go back there.

Not yet.

If you're not going to go back until the guilt goes away, then you're never going back.

His mind immediately rejects the notion of not returning.

But he can't bring himself to go back *right* now.

He just can't face him.

When he isn't focused on hunting, his experienced fingers skillfully cocking his weapon as he hides behind trees, crouches behind rocks, all he can see is that look on his face.

That look he had before he went into the basement.

So much for being scared of the dark.

But maybe he found something scarier than the dark.

He crouches behind a fallen tree.

Carefully sets his rifle up, aims it at the frozen water.

Is content to simply wait now, even though his stomach feels like it's caving in, he's so hungry.

But the contentment fades away as he begins to think again.

He blinks and sees that face.

Such a plain person.

Such a plain face. Unremarkable.

Crooked nose, broken a few times.

Narrow mouth that hesitated to speak.

He's not pretty.

Or handsome either, although, the dissident imagines that if he were one of the elites, an artist, a singer perhaps, and a talented one at that, then any gossip magazine would find him acceptable enough.

His only really interesting feature is his eyes.

Dark eyes.

Mysterious.

Even when he's afraid, his emotions lurk just out of reach, hiding beneath a surface, only the first layer of intrigue.

Even when he's laughing, there's a closed door, a gate, keeping those eyes guarded.

How he'd longed to tear down those walls just once-

To forcibly take what is not yours.

He tries to force the image to go away, but he can't force himself not to blink, and every time he blinks *he sees those plain eyes.*

It's circumstance, nothing more. You wouldn't think twice about him if you met him in a bar.

So circumstances were special, that's irrelevant.

He's attracted to him.

In more ways than one, perhaps.

There's no denying that.

But you acted on your attraction, the same way you always do.

It backfired.

Why did it backfire?

Because the prisoner didn't…want him.

He doesn't want to be here.

Why not?

How could he still long for his home?

How could he not see…the joys of being alive, the value of their lifestyle over his old one, all of the sensations, the full spectrum of the human experience?

Not one of you.

But human.

All humans view the world through different eyes.

See in different shades.

Comprehend in different languages.

They have wants and needs, just like us, but they're not the same as ours.

And if they are, then it's slanted differently, it's tightly intertwined with their own cultural system.

They like…stability.

Impartiality.

Commitment.

Is that what he wants from you?

Or does he want nothing from you?

Does he even want at all?

The dissident shakes his head.

It's not his business, if the prisoner wants him or not.

He shouldn't have crossed the line again.

The prisoner has made it so clear…how could he have slipped up again…

Because…because here we do not have to hold back.

With him…*we do.*

The dissident abruptly takes his gun off of the log.

That night he goes without eating again, but curls into a ball, pressing his hands into his stomach to quell some of the hunger pangs.

It's time he got back to the prisoner.

He deserves an apology.

A…promise to never do it again.

A…reassurance that he understands now.

And it won't be a problem anymore, not once they leave the cabin.

He can control his urges when he isn't locked up in a cage with just one other living creature.

He hadn't had this problem at all before they arrived here, right?

It will pass.

In the meantime…the prisoner is alone.

All alone in that house.

Perhaps running out of food supplies.

Perhaps afraid that he'd left for good.

Or that he had left in a rage, rather than leaving because he needed space and time to think.

He needs to get back.

More than anything, he needs to get back, it's been, what, two weeks?

He wants to see him.

So he begins to head back.

Re-tracing his steps.

Each step just encourages him, invites him home, where food is probably running low, and the prisoner will be relieved to see him, and he'll accept his apology, and be happy to see he's brought *meat,* which he'll cook to perfection and they'll eat by the fire, sitting on the floor in companionable silence or in gentle, quiet conversation.

The dissident blinks, little daydreaming grin on his face, and instead of the prisoner's eyes, he sees…

A rather large, somewhat threatening blur.

He flinches and points his gun.

It shuffles over the ground.

Looks curiously at him.

A bear cub. Had to be close to a year old.

But the implications of what the bear cub implies are lost on him for a moment.

Maybe it's due to his stomach, his hunger, gurgling away in his gut, maybe it's due to his mind, garbled by thoughts of his prisoner, by memories.

But he doesn't see the threat as it's staring him in the face.

All he's thinking about is how he doesn't want to come back empty handed, how he needs something else in order to make his fantasy real, and a target just presented itself.

So without a single thought in his mind, on impulse, he quickly aims. Fires.

The bear cub immediately goes limp.

He sighs.

He'll feel bad about it later. Right now, he's hungry and if he walks quickly, he can make it home and start preparing its meat before he drops dead from starvation, and how embarrassing that would be, *just* making it home and collapsing on the porch, with meat in his hands-

He hears a loud, angry huffing sound.

A familiar sound.

One he's heard before, but not quite so…large.

He stares at the cub's corpse, instantly filled with regret, for an entirely different reason than before now, and he's still staring when he's thrown onto the ground.

The gun feels abnormally warm in the prisoner's hands.

But he hasn't fired a gun in a long time.

And certainly not a rifle.

It burns his palms and he drops it, fingers shaking. When he blinks, for one heart-stopping moment, they're soaked with blood. When he blinks again, the blood is gone, but the image still haunts him as he stares at the carcass of the huge, hulking beast he'd just killed.

He's never seen a bear in person.

He had no idea they were this huge.

The prisoner sees one of its children scuttle away, into the bushes, but barely registers it as he falls beside the bear's body and immediately pushes as hard as he can against it.

The body rolls over with a thump, its bloodied head, shot multiple times by the prisoner's swift, but accurate bullets, flipping over with it. Its mouth falls open in the parody of a snarl, its huge tongue lolling out and its thick bloody teeth bared as its lips flop.

It's dead.

Yes.

So is he.

No.

"Dad, there's so much blood, I can't-I can't, I'm gonna be sick!"

He can see the baby's corpse out of the corner of his eye.

Then he's jerked back and forth so hard his teeth rattle, his neck snaps to and fro so severely that he thinks that he can hear his brain sloshing up against the confines of his skull, so shaken it's nothing but liquid now. He feels like a toy in the jaws of an enormous, energetic dog.

But this is no dog, this is-this is a-

"Bear with me for just one moment. Just...distance yourself. Don't look at it like it's human. Just think of it...like a broken piece of machinery. No, don't look away. Get rid of those churning gut feelings. You don't need them to help this man, and you want to help this man, don't you? Go on, nod for me, my boy, nod. There's a good boy."

He opens his mouth to scream, but it's immediately stuffed with snow as his head is slammed into the ground, as his entire body is battered by the force of the bear's thrusts.

The bear sniffs him, her huge head bending over his head, panting hot and acrid breaths in his ear. Its nose tickles the back of his neck, cold and wet and not unlike the friendly, gentle snout of his father's favorite hunting dog, Connie.

He doesn't move.

He's not sure what kind of bear it is, all he knows is that if it was protecting its cub, then it might leave if he plays dead.

But if it was hungry...which was likely, as... he himself knows, there's not much food running about...

The bear moves off of him.

For a moment, he thinks, a jolt of hysterical hope unsettling his belly, that it's going to leave.

But what happens next smothers any hope that the bear isn't hungry.

It sinks its teeth into the juncture between his neck and his shoulder.

This time he screams.

It hurts more than anything he's ever felt, more than breaking his leg skydiving, more than all of the concussions he'd gotten playing football, more than being backed over with a tractor and breaking his ribs.

All of those things had occurred during a moment of excitement, a "boy's moment," his dad had called it, when a boy gets so ahead of himself that he forgets he is mortal.

He's never felt more mortal in his life.

All he can do is twitch weakly as it pulls him away.

Its other baby following cheerfully behind.

Mocking him.

His eyes hurt as he strains them to get one last look at its sibling's corpse.

"This is your fault," the corpse seems to say. "I'm dead because of you."

I was hungry. It was nothing personal.

He closes his eyes, forcing the corpse to go away.

But it persists, it appears, dark and motionless against the white background of his mind, which is splashed with blood and red flashes of pain as his body is dragged across bumpy terrain and through pin-pricking snow.

It opens its baby mouth, but it's not a bear's growl, it's a baby's cry-

"There are no unwanted children."

He'd drowned them because they were not ready yet.

Not ready for life.

It happened.

She would come back.

She would come back someday, he had to believe that.

As he lowers his baby sister, small and weak and not ready for life yet, into the tub, he could've sworn he saw her smile. She reaches out with her small hand and grasps his sleeve playfully.

He stops for a moment, amused.

Her weak, tiny fingers brush over his clothing, then fall off.

She kicks her stubby little legs, and for a second, he doesn't want to do it.

He entertains the idea of hiding her in the barn and taking care of her himself.

It couldn't be that hard, right?

His own personal pet project.

Dad always said he needed to dedicate his time to more projects...

Ah, but he doesn't really know how to take care of a baby...and his little sister deserves proper parents to take care of her. He isn't a proper parent.

He smiles at her happily gurgling face as he lowers her into the tub.

He lets out an airy groan, a plea to no one, begging for help.

The living bear cub runs up alongside him.

It playfully swats at him with its tiny claws.

It too speaks.

It opens its mouth, its little tongue curled, its bottom jaw lined with perfect white fangs, and says, "I said no."

Monica said no, but she didn't mean it.

Women are complicated, his dad said. They don't know what they want. Not until they've got it. If you want a girl to want you, you gotta give yourself to her, and then leave. If she's the right one, she'll come back begging you to take her again. And if not, she's just playing harder to get than most. And then you'll really *know she's the right one.*

She said no.

He backs off, but she's just being playful.

Next time, surely.

She pushes him away, and he thinks surely next time, she'll be begging. The offer is enough, isn't it? That's "giving," isn't it? Why did women have to send out such mixed signals? Why couldn't she be like Janice, who Cody said wanted it all the time? And had asked him for, no less? Couldn't she be less complicated, like Janice?

Like all the other girls he knew, girls who would be perfectly happy to...

Ah, but he likes this one.

She just doesn't know what she wants.

The next time, he decides, is going to be their first time.

He asks her very politely.

She says no.

But he expected that.

A theory comes to him when it's all done, as she's panting, flushed and pleased, or at least he thinks so, since she moaned quite a bit, especially near the end.

It's not her fault that she's not aware of what she wants.

The bear stops.

He lets out a choked gurgle.

The cub tugs at his sleeve.

He stares up at the sky, face swollen and bruised from being slammed into the ground, back and neck on fire, cut and chewed up and bleeding heavily.

His everything aches.

The bear's paws bat at him.

He has only a moment to consider putting all of his remaining strength into one last ditch effort to get up and run, but it's so short, too short, because it's on him, its paws are so big and heavy on his chest, and he gasps, he can't breathe, it hurts so much, it's so heavy, so strong, thick with muscle and superior physique, and he bizarrely thinks of Monica again, of her face when he was on top of her, and then her face changes, and he's staring at the prisoner.

If only he were here.

If only he hadn't left on his own.

Left the prisoner by himself.

Now the prisoner will think he just up and left and just never came back.

Maybe he didn't even wait for you.

Maybe he just left on his own the moment you were gone.

Maybe he wasn't playing hard to get.

Maybe he just didn't like you.

Or want to be around you.

It lets go.

He squeezes his eyes tightly shut.

Snap my neck.

Bite through my throat.

Please just don't eat me alive.

Monica.

Sister.

...my...friend.

If you were scared...I'm sorry.

Suddenly, there's an explosion of noise just above his head.

The bear snarls in pain.

He gasps as its paws dig into his chest, its weight so overpowering, so crushing, that he damn near passes out.

He struggles, shoving against its powerful, broad chest, as immovable as a statue, but he's weakened by his injuries and the thing is just too strong. It's not even fazed; it merely lurches forward and bats him in the face with its paw.

Its claws rip lines of fire right through his skin, splitting his eye in half, narrowly missing the other one, slicing through the flesh of his face like paper, and blinding him.

He screams out in shock and pain, his hand instinctively clutching the parts of his face that've been set on fire, that feel engorged and lumpy and *peeling.*

He wants to pass out.

He's going to.

He won't wake up.

And he's fine with that.

He falls again, his back hitting his snow cushion for the last time, grey finally overtaking the screaming red of his vision.

He's barely clinging to consciousness, the pain pulsing like a heartbeat inside his damaged eye, shock waves of agony spasming throughout his abused body, when he hears another explosion of sound, right above his head, so it seems.

A rifle, he thinks dazedly.

His rifle.

The cabin owner's rifle, technically, but his.

He feels a heavy, suffocating weight drop on him, gasps, but then it moves, it's pushed off of him, and suddenly, blessedly, (perhaps it's an hallucination, his rapidly fading mind says), there are hands on him.

It hurts, but damn does it feel good having someone to confess to.

His head and neck strain, he reaches out, feels the other person stiffen, tense in his grip, but he doesn't care. He grips his arms tightly and opens his mouth to thank him.

But he can't.

His body is torn up, and there's blood rolling down his cheeks like tears, warmly gushing over his chin like a waterfall.

The prisoner, because of course it's him, is saying something, probably staring at him with concern in his lovely, complicated, mysterious eyes, but the dissident merely smiles, touches his cheek gently, with bloody fingers, and lets his head fall backwards.

Into the prisoner's arms, which hold him like his mother used to.

68

Please don't die.
Please don't die.
Please don't die.
Not like the others.
All of those people I saw…in the hospitals, in the morgues.
Please don't be another corpse I have to bury.

He's never known terror like this.

His life has been threatened more times than he can count, more times than he can remember, or even care to remember. He'd been trained and conditioned to suppress any feelings of self-preservation that might interfere with a mission, because fear of death is irrelevant, insignificant when one's life belongs to the Empire, and to lose it in service was to award one's self with the ultimate purpose. The Empire's victory was your victory, life forfeited or not.

The times he felt true fear had been when he was afraid of dying a failure. When he'd been shot down and swimming away from hostile territory, knowing he had failed and would die with the Empire's loss over his head, damning his name, his body, to obscurity and shame.

When he was tortured, used as the sick conduit of another man's sadistic whims, for no purpose, no purpose at all.

He had known fear. If not fear of death, then fear of failure. Of pointless suffering.

But this fear has never touched his heart, frozen his blood, slowed his pulse to a stop.

This fear for another person.

He tears off his jacket.

Pulls off his shirt.

Tears it into strips.

He wraps it as gently as he can around the dissident's eyes, wincing as he moans, but knows he has to tighten it, has to at least slow the bleeding.

He's barely aware of how cold it is, how his own skin, his own heartbeat, might be in jeopardy as he sits, shirtless and kneeling in snow, patching the dissident up.

He can barely feel his fingers.

He's clumsy, he's always been a clumsy medic. He presses another rag to his neck, trying to slow some of the worst of the bleeding there.

His shirt is not enough.

And he can't prevent an infection from developing in his eye if he doesn't go back.

The prisoner's fingers curl in his shirt.

He doesn't want to leave him.

He doesn't want to leave him alone.

But he can't risk moving him, not yet.

He'll have to go back.

But he can't…

He doesn't want to…

And what if there are other animals lurking out here?

He looks upwards automatically, remembering the vultures he'd seen as a child, on a moving screen, descending in lazy, unhurried circles onto dying or dead animals.

What if there are other animals?

Another bear? Things he's never seen before?

Can he leave him?

The prisoner looks down, conflicted.

He knows he has to make his choice fast.

If he tries to move him, he might die, or his injuries might be exacerbated.

But the thought of leaving him weighs him down, turns his legs and feet into lead.

He doesn't want to leave him.

Even if the dissident had left him, he hesitates to return the favor.

But time is moving fast, so he bites his lip and makes his decision.

Even though he doesn't want to, even though it feels like something inside of him is tearing itself apart, he pulls his jacket back on.

He stands up.

Or tries to.

The dissident seizes him by the wrist.

Caught by surprise, the prisoner is yanked down to his level again.

"Don't leave," he croaks.

The prisoner grasps his arm.

"Don't. Please."

The prisoner gently pulls away from him.

"I have to," he whispers.

The dissident, his once handsome face torn up almost beyond recognition, his hair stuck flat to his head with blood, his clothing in tatters, his built, muscular body small and helpless, broken up and mangled, lets out a gasp.

The prisoner pulls his jacket back off and throws it over him.

"I'll come back. As fast I can. I promise. I'll come back," the prisoner says.

The dissident slowly falls back onto the snow.

"Don't fall asleep," the prisoner warns him.

But he doesn't expect the dissident will be able to listen to him, not for long.

So he runs.

Runs faster than he ever ran for any officer, for any physical exam, where they prized resilience over sheer speed, stamina over swiftness. Runs faster than he ever did on any mission, even when ordered to be as timely as possible.

Pushes his muscles harder than he's ever pushed them, feeling adrenaline pulsing through his veins, his heart in his ears.

And the dissident's face, mangled, but still able to convey regret, a sorrow he does not understand, and the desperate desire to say something, fueling his frantic heart.

He wants to hear what he will say.

So he runs even faster.

He feels rather than sees the prisoner.

His hands cradle his head, they're so gentle, running through his hair like his mother's used to it, and his fingers are so warm and gentle on his throat, they brush passed his chin, they caress his face as they move, and he opens his mouth, wanting to thank him, to beg him for forgiveness.

But then the moment is over.

And the prisoner is *leaving*.

Don't leave.

The prisoner is speaking.

He can't hear a word he's saying.

All he knows is that the prisoner is leaving.

Don't leave.

But of course he's left.

He's left because that is what the dissident had done.

The dissident opens his mouth, but he doesn't have the air to spare.

Instead, he lays his head back and fights to remain alive.

He must live.

He must tell him.

Even if the prisoner never comes back, if he's left him here, abandoned him, he must live as long as possible, just in case he does.

He must tell him.

He grits his teeth and forces himself to keep breathing.

70

"Don't you want to look at the stars tonight?"
"No, we're going out to the city, don't you want to come?"
"I think I'll go canoeing."
"Suit yourself, Grandpa."
"Very funny. Have fun."
"We will, drinks are on Monica."
The lake is so beautiful at night.
No one out here but him.
And the stars of course.
On clear nights, they leave the heavens and swim beside him.
He can reach out and touch them.
It's dark.
He can't see anything.
It's cold.
There's something around his head.
He tries to tear it off.
Someone stops him.
He tries to fight back, but he's too weak.
The dissident tries to say something, but then he blinks, suddenly completely drained.

He falls back, the person's arms slowing his descent, lowering him back into nothingness. Into the lake, swimming with stars.

"We will live gated no longer!"

"No longer!"

"There are others out there with more resources than us!"

"No longer!"

"We are stronger! We have hidden within our walls for long enough!"

"No longer!"

"We own this continent! It has always been ours! We must take back our resources! No longer shall we suffer!"

"No longer!"

"And we will take back our land! We will expand it so that our children may live in prosperity! In our descendants' names, we will take back what is ours! We will be oppressed no longer!"

"No longer!"

"They're trouble."

"They know what they're talking about!"

"They're trying to stir trouble with the southern nation. Leave them be, let them live in peace! Our entire system rests on the foundation of the Border system."

"It's crumbling. We need to fix it before it collapses under our feet."

"Don't do this."

"I'll come home again."

"Mom! Mom! Mom!"

He needs to go home.

His mother will be worried. His father is probably out looking for him, and he's so old, he hasn't been well.

He needs to get home.

Who's holding him?

Let go.

Why does he hurt?

This pain in-in everything, someone's holding him, he's the one that did this-

A solid hit.

The person holding him cries out.

Get out get out get out get out-

Tired.

Too tired.

Sinking…sinking into…

The person's hands on him again, but he's too weak to fight them off…

Every time he opens his eyes, it's to darkness.

There's something tied over his eyes.

He grabs at it again, but is *stopped* again.

The hand that stops him is warm.

It strokes his hand comfortingly, squeezing his fingers, his knuckles. Its palm is rough, it feels calloused, but it's also kind, protective. Tender, but firm.

He stops trying to move his own hand and lets it fall to his side.

The hand remains over his.

The prisoner hasn't slept in four days.

He can't.

The dissident wakes up at the strangest times.

Usually delirious, disoriented, afraid of nothing *he* can see.

But insistent.

He seems to find the bandages around his eyes itchy or in some way undesirable, because he keeps trying to rip them off, and the prisoner has to force him to stop.

The prisoner had wrapped him up in blankets and crouched against a nearby tree, spending all day and night watching him, his exhausted eyes occasionally flickering to the fire.

The flames never cease to be a source of comfort.

He rubs his weary eyes, eyelids twitching, drooping with tiredness.

The dissident jerks.

They shoot back open and he watches him anxiously.

If he rolls over, he'll be too close to the fire for the prisoner's comfort.

But he also needs to keep warm…

The prisoner crawls over to him.

He presses himself against the dissident's body, putting a barrier between it and the fire, and wraps his blanket around the two of them.

For a while, he just listens to the fire crackle and watches the dissident sleep with unseeing eyes.

But then, for no reason he can think of, he looks up.

The stars are out in vast quantity again.

He puts his hands in a rough square around his eyes, pretending to look at them through his skylight.

He longs for the bed, for the room, the safety of the cabin.

The dissident shifts, and his sleeping hand touches his thigh.

The prisoner holds it there absentmindedly, rubbing his scarred knuckles and the back of his hand without thinking.

The next thing he knows, he's jerking back awake, having accidentally drifted off to sleep. The dissident's arm is around his neck. His face is in his shoulder, his hair tickling the prisoner's cheek.

He pushes him off, feeling strange.

The prisoner lies down next to the dissident.

Pulls his far leg over his own.

Takes a hold of the dissident's far arm by the wrist, pulls it over his shoulder.

And as smoothly as he can, he rolls over, pulling the unconscious man onto his back.

As he stands up, his knees buckle.

But he forces himself to ignore the pain, the screaming of his muscles, merely gripping the dissident's wrists tightly around his neck as he begins to walk.

He's hoping he isn't worsening the dissident's injuries.

He's hoping the dissident's breath, hot and faltering on his neck, doesn't stop.

He's hoping the dissident's heart, beating hard and wild at his back, the man's larger frame encompassing him completely as he struggles to move through the snow and see through the rapidly increasing falling snowflakes, doesn't stop.

But the hopes do not outweigh the fears he has, the fears burning in his trembling hands, shuddering through his chest, shaking apart his stomach and vital organs, cracking his fragile bones.

He is hurting him.

He will lose him.

It will be his fault.

He has…betrayed him.

Betrayed the dissident.

Betrayed him with the body too weak to lift him properly, too weak to run faster, to take care of him properly, to save his life.

He betrayed his Empire, and now he's betrayed the only other thing he had in this world, the only other person who gave him a purpose.

The dissident's head lolls, his hair tickling his neck, his nose and mouth pressing into his shoulder. They feel cold.

He pulls his arms tighter around his neck.

The dissident is bleeding through the bandages again. His blood is sickeningly sticky and wet as it creeps down the prisoner's throat, lovingly caressing the flesh wall separating it from its foreign brethren.

He swallows.

He cannot lose him.

He carries the dissident on his back, his body limp and unresponsive, walking with as much speed as he can muster. He's filled with a borderline hysteria as he carries him, the unconscious man's feet dragging in the snow, feeling like sandbars as they force him to walk slower.

He'd run out of supplies, but before he could go back to the cabin, it had begun snowing.

And he'd been terrified that he would lose the dissident to frostbite or hypothermia, or worse, get lost in a blizzard. He isn't sure if the dissident can be moved, but he's at least more ready for travel than he was days ago.

The prisoner wrestled with that decision for almost a full day.

By the time he made up his mind, the snow was falling so thick his vision was almost all white.

He can barely see now.

He blinks away snowflakes.

They sting his cheeks.

He grips the dissident's freezing hands as hard as he can, pulling his arms even more tightly around his neck as he marches on.

All he can hear is his own breathing and the lonely thud of his heart, pounding away in his ears.

The wind, howling, a blanket white noise as empty as silence.

The snow, deathly quiet, as it piles up around him.

He's never felt anything like this before.

His comrades dying had never affected him.

He did not fear for their lives.

Even when they were in danger and he needed to help, to save them, he never felt fear, just an icy calm, a certain iron determination to come to their aid.

But the dissident?

Heavy, much too heavy against his back, his arms choking him, it feels like.

If he dies, the prisoner will know it was his fault, because he was too weak to save him, and he will become a murderer, a traitor of body once again, betraying the objective by being inadequate.

You've betrayed everything you stand for.

You've betrayed countless men and woman, dutiful, obedient, honorable people who dedicated their lives to that which you once held dear.

What makes him so special?

Not even a member of your own kind.

You never gave the others this fear, this personal concern. This...determination to save someone.

Did they mean nothing to you?

Perhaps you aren't just betraying in body.

Perhaps you are betraying in mind as well.

The prisoner ignores the voice.

He can't think straight, and the voice's words sting too sharply, dig too deeply.

Besides.

They are irrelevant.

He must not lose the dissident.

He must not.

His own weakness cannot betray him.

He will not lose him.

Not again.

He needs to tell him.

He needs to.

The snow is so beautiful.

It sparkles around him, bright as stars, gleaming like the sun, dancing around him in blinding purity.

He's carving a blood trail through it.

He can see flashes of ugly red on the pure white ground as he drifts in and out of consciousness.

Ugly.

So ugly.

He wants to cry out to the prisoner to stop, he's ruining God's masterpiece, but he doesn't have the energy.

Instead all he can do is feel the prisoner moving underneath him, struggling with all of his might, breathing hard.

So firm and warm underneath him.

Almost as if they were back at the cabin and he was-

No no no no no no no no stop right now, stop this instant-

He forces the turbulent, roiling emotions to abate, to settle in his chest.

The prisoner doesn't deserve that.

He doesn't deserve to feel the fear of being crushed, of being suffocated by the weight of another, of having his will ignored, and being pummeled and torn apart for the satisfaction of a stronger being.

He might be underneath him, but he's not *beneath* him.

The prisoner's carrying him this time, the prisoner's supporting *him,* and he will not be tainted by his sickness, not like the snow, painted red as the dissident soils *its* purity.

He lets out a noise, a pained choke, a gasp of air that was meant to have words in it.

The prisoner stops immediately.

He falls to the ground. Comes to his side.

Begins to change his bandages.

He doesn't seem to notice the dissident trying to speak to him.

He wakes up blind again.

He lets out a gasp and tries to get up, grasping a soft material, a sheet, or no, it's the couch, he's touching a leg, it's made of wood, he tries to open his eyes, but one won't open, it won't open, and the other seems to be fused shut, he can't open that one either, why can't he open his eyes, where is he, there's someone holding him, someone touching his shoulders, he shoves them back, hears the person yell, and it's familiar, but he can't stop, can't think, he scrabbles to his feet, or tries, because he falls back, and the other person is on him again, holding him down by the shoulders, it hurts, his shoulders hurt, his neck hurts, everything hurts, his spine arcs in pain, it hurts so much, his back, why can't he see-?

"Stop. Stop. Please. Stop."

He does.

He's tired.

The voice is tired.

He feels sorry for it.

If he sleeps, maybe the voice will sleep too.

They'll both sleep and be ok.

He'll wake up and be able to see again.

"I wanted to see, I wanted to see, I wanted to see!"

The prisoner is once again jostled from his light sleep by the dissident, whose hands are firmly pressing into his heavily bandaged eyes. The prisoner stands up and grabs at his arms, but the dissident wrenches them away.

"I wanted to see the outside world, I wanted to see new people and things and expand our horizons and see how others lived and looked like and I wanted to hear new music and see new plays and movies and I thought the Borders had to come down, I thought we'd been hiding for long enough and I was right, wasn't I, you're here, you're here, and you're not so bad, the rest of the world must be the same, it must be the same, we-we shouldn't hide from you, from one another, no longer, no longer!"

The prisoner, a little disturbed, tries to push him back down.

But the dissident fights him off, shoving him away and trying to stand up. He staggers, falling to his knees immediately. The prisoner rushes to his side.

"I wanted to see! I wanted to see!" the dissident cries out. He lets himself be pulled up and put back on the couch. But as the prisoner moves away, the dissident's hand shoots out and grasps his sleeve.

He yanks him back down to his level.

He can't see the prisoner, just feel his soft breath on his face.

"I need to tell you something."

"It can wait," the prisoner says softly.

"No...no...if I die-"

"You won't die."

"Everyone dies," the dissident whimpers. "We all die. I just wanted you to know, before I do...I'm sorry. I'm so sorry. I'm sorry."

The prisoner sways slightly in his grip.

"It's okay."

"It isn't."

The dissident lets go of him. Falls back onto the couch.

The prisoner pushes him more firmly onto it, wrapping him back up in blankets, checking his bandages to make sure he didn't irritate anything.

He keeps murmuring it isn't, saying it over and over again, curling onto his side, whispering it isn't, it isn't, and he's still mouthing it when the prisoner begins to nod off again.

"I want to help."

"You're in charge of food supply. The resistance needs you."

"But I want to do more."

"Feeding all of us and coordinating with new members is a lot, it's everything!"

"But I can do so much more, I'm qualified to do more than just keep track of how much food we can export. Come on, I know I won't disappoint you! Just keep me in mind in case any special assignments come on, anything I would be suited for?"

"Oh, fine, fine. What kind of skills do you have?"

"...well...I'm a decent medic, and I know computers. I'm a decent shot. I've been trained in close combat. And uh..."

"And?"

"I know how to survive in the wilderness. I like to camp, and I can handle all terrains."

"...well, I'll keep you in mind, I guess, but I don't know if we'd ever need a guy like that."

He's so tired.

The prisoner rubs his eyes furiously. He's sure they're puffy and red *and* heavy with bags from too many sleepless nights.

But the dissident is looking better.

Some color has returned to his face.

He's able to *see* a little, his untouched eye strained, but functioning normally.

He can actually *recognize* the prisoner when he wakes up.

He can sit up.

The prisoner can get him to drink.

Eat a little.

He doesn't say a word, but he does sometimes stare at the prisoner like he's thinking of something to say, but is still too tired to do it.

He sleeps less fitfully.

Can move on his own, albeit stiffly, painfully.

The prisoner still has to help him to the toilet, the dissident clutching his arm like a life preserver, but he's getting stronger.

He stares at the dissident's sleeping body.

Sunlight streams in through the windows, blinding and unimpeded by clouds.

The snow is finally melting. Patches of dirt are finally peeking through the layers of white.

The lake has thawed. That's where he goes now, his weary eyes darting to the dissident one last time before retrieving the rod from the basement.

He always does his best to come back before the dissident wakes up. The first time he'd gone fishing, he'd been so anxious about leaving him alone that he hadn't caught a thing, opting instead to rush back to the cabin after a mere ten minutes.

After ascertaining that the dissident was sleeping, safe and comfortable, he'd returned to his spot. Only to rush back, fifteen minutes later, to do it again.

Now he knows the dissident will be ok.

But he still tries to come back as quickly as possible so the dissident won't have to wake up alone.

The two times he doesn't make it, the dissident looks up from the couch, his face so relieved the prisoner feels guilty.

Don't leave.

He enjoys fishing.

He can't stand for that long, as he had pulled quite a few muscles running and carrying the dissident as far as he had, his weak ankle more hobbled and wobbly than ever, but he sits rather comfortably on a smooth, large rock and waits for a fish to bite.

As soon as the dissident's condition had stabilized, he'd gone back for all the items he'd left behind. The bloody bandages had been blown away, as had some articles of clothing, a blanket, and an empty bottle of antibiotics, but he finds the rifle carefully wrapped in blankets where he'd left it.

He'd been worried it might freeze or moisture might have infiltrated and broken a mechanism inside of it, but he fires it a few times to test it. It seems to be in working condition.

He brings it back to the cabin and leaves it in the basement. The fishing rod is his weapon of choice. He knows how to prepare fish.

The animals that come to drink from the thawed lake sometimes wander very close to him. But he has no desire to kill or eat any of them.

For now, the fish is enough.

For now.

The prisoner absentmindedly strokes a rock between his fingers.

An image of the dissident sleeping peacefully flickers across his mind, temporarily blocking out the weak, early morning light and the pale sky.

He smiles. Thinks about touching his forehead, checking for fever.

Brushing his hair out of his face.

Checking the wounds on his neck and upper back.

Touching his shoulder when he wakes up and telling him to try to eat, to drink, and feeling a pleasant satisfaction as the dissident obeys and smiles weakly but gratefully at him.

He feels…a sensation like an ember growing in his belly at the memories.

It is… pleasurable.

As is the feeling that sometimes flips his stomach, twists it into uncomfortable knots, when the dissident is conscious for a little longer than usual.

When the dissident thinks the prisoner isn't looking, he'll stare.

He'll stare while he's cooking, cleaning dishes, or washing the floors.

Packing.

Carefully sorting through trash for everything burnable and burying anything that isn't.

The prisoner can feel it when he does that, but he pretends he can't.

At first it was unnerving. It reminded him too much of the training camps, being constantly supervised by a commanding officer.

But the dissident's gaze is nothing like *their* gazes.

It isn't critical or sharp.

It's merely…

Fond.

The prisoner flushes, perhaps in response to the cold, perhaps with something else.

That wormy feeling.

That feeling of…unease mixed with…a rush of…

Is it affection?

He closes his eyes.

He doesn't want to answer the question, not even to himself.

He feels the line twitch.

He grips the rod tighter.

I am unhappy.
I am unhappy.
There is nothing here.
I do not understand.
Where are people?
What do they look like?
What do they look for?
I am writing.
I do not write.
Will he come back?
Is he gone?
Is he safe?
Why did he say goodbye?
Where do I go?
Where shall I belong?
Empire. Empire. Empire.
What was the ink man's name?
The woman's?
When will he come back?
Soon?
I hope.
If not, goodbye.

The dissident shouldn't have done it, but the prisoner is gone when he wakes up, and he's so bored, lying on the couch, waiting for him to come back. He'd painfully hobbled over to the bathroom, then sat outside of it, having lost the will and strength to continue the journey. On the stairs, he'd found a notebook full of scribbles. The prisoner's scribbles, he assumes. His handwriting is neat, small, efficient comes to mind, but his words are rather confused, fragmented.

Still, the phrases jump out at him.

Sad ones, mostly. The confused, lonely ones.

Will he come back?

The dissident brushes his fingers over that line over and over again.

But by the time the prisoner is back, two fish hanging from hooks in his hand, he's back on the couch, out cold again. He dreams of being lost in a snowstorm, his hair falling out, his teeth rotting. And a lantern, somewhere up ahead, dancing tauntingly, offering food and comfort, but never getting any closer. He reaches for it, but then stops, because someone's touching his back, someone's holding his jacket, whispering (which he can hear perfectly, because it is a dream after all) "Goodbye."

The dissident wakes up screaming.

The prisoner tries to soothe him, but he's inconsolable, he can't suppress the feelings of panic surging up inside of him.

He leaps to his feet, staggering a little, and bolts, the prisoner hot on his heels.

But due to the change in depth perception and the low lighting, he finds himself sprawled on the floor, having hit the stairs earlier than he thought he would. The prisoner falls over him and ends up right next to him, grunting as his stomach is winded by the hard wood staircase.

The dissident scrambles back to his feet and leaps up the stairs in bounds, ignoring the jolts of pain in his back.

"What are you-?"

He fumbles for the light.

And stares at himself in the mirror.

He can't see a thing.

The prisoner is walking ahead of him, he can hear him.

He just knows it's him, knows it in his bones, in his blood.

He reaches out for him, trying to feel him, trying to touch him.

His fingers brush against fabric, but it feels like air; it might as well be wind, slipping through his fingertips.

"Don't leave me!" *he cries out.*

"You're useless," *the prisoner's voice, listless and clear, says flatly.*

"No I-I can help you!" *the dissident calls back.*

"You can't even help yourself," *the prisoner sighs.*

The dissident feels him slipping out of his reach, but he can't open his eyes, he can't open his eyes and see where he's going, why can't he open his eyes, why can't he see, open your eyes, open your stupid-

He feels for them, but they're not there.

His eyes are gone.

Nothing but flat, smooth patches of skin where his eyes used to be.

He opens his mouth to scream, but finds it's sealed too, a patch of skin binding the chasm where his mouth used to be.

"Let me in please."

"No!"

The dissident stares at his reflection in the mirror.

Not exactly like his nightmare.

But close enough.

"…are you ill?" the prisoner asks softly.

The dissident punches the door in response.

"Leave me alone."

He's ashamed.

Sickened to his core, thinking about how the prisoner had been leaning over him for days, changing his bandages, touching his face, tenderly dabbing his wounds with antibiotics.

And all this time, he'd been staring at *this*.

This angry red and purple and white mass of scarred flesh wrinkled around a pale, sightless eye.

An eye he gingerly touches now.

He'd been able to avoid the truth until now.

Attribute the blindness to the bandage.

Cheerfully tug at it, rub at it, scratch at it until the prisoner slapped his hand away like a scolding mother.

But now, it's off.

It's off and he has to look at himself in the mirror.

The claw marks.

Still nasty and red, but he knows, he knows they'll be lumpy, uneven pink and white flesh for the rest of his life.

And his vision.

Halved.

Impaired.

One eye completely damaged, the other blurry; it hurts to focus, and when he does, he can't see the way he used to, has a harder time seeing things far away.

There's nothing he can do about it, he simply can't see out of that eye ever again, and he'll never see with this one the way he used to.

The finality of it, the inescapable, unalterable rigidity of this fact stares him in the face in the ugliest manner possible.

Alone in the bathroom, the prisoner hovering outside the door, distraught but unsure of what to do, he backs away from the mirror.

He feels an overwhelming panic that threatens to destroy any sense of rationality he has left.

He despises his own body.

He's never looked so ugly.

Never been so damaged, diminished. *Disabled.* The word burns through his tongue, trickles down his throat in caustic, flesh-eating trails.

He's never…lost control of his own body this way.

With the door shut, with only the prisoner to bear witness to his shame, and all of it too, all of his degradation, he allows himself to cry. The tears burn as they squeeze out of the corners of his eyes like blood.

83

"You're going the wrong way."

The dissident turns abruptly.

There's no one there.

He spins quickly, trying to catch a glimpse of the prisoner, but he doesn't see anything.

Just darkness.

"Are you coming or not?"

"Tell me where you are!"

"I can't do that," the prisoner says.

"If you could just tell me!" the dissident yells. "Help me! Please, if you just-if you just helped me, I-"

"I don't want to be trapped in here. I have to leave," the prisoner says flatly.

"Don't...don't..."

"I'm sorry. You simply cannot follow."

The dissident opens his eyes.

It's night time.

He'd fallen asleep on the floor of the bathroom.

His neck aches and a spasm of pain wracks his spine as he forces himself onto his feet.

He doesn't dare look into the mirror.

Instead he opens the door.

He peers cautiously out.

The prisoner is asleep at the top of the stairs.

He feels a flicker of guilt upon seeing him.

He must've been waiting all this time.

The dissident tries to ease passed his sleeping body, but sees a roll of bandages next to him.

He bends down to grab it, since his bindings are feeling a little wet, but the prisoner's eyes flicker open the moment he touches it.

The prisoner meets his gaze and the dissident is struck by how utterly exhausted the other man looks.

This time a *wave* of guilt crashes down on him.

He grimaces at his companion, who reaches out and grabs his hand.

The prisoner carefully extracts the roll from him.

And the dissident allows himself to be pulled into the bedroom.

He sits down on the bed and lets the prisoner wrap fresh bandages over his wounds.

And even though he's just woken up, he finds himself tired once more.

As soon as the prisoner presses down the last strip of cloth, his hands lingering a little longer than usual (or perhaps he's merely hoping), he sighs and falls onto the bed, his sore back cushioned comfortably by the mattress.

He's asleep almost immediately, but if he has any nightmares, he doesn't remember them.

Which might be coincidental.

Or have something to do with the fact that when he awakes, the prisoner is curled up beside him.

84

They don't talk about it.

But it puts them both at ease, sleeping together in the upstairs bedroom.

The dissident's nightmares seem to go away, or at least, fade into his unconsciousness before he wakes.

And the prisoner doesn't have to worry about being too far away from him if he needs medical care. Or about him thrashing wildly in his sleep. Something about his own presence seems to help.

And if he's honest with himself, the dissident's presence…helps *him* sleep longer and better as well.

Although he's finding the dissident to be a very…friendly sleeper.

Often times he wakes up with the dissident's arms around his neck or waist, and he's forced to push him off as gently as possible. Sometimes the dissident wakes up as he does it, proceeds to look embarrassed or horrified, and then scuttles as far away as possible, but the prisoner just shakes his head.

It's not his fault.

But when he assured the dissident of this, the man just looks even guiltier.

Still, every night, he does hesitantly scoot into the bed, keeping a formal distance between the two of them, despite knowing he'll probably breach it sometime in the night. And the prisoner joins him despite knowing this too, because it's become something of a comfort to him as well.

He should admit this to the dissident to relieve some of the guilt etched so obviously on his face, but something prevents him from doing it.

Perhaps it's a relief to *him,* knowing the dissident is trying to respect his boundaries.

And that guilt is proof that he's not doing this on purpose, and won't, not again.

But there are other forms of guilt that he does need to address, and soon, since it's becoming a hazard.

It's clear from the look on the dissident's face that he can't stand being taken care of. He fidgets when he's being bandaged, he often stubbornly walks into furniture, refusing to let the prisoner lead him around by the arm despite his distorted depth perception, and once he even tries to chop firewood, the axe repeatedly missing the log he was aiming for. The prisoner is forced to stop him when the axe bounces off the log and sinks into the soggy earth just inches away from his foot.

The dissident's also a little restless.

The prisoner tries taking him fishing, but he just fidgets and starts babbling almost incoherently, and with a hint of frustration, about rifle maintenance or some other unbearable topic. In the end, he can't sit still for ten minutes and begins to pace, still talking rapidly about white water rafting or canoeing or some other water-based riding activity. Within an hour, he's off for a walk and he doesn't come back until he's sure the prisoner is cooking dinner.

And that's something he keeps trying to do too.

The prisoner has taken to hiding the knives from him.

He much prefers the dissident glowering at him as he's cutting off fish heads to the dissident cutting off one of his own fingers.

It's not that he doesn't think the dissident is capable of compensating for his weakened vision; he just gets the feeling that the man is rushing things because he's afraid that his impairment will take over his life and he needs to prove to himself that he can go on the way he was before.

The prisoner *would* allow him to do that.

If he didn't think the dissident would over-do it and only hurt himself more.

But still, he *is* recovering.

The worst of his injuries have closed without any sign of infection, although unfortunately, with the crude technology and poor medical expertise at hand, the scars and patches of distorted, twisted skin will always remain. But the bandages on his chest, neck, and arms can be removed soon.

He complains that his head still aches, but also reports the nausea has dissipated.

As for his eye…

The prisoner still needs to check for infection and continues to wrap it, but it's becoming apparent that although the eye is no longer functioning properly, it will at least not need to be removed.

It's whitened and distorted, reduced in size, but it's no longer dangerous.

For the most part, he is also regaining his independence.

The prisoner often finds he's left the house, if only to go for short walks or a sit out in the slowly, but surely warming air.

At first, this unsettles him, and he scolds him when he comes back.

He pesters the dissident to eat more, to sit or lie down a certain way, to drink more.

As the dissident gets stronger, he finds himself paradoxically worrying more about him.

It's on one of the dissident's little walks, this one slightly longer than usual, that the prisoner begins to realize why.

He's…disappointed.

He… rather…*appreciated* the feeling of being needed.

He…*liked* giving someone things.

And as tired as he was, as he had been, staying up for almost an entire week, the feeling of relief that came from sleeping afterwards was almost transcendent. He woke up feeling…something like happiness, but…higher. Elevated.

Triumphant.

That was the word.

Because though it was demanding work, taking care of someone else's needs…it was also proportionately rewarding.

But now that the dissident is mostly back on his feet and not needing his care anymore…

The prisoner tries to tell himself that he is glad.

And he is.

He's glad the dissident is better.

He truly is, because when he'd first seen him, it had felt like a rock had been dropped into his throat and come rolling down into his stomach, where it smashed up all of his organs.

He doesn't want to see him like that.

He doesn't want to see him suffer.

He just… also doesn't like to see the dissident over-exerting himself. Perhaps for that exact same reason.

Walking too much.

Going up and down the stairs more than absolutely necessary.

Going out late at night to stare at the stars, standing when he should be sitting.

Not coming home as soon as he'd expected and making him worry.

Silly. He's a grown man. And he is well.

Why would you want him to remain hurt?

That's not it at all.

The prisoner just feels…

Validated.

But only the Empire validates.

The only thing that gives one purpose…just as the Republic gives this one purpose…

Nonetheless, the dissident is all that he-the only purpose…

That you have?

The only thing that needs you?

He won't always.

Not for much longer.

What will you do then?

"I did not cease to exist the moment the Empire no longer needed me," the prisoner murmurs. Saying it aloud makes him feel better.

"Eh?" the dissident yells from the porch.

The prisoner clutches his tackle box closer to his side.

"Are you alright?" he calls.

"I'll survive," the dissident grunts. He yawns, leaning against the wooden support pillar on the porch. It's rather warm, so he's unbuttoned all of the buttons of his shirt, revealing the ropey red scars on his throat, bumpy and misshapen and so out of place on an otherwise flawless form.

The prisoner sees the scar formation even when he closes his eyes.

He looks away, but it still follows him.

"…you ok?"

The dissident frowns.

"..Hey?"

The prisoner shakes his head.

He hands him the tackle box.

"Yes."

He doesn't say another word.

But that evening, when the dissident goes to bed, he does not follow.

He sleeps downstairs, on the couch.

And when the dissident wakes him up, sleepily and loudly tromping down the stairs, he merely curls into a tighter ball.

To his shock, the dissident taps him on the shoulder.

"My snoring getting too much for you?" the man laughs. Although his eye is kind and humorous, there's concern there too.

181

The prisoner sits up.

"..."

"...you can sleep in there if you want," the dissident says more gently. "It's more comfortable than the couch. I'll just go to the other room."

"No," the prisoner protests immediately. "I mean. I just..." *Wanted to distance yourself?*

Because you know he won't always need you.

And probably doesn't, not even right now.

"The couch doesn't feel...as...alone. As the other bed would," the prisoner finishes lamely. "When you were gone, it...it was..."

He can feel heat creeping up his neck, and he's utterly bewildered by it.

Why is he perspiring?

It's not that warm.

He pulls at the neck of his shirt.

"The couch just makes me more comfortable," he adds feebly. A poor excuse, but accurate, at least.

"Well if that's what you don't like...the other bed is big enough for both of us," the dissident says casually.

The kindness he sees in his eye is crippling.

He's not sure why that word comes to mind first and foremost; he just knows it's fitting, and it most adequately describes the feeling he has right now, staring into his scarred, but still beautiful face.

Beautiful.

Why that word?

What would you know about beautiful?

Such an irrelevant word.

Meaningless.

What meaning could it possibly have for the likes of you?

"But if you don't want to share a bed, I completely understand," he whispers apologetically. "I wouldn't...if I were you."

And it's precisely because he says that, and the way he says it, voice aching with unspoken regret, maybe even embarrassment, that the prisoner shakes his head.

"I don't mind if you don't."

And he returns to the bed.

Where they lie down to sleep a cordial distance away.

The next morning, he wakes up without the dissident touching him or encroaching on his side.

He rolls over to find him tightly curled against his pillow.

So close to the edge, as far from the prisoner's side as possible, that he looks like he's about the fall off.

The prisoner smiles.

And then thinks about why he'd even offered.

When the dissident had the bed to himself, he had as much space as he wanted.

He didn't have to worry about trespassing on his.

And he definitely didn't have to care where the prisoner slept, on the less comfortable couch or in the adjacent bedroom.

So why had he offered at all?

But then it occurs to the prisoner that perhaps the dissident had offered because, in that bed, in that room, under the skylight, he too felt alone.

85

The dissident stares at him in horror.

The prisoner gently lowers the body to the floor, his hand cradling the back of its neck.

The other still clutched around the blood-drenched kitchen knife.

The dissident feels his stomach lurch.

He'd killed men before, of course.

He'd killed at least a dozen rescuing the prisoner.

He'd been trained to do so, was good at it.

No one had ever managed to subdue him while he was training with the resistance.

Fighting the ministry's interrogation officers had been a piece of cake compared to training with his superiors at the base.

They went down easily, and he, mindlessly, almost automatically, hadn't even hesitated before putting their own guns to their heads and blasting out the backs of their skulls in a whirl of violent color. The euphoria was exhilarating, more adrenaline and pressure than sadistic killer instinct, but enjoy it he did.

It felt too surreal, like an exciting daydream, like a real life video game for him to feel guilty.

Swipe that one's arm to the left, slam it into the wall, take the gun, kick him in the knee, hear it crunch, and as he falls to one knee, shoot him through the face, watch and hear the blood splatter onto the tile.

Keep moving.

But now…

The dissident watches the prisoner pull the body outside, his blood dragging along the previously spotless floor, his mouth still moving, his chest heaving.

The dissident watches the prisoner's face for emotion, but there is none.

Just cold, clinical calculation as he drags the living corpse out back.

The dissident feels a shudder of unease, but isn't sure why.

The prisoner had not done anything wrong.

This man might've even killed him if the prisoner hadn't been so quick on the uptake.

But something about his face bothers the dissident, and it's not until he mechanically walks out to the yard with him and begins helping him dig a hole, that he realizes what it is.

As he begins digging with his bare hands, the prisoner beside him, he thinks that the look on the prisoner's face, when he slit the man's throat, opened a gash in his veins, ripped the breath from his body, was the same look he'd had when they'd first met.

Empty.

Devoid of any life, despite being alive.

He'd been ready to die.

And here he was.

Killing.

With that same hollow look in his eyes, as though he had been given orders and that was the only thing keeping him alive.

When the dissident looks into those eyes, he sees the Empire.

The eyes of the Empire, staring through him, not at him, but right on passed his skin, his muscles, his organs, his soul, and out into eternity.

He has those eyes now.

The dissident has just been reminded that the Empire still lurks within him, after everything, after all this time.

As the dissident digs, throwing aside rocks and dirt clumps into a pile, the prisoner working faster than him, he can't help but look at the dying body from time to time.

That could've been him.

He could've died out here.

Easily.

Almost had.

The prisoner could've easily been digging his grave.

His friends would never know what happened.

Maybe they could've guessed, but they wouldn't know for sure.

And his friends in the resistance would've done their best to erase him completely from their database.

And been completely forbidden to speak about him.

If it weren't for the prisoner...

"Hey."

The prisoner doesn't stop, but he does tilt his head to indicate he's listening.

The dissident forces himself to the look at the body.

The throat is slit.

Blood is still gushing out of the wound, pouring down the man's front as he twitches, his muscles still spasming as they die and lose function.

"Thank you," he says. "For saving me."

The prisoner pauses.

The body clutches at his knee and he pushes it away almost absentmindedly.

The Empire.

In those eyes.

He watches carefully.

And he sees it.

It's fading.

The warmth is returning.

The prisoner who held him against his chest when he thought he was unconscious, who stroked his hair like his mother used to, absentmindedly-who knows what he was thinking at the time?- who held his head as gently as he could while dripping water into his mouth, has his own eyes.

Mysterious eyes, the dissident thinks.

"...I never thanked you either," the prisoner says quietly back. "...thank you."

The dissident, feeling the slippery wet mud in his hands, smiles and looks down.

He squeezes the ground between his fingers, feeling rather glad to be alive, with the sun on his back, the blue sky above, fresh earth under his knees, and the prisoner, thanking him for saving his life. The prisoner, who hadn't wanted to live. To be saved. Who had wanted to be left behind to die.

"We're even, I'd say," the dissident grins.

Except, not really.

I saved you because you were...all I had to show for myself.

I was using you.

I needed you.

As I still need you, to complete my mission.

But you saved me... because you wanted to.

Because you saw me dying and your first instinct was to save me.

You, who believed in giving the Empire everything, who believed there is no purpose in doing anything that does not suit the Empire's needs.

Who could have easily left me to die.

I owe you more than you owe me.

86

It's one of the trucker's easiest jobs.

A friend of a friend had mentioned the old man, late one night, after a few drinks had brought down the barrier of discomfort that often arises during a meeting between friends of friends.

He'd rambled that his neighbor often divided his time between homes, and when he was away from the house near his house, he paid the friend to take care of it.

Idly, the trucker had asked him about the other houses he owned, and the friend of a friend had mentioned houses in all four zones, two mansions, one modest little house in the tropics, and one small, humble little cabin out in the middle of nowhere, on the Trail.

He'd then proceeded to explain that the neighbor was rather displeased with the state of the cabin and the near constant repairs he had to make after leaving it alone and unattended for too long.

The trucker, drunk and bold, says he wouldn't mind going out to check on the house at the end of winter, making sure there weren't any broken pipes, inspecting for any animal invasions, or just brushing the dust off the shelves.

The friend of a friend laughs as the friend comes back from the bathroom.

He had then taken the trucker's number, telling him he'll call him.

He doesn't, of course.

And the trucker actually forgets about the offer himself, since he wakes up with a splitting headache and a stern reprimand from his boss for being too hungover to drive a new shipment out.

It completely slips his mind until, to his shock, the friend of a friend does call.

He says that he'd been chatting with his neighbor and that the old man had once again lamented that he was wasting a fortune on repairs.

And then the friend of a friend had remembered him and mentioned him to the old man, and he'd immediately offered him seven thousand dollars to go out at the end of each season to make sure things were working properly and make any repairs he was capable of.

He'd of course accepted immediately.

Seven thousand was a lot of money and it was practically a vacation. His only duty was to keep the place warm while the old man was gone.

What a perfect gig. The only downside was that it was completely boring out there. No internet connectivity, no neural interface, no verbal interface either, no moving screen, and worst of all, no TV.

But no problem.

He brought a book and a holo-imager of his own, one that could at least project a couple of recorded programs on the glass or walls.

The drive takes a few hours, and he has to pass through quite a few inspection stops, but for the most part, it's a calming, scenic little trip.

After a while, the roads begin to disappear, though.

He has to turn off one of the last remaining roads, and begin driving through undergrowth, doing his best to dodge trees.

Because the cabin hides within a bowl-shaped valley, he never brings his car all the way to it.

He parks just outside of it and hikes the rest of the way up.

There's no one out here to steal it.

Besides, he doesn't want to ruin his tires any more than they've already been ruined driving through undergrowth. If there had been snow, he would've taken the car further, but since it's not horribly cold anymore, just a bit frigid, he decides the walk could do him some good, and with a backpack on his shoulders, he walks the rest of the way.

It's a gorgeous valley.

He can see why the old man keeps the cabin even though he spends much more time between his other homes.

With a view like this, a man could get lost in this place.

Especially in spring.

In summer, it was bright and green; in autumn, it was splashed with lively orange and red leaves; in winter, it was fresh and white and the frozen lake was a thing of perfection, but he most enjoyed the place in spring.

When it was speckled with flowers and trees reborn, baby animals just coming into the world by God's grace, and old ones returning from sleep.

It's like a paradise, the last haven untouched by man.

Which is another reason he doesn't like to bring his car into it.

It ruins the aesthetic of the place.

But he'd never admit that aloud.

His friends would mock him.

If he mentions this job at all, he makes sure to gripe and complain about how these rich people are too lazy to do this themselves, how the pipes moan, and the floorboards creak, and there's nothing to do out there.

But as he's rounding the lake, watching ducks land in the water, swimming about with little ducklings, a deer drinking all the way across, on the opposite shore, his friends and what they would think of him enjoying this job and loving this valley vanish.

They become irrelevant out here.

Everything does.

It's a place out of time and space.

He drops his backpack on the porch and fumbles for the keys.

He finds them and pulls up the correct one, the front door key.

Very old fashioned. Most people have voice recognition locks. He supposes the cold weather might mess with an automated lock, so the owner had opted for a traditional lock.

He tries inserting it in the keyhole and turning it, but the door is…already unlocked.

He frowns.

Did he do that?

No, he's pretty sure he locked it last time.

Odd.

His first immediate thought is that someone must've broken in, but who would come all the way out here to break into an old man's cabin?

Had the old man lost his keys and broken in? Perhaps left it unlocked?

The trucker, feeling uneasy now, slowly walks into the familiar hallway.

He cautiously looks about.

The lights are off, but there's fresh wood in the fire place, and wood stacked up in the corner, which definitely hadn't been there when he'd left in autumn, and the basement door is open, and-

Someone sits up on the couch.

"I think you like fish because you're both cold blooded-" the man's mouth stops moving out of shock.

They stare at each other for a moment, both too stunned to react.

There's something caught in the gears of his mind, grinding them to a stupefied halt. He stares at the man, who leaps to his feet, looking wary. A very tall, very muscular man who looks like he regularly works out, or perhaps hikes, which he clearly does if he's all the way out here.

A man whose right eye is covered by bandages.

"Uh…hello?" the man says.

"…who are you?" the trucker asks, his voice shaking slightly.

"I…I'm sorry, I uh…got lost hiking. And uh…this was where I had to take shelter," the man says slowly.

He sounds sincere, but the trucker doesn't trust his face.

It's too…tense.

Like he's trying hard to sound…well, sincere.

And his eye keeps darting around, as though he's looking for an escape route.

"What happened to you?" the trucker asks, gesturing at the bandage over his eye. It seems recent, as do the bandages on his neck, which seem to trail down to his chest, under his shirt.

"Uh…a bear attacked me. Almost killed me. It was really cold. Really cold out there," the man says very awkwardly, forcing a pained smile on his face.

"A bear? You're lucky you're not dead," the trucker says, inching forward.

The man's eye keeps darting to the kitchen.

What's in the kitchen that he keeps looking at?

"Lucky, oh yes. Lucky your, uh, cabin was here. I'm really sorry, man. As you can see, I've gotten better and I'll leave as soon as possible." The man forces out a little chuckle, his face clearly not amused by the situation.

"S'not my cabin," the trucker says. "I'm just a caretaker. I'm here to make sure everything's in working order."

"Well I've done that for you," the stranger laughs rather shrilly. "I am sorry for trespassing, though."

"No problem, I'm sure it was urgent. I'm sure the owner would understand. But if you wouldn't mind giving me your name, rank, address, and phone number or interface link, I think I'd like to make sure he knows about this and can take any actions he deems-"

He quickly turns into the kitchen.

But there's nothing in there.

Nothing on the counter, nothing out of the cabinets, everything is in place.

Except…

He looks in the sink and sees water droplets clinging to the edges.

A droplet hanging from the faucet.

He hastily walks out of the kitchen, the man now on the other side of the couch, looking up in trepidation as he approaches.

"Who else is here-?"

But he chokes.

One moment his throat is in perfect working order, passing air and words through his mouth as it had been his entire life.

The next, a soft, hard, cold steel is there.

It gently breezes through, so quickly there's no pain.

He barely registers its presence.

But then it begins to gush.

Then it starts to pour.

It's so warm.

It splatters down his front.

He turns his head.

One moment, he'd been talking, and the next, a hand is touching him, the steel cuts through, and now he's staring at the owner of the hand, the owner of the steel.

The steel is thrown to the ground.

The man's hand is warm on his neck.

He looks into the new man's eyes.

Dark.

Mysterious.

Unbearably, chillingly empty, like how he imagines the ocean would look.

He drowns in those eyes before he drowns in his own blood.

The hand is gentle though.

It holds his neck, another supports his back, and he feels like a child, like he's being lowered into a crib, this man, this mysterious-eyed stranger, passing him from his own welcoming, benevolent arms into the arms of God.

87

Blood spills all over his lap, in his hands, slipping through the cracks of his fingers in thick, crimson cascades.

He uselessly touches the dissident's throat.

The blood is gushing warm and sticky and wet on his palms.

He wants it to stop.

Why had it started?

Who did this?

Something glints out of the corner of his eye.

He turns his head.

A knife.

His knife.

He's holding the dissident's neck and sliding steel through muscle.

"And what a lovely thread of scarlet."

The prisoner jerks awake.

It's completely dark out.

The moon is hidden by clouds or trees or perhaps it's simply gone, swallowed up by the ravenous sun, nothing but an endless black expanse overhead.

The prisoner shivers.

He pulls his blanket tighter around himself.

He doesn't like when the stars vanish.

Are you afraid of the dark?

No.

Two people had asked him that in his whole life.

He is not.

But a sky without stars.

He finds it…disquieting.

He can hear the trees rustling.

He can hear the grass rippling.

Things moving about, out of view.

Everywhere, he can hear signs of life, of a living, breathing world just outside of his perception, and yet despite this rationality, fear still shakes his hands, grips the rifle like a lifeline, an anchor to reality.

The thought of being alone jerks him again, this time to his feet.

The prisoner fumbles in the darkness.

His hand reaches and eventually finds the tent.

The tent he had set up, the dissident attempting to help, but his impaired vision only hindering progress with the stakes and mallet.

He gently touches the flap of the entrance, but does not attempt to enter.

He just holds his hand to the tent, relieved to find it there.

Maybe he's scared of you.

Do you remember his face, when you slit that man's throat?
So easily you did that too, so smoothly, professionally...
How proud your Commander would have been.
Do you remember him?
What about me, do you remember me?
I asked you too.
I asked you if you were afraid of the dark.
And if you weren't before.
You are now.
No.
No, he isn't.
What you conceive as fear of darkness is rudimentary.
The fear of the dark is juvenile.
Only small children fear blindness.
If you truly believe that, then perhaps that's why you don't understand why he is

upset.

The voice, slippery and insidious as always, actually makes him pause.
The dissident *is* upset.
He has been, all day.
He hadn't given it any thought. Not until now.
You've been around us for too long.
Selfishness.
It's one of our unique egotistical little traits, isn't it?
You're learning.
Why did it have to be *his* voice?
The prisoner hates his voice.
But there's no other voice he can conjure in his mind.
Why...why is no other voice so clear, so vivid in his mind, so sharply clarifying,
bitter and sly, honest and cutting, right to the bone?
The voice says nothing.
But even dead silent, its noise is deafening.
It asks him what he's going to do, when he finally shares a tent with the dissident.
When he willingly puts himself beside the man.
In that small, dark, confined space.
An impregnable fortress, blotting out the stars, blocking off the sky.
But why is he thinking of it this way, it's merely a tent, a configuration of cloth and
stake. Why does the thought of entering it make him nervous?
Go inside.
You frightened little lamb.
Go ahead.
You're going to have to eventually.
He'll be expecting it, won't he?
No.
The leer in the voice makes his mind up for him.
No, he won't hurt him.
Not like before.
He'd changed, and the voice is wrong.

191

It *is* wrong, sometimes.

The prisoner does not enter the tent, however.

The dissident finds him in the morning, lying in front of it, sprawled out like a faithful guard dog on the welcome mat.

The dissident doesn't ask, and the prisoner doesn't tell, but the next night, just thirty or so minutes after the dissident does, the prisoner crawls into the tent.

88

It is not a prison.
It feels like one.
It's no different from the cabin.
Can you see the sky?
It's safe in here.
Can you see the fire?
It's safe in here. Who needs either one?
How do you know it's safe?
The prisoner glances over at the dissident.

He's taken to completely zipping up his sleeping bag and positioning himself as far from the prisoner as possible.

Whenever he wakes up and finds himself even remotely close to the prisoner's bag, he jerks away and rolls to the furthest possible corner.

The prisoner knows this because he'd once woken up to the tent shaking, the fabric rustling in the dissident's haste to get away from him.

It makes his stomach lurch.

Why would that bother you?

You don't want him to be close to you, do you?

The voice is taunting him somehow.

It sounds amused.

You'll figure it out.

But the voice laughs a chilling laugh, and the prisoner remembers how the dissident had touched him, had kept doing so even when he'd asked him to stop.

He stares at the dissident's body, asleep and peaceful, but more and more menacing the longer he looks at it.

It's heavier and stronger than his.

He should be warier, shouldn't he?

He's trapped in a small space with him again, isn't he, maybe he'll snap again, maybe he'll-

The dissident rolls over.

The prisoner flinches, but the dissident is still asleep.

The scars on his face and neck catch the morning light, angry and twisted, made by a wild animal. The prisoner thinks of his own. Angry and sharp, precise, calculated. Made by a human animal.

The prisoner, against his better judgement, creeps forward.

He hesitantly gets within touching distance and looks closely at the injuries he himself had treated, slaved over day and night to bind, and re-bind, and why?

Why had he done this for an enemy?

He blinks and see rivulets of red gushing down the valley of his soft throat, and battered flesh, purple and black and swollen, and remembers being so tired he could barely keep his eyes open, but keeping himself awake by plunging his hand into snow, or standing up and pacing when they were back at the cabin.

Why had he done this for an enemy?

What has he become?

When had this happened?

When had he begun…feeling like this?

Feeling strongly.

Painfully.

Pain?

A different kind of pain, different than Teacher's.

He stares at the dissident's sleeping face.

This is a pain I don't understand.

Without thinking, he reaches out and brushes his palm thoughtfully across his cheek.

The dissident's eyes drift open.

The pale, injured one stares unseeingly forward, into nothingness.

The other is unfocused, groggy with sleep.

When it begins to slide into focus, it merely blinks with confusion.

"Something wrong?" he murmurs.

He doesn't push the prisoner's hand away.

And the prisoner doesn't take it away.

"No. I don't think so," he says softly.

The dissident nods.

"As long as you don't think so."

And he closes his eyes again, drifting back to sleep.

The prisoner lets go.

But he doesn't want to.

And that's when he realizes what the voice had been taunting him about.

And where this pain comes from, why it burns every time the dissident flinches away from him, whether that's at the camp fire, when he tries to share his blanket with him, or when they're walking side by side, the prisoner lightly holding his sleeve, guiding him away from any hazards his weakened vision doesn't see.

He doesn't want to let go.

The tension is palpable.

It hadn't been there when they'd been traveling before.

But he'd crossed a line, and now the prisoner is…confused.

Or perhaps oblivious.

The dissident hasn't figured out which yet.

He has so many regrets.

He's made so many mistakes in his life, mistakes that are now beginning to haunt him, every single one, big or small.

But he'll regret making *that* mistake the most, when he was suffering from a little cabin fever, from a frustration that manifested itself in the worst way.

Don't you dare.

He concurs with himself.

He will not.

Even if it seems to him like the prisoner is…hurt by his distance, by his refusal to sleep close to him, to let their skin touch, or make any unnecessary contact, he refuses to allow himself the indulgence of self-delusion.

He doesn't want it.

You will not take anything from that man.

Not after he gave you everything.

Put everything he had into making you well.

You will not delude yourself, you damned fool.

Not again.

The prisoner lets go of his sleeve.

They're walking together, out in the wilderness, looking for all the world like two normal people, two *friends,* and the prisoner has taken a hold of his hand and isn't letting go.

The dissident's heart jumps.

It scares him.

He immediately pulls his hand away.

He berates himself as he falls back.

Don't you dare.

He doesn't know what he's doing.

You do.

Don't mistake his kindness for something it isn't.

The prisoner doesn't try again.

"What do you think of?" the prisoner asks him.

"Why do you ask?"

"...you and I are so different," the prisoner states. "I was just...thinking."

"That's what you think about?" the dissident asks, a muscle in his cheek twitching. "What *I'm* thinking about?"

"...what else could I be thinking about?" the prisoner asks.

"Home?" the dissident suggests. "Do you miss home?"

The prisoner, sitting across from him, holds a stick in the flames of their fire. The temperature is getting warmer. He sits without a blanket, his back slouched, his body bent forward. He's so different from the stiff, steely-eyed, strict-postured prisoner he'd rescued months ago. Or perhaps he's just imagining it. The same way he'd imagined the prisoner touching his face the other day, in the early morning light.

"...I don't know," the prisoner says honestly.

"Let me...put it this way. Is there anything you want to see? Anything you want to hear? Anything at all that you can only experience or savor back there and not here at all? This place can't feel like home to you."

"What does home feel like?" The prisoner withdraws the stick and holds it aloft.

The fire burns at the end of the wood. The dissident smiles.

He looks like one of the wizards from the story books his mother used to read to him, one of the people who waved wands about, said funny words, and made things mysteriously appear. "It feels like...nowhere else could be more peaceful. Nowhere else could make you feel...I guess...comfortable. Happy. It's a...place you need to get back to, because you feel like it's where you can rest, return to when the rest of the world feels a little too...rough. Lonely," the dissident adds.

The prisoner puts the stick out in a mud puddle. "That doesn't sound like *my* home," he murmurs.

"But...it's at least *familiar*, isn't it?" the dissident presses. "The Republic has to feel alien and strange to you."

"...no more than the Empire did," the prisoner sighs.

"...so...where can you call home?" the dissident asks, feeling rather sorry for him. "There has to be somewhere where you felt like you belonged. Where you felt like you could stay there forever because the outside world might as well not exist while you're there."

The prisoner, inexplicably, stares at him for a long time.

"When you put it like that," he murmurs. "I suppose...the place we just left."

As warm as it is, the dissident feels himself growing rather cold. The prisoner begins to draw circles in the dirt as he excuses himself to urinate. After he does so, he comes back and finds the prisoner has gone into the tent.

He stares at the fire for a long time before joining him.

"What will you do when you get home?" the prisoner asks him out of the blue.

The dissident, sitting by a creek, rod in hand, stares at him.

One eye, weaker and strained, but still functioning focuses on him, but the other he can only *feel* moving.

He feels a little self-conscious.

He catches the prisoner looking at him, and it embarrasses him. He knows he looks awful, with the drooping, sightless white eye and the angry red and pink scars. Three cross his face, one cutting down the bridge of his nose, one slicing through his cheek and splitting his eye in the process, and the last going through the other cheek and trailing further down his chin than the other two. He'd studied himself in the mirror before they'd left, and known his social life was over. He'd be a pariah when he got home.

Because of his fuck-up, he looks like something right out of a horror movie, the kind of man parents would pull their children away from. Or flinch at, upon meeting his gaze.

He looks at the prisoner.

And feels bad, remembering how the man had looked when he found him.

And how disgusted the dissident had been by his mutilated body.

How he'd made no effort to hide his distaste.

"I'll… I'll wait for the resistance to contact me for another mission, I suppose," the dissident murmurs, trying not to look the prisoner in the face.

He hadn't recoiled.

There had been no disgust in his hands, eyes, or body as he saved the dissident's life.

"Do you…look forward to that?" the prisoner asks.

"…Not really. It was boring," the dissident admits. "All I did was manage food storage and waste removal, sometimes."

"What about your friends? And all of the…activities you told me about? Don't you want to enjoy those?" the prisoner asks, his voice…earnest?

The dissident squints at him, a little confused.

"I mean…my friends haven't really been hanging out with me lately. I guess I've been drifting away ever since I joined the resistance. Well. Ever since my parents died, actually. They happened around the same time, so…"

"Is that why you joined them?" the prisoner asks.

The dissident thinks about it.

"No," he says finally. "I would've joined eventually. My dad was against it, but I probably would've joined without his approval anyway. I guess after he died, and after Mom retired herself, I didn't have a reason…*not* to join."

The prisoner's head shoots up.

"Retired herself?"

"Yeah. Killed herself," the dissident clarifies helpfully.

"Killed herself? She killed herself?"

"Yeah," the dissident says, a little surprised by his reaction. "Why?"

"She killed herself," the prisoner says flatly. "For what purpose?"

"She…didn't want to be alive anymore," the dissident says, rather flummoxed.

"That's not a purpose. Why would she…waste her own life like that?"

The dissident frowns at him.

"She didn't waste her life. She just didn't want to go on without my old man, so she decided to join him in heaven."

"Didn't that hurt you? You spoke of her fondly. You cared about her a great deal, didn't you?" the prisoner asks, his voice more agitated than the dissident has ever heard it.

"I…I loved her and I was devastated, but-"

"So why aren't you more upset that she chose to do that? Chose to leave you? And what if…what if you never meet her again?"

The dissident scowls for the first time in a long time at the prisoner, remembering those earlier fights they'd had, where their positions had been reversed, and he'd been the one demanding answers from the taciturn, reserved captive.

"I will."

"How do you know that for sure?"

"It's a gut feeling."

"It's not enough."

"Why are you so concerned about this? It's none of your business," the dissident snaps.

The prisoner opens his mouth as if to say something, but the fire spits.

He closes it abruptly and looks back at the flames, his eyes full of flickering orange embers.

"I'm sorry," he says quietly.

"What, you think suicide is wasting a body that could be used to serve its government?" the dissident asks wryly.

"… I don't believe in God," the prisoner says, ignoring his last statement. "So forgive me if the thought of…a person sacrificing the only life they have in the hopes of seeing someone who is gone while ignoring those who are not…disturbs me."

The dissident feels like if he'd said this months ago, he might've been angry.

He might've scoffed and told him how sad it was, to not believe in a higher power when His hand was so clearly guiding all things, moving the world in mysterious, but beautiful, palpable ways.

But now, the dissident imagines what it must feel like not to believe in God.

And to only believe in an Empire, in a government, as your path to immortality, an organization dedicated only to the survival of its viability.

He grimaces and feels nothing but pity.

"Don't apologize," he says. "I was upset with her too. I was hurt that she could leave me behind. But I understood. God took her into His arms and carried her away, just like He will carry all of us to heaven where we'll meet again."

"Not people like me, though," the prisoner says ruefully.

The dissident's stomach drops unpleasantly.

"No," he says slowly. "No." *I'm sorry.*

"When I die, I won't see you again," the prisoner says, so quietly the dissident almost doesn't hear him.

Almost.

The dissident lets his head drop into his hands.

"That's not such a bad thing." He grins apologetically into his palms.

He looks up again, hands sliding over bumpy skin tissue, and finds the prisoner studying him carefully.

He leans back, feeling uncomfortable, not wanting the flames to illuminate his sorry face.

"We die. We become nothing. That's what I was taught. The best thing you could hope for was dying in service. But…"

You took that from me.

The dissident, once again, feels his stomach lurch, a chill jolting through his lower belly.

"Now what'll happen to me?" The prisoner closes his eyes.

The dissident can't answer him.

92

He's quiet for so long, the dissident wonders if he'll ever speak to him again.

Not that he would blame him if he didn't.

But he's tying and untying a snare, leaning against a tree, his legs crossed, when he finally breaks their silence.

"The resistance you fight for. What is it you want?"

"We…we believe in…expanding our borders. Moving into the southern hemisphere. Taking back what's ours."

"And the people living there?" the prisoner asks.

"They'll…need to move," the dissident says.

"How? Where could they go?" the prisoner asks. His voice is impartial, nonjudgmental, and yet the dissident can't help but feel defensive.

"That's not our problem. Our problem is that we can't remain caged any longer. The government has been lying to us our whole lives, telling us everything's fine, but we're dying. Our population is growing too fast, it's exceeding the land we have. It's only logical. We have no other option but to expand our resources," the dissident says.

"…alright," the prisoner says, taking him by surprise. He'd been expecting the man to fight him, but he seems to have accepted this answer. "Why not try and negotiate with them? Share resources. Perhaps…exchange something they want for something you want."

"That won't work." The dissident is shaking his head before his companion is finished speaking. "They would never agree to that."

"When was the last time you spoke with them?"

"It's been two centuries, at least, but it won't work. It's never worked, historically." The prisoner blinks.

He doesn't say anything, but the dissident inexplicably feels even more irritated.

"What? Have you ever 'negotiated' with another country? Is that something *you* do?"

"No," the prisoner answers dully. He doesn't sound upset, but his eyes are a little flat, as though he were shutting himself off from the dissident's hostility as a defense mechanism.

The dissident backs off.

He shouldn't be getting so angry.

The prisoner doesn't understand, but it's not his fault.

He needs to remember that they're…

Fundamentally different.

"But I've...never talked to a person from another country. Not like this," the prisoner points to himself and then to the dissident. "I've never been…saved by one either."

The dissident looks away.

"That was…my mission. It was in my own self-interest. In my resistance's interest. It was nothing more than a battle tactic."

"Perhaps. But…you think…" the prisoner stops.

The dissident, picking through berries he'd foraged, looks back at him.

"What?"

"…yes. Maybe it is what this…but perhaps we need…" the prisoner says.

The dissident's brow furrows in bemusement.

"What?"

But the prisoner says nothing more on the subject.

He asks the dissident to tell him about his family and his friends and his teachers and the people of his town. And the dissident, realizing that he's asking because he has no stories of his own, no fond memories of home, of hobbies, of friends who shared both of these things, is happy to oblige and steer them back into comfortable territory.

93

It's raining.

It rains here a lot.

He misses his old district.

It was usually overcast, but the clouds always flew right on over.

The wind felt refreshing.

Here it seeps through his soaking wet clothing and freezes him to the bone.

He looks up as a Commander passes by, but does not make eye contact.

Water slides down his forehead, slipping over the edge of his nose and off his nostrils when he shakes his head.

It glides down his cheeks and gets caught in his stubble.

He scratches the hairs on his chin absentmindedly.

It's been a long time since he's been able to shave.

There aren't any razors left on base.

His partner, standing on the opposite side of the entrance to the strategical tent, doesn't look at him, but he feels a small connection to him, a link based on mutual suffering.

Camaraderie is to commiserate.

It rains here a lot.

Involuntarily, he shivers.

Something fleeting passes through him, a sense of inadequacy, but he does not dwell on it.

He does not dwell on the past, on the days he's spent in these same conditions, nor the future, where he will spend countless days waiting, guarding, standing still, soaked to the bone, and buffeted by wind.

Even the present becomes irrelevant after long enough.

Every minute that passes becomes a minute lost, a minute insignificant.

His companion moves ever so slightly.

He does as well.

He imagines his companion saying that he too is cold, stiff, and uncomfortable.

This is the closest thing to a conversation that they ever share, because his companion is sent out, weeks later, to the southeastern Border, and is blown out of the sky by an aerial mine.

Another guard replaces him.

This one does not move.

He does not acknowledge him in any way.

It rains here a lot.

The dissident jumps as the zipper of the tent is abruptly pulled up and the prisoner slides in, soaking wet and agitated.

The dissident pulls his legs up to give him more space.

The prisoner yanks off his coat and throws it in the corner.

He struggles with his shirt, pulling it off clumsily, almost savagely, and throwing it into the same corner.

The dissident hastily shuts his eyes.

But he opens them again and his functioning eye takes in the prisoner stripping off his pants and bending over as he twists and squeezes water out of them just outside the tent.

The dissident rolls over and buries his face in his sleeping bag.

He stays like that until he feels a weight drop beside him.

He turns to that side.

And winces.

"Get another shirt," he sighs.

The prisoner, in just his underwear, blinks.

"I'm sorry, I left my backpack outside," he says.

But he makes no move to get it.

The dissident closes his eyes and turns away again.

But to his shock, the prisoner touches his shoulder.

He jerks back towards him, a little irrationally upset now.

"What?" he asks curtly.

He keeps his eyes firmly on the ground.

"I don't like rain," the prisoner says.

"Me neither."

He sits up and rolls over to his own backpack. With some difficulty, he extracts a shirt and gives it to the prisoner, who slips it over his head and pulls the excess fabric tightly around him.

The dissident can't help it; his eye roams over the scars of his legs, the skin distortions where a needle or a knife had cut through, lacerations that hadn't healed properly and left history etched in flesh.

He sits on his sleeping bag, the dissident's shirt almost comically large on his smaller frame, pulled around him like a blanket, his knees pulled protectively up to his chest.

Twenty six.

He's older than him, but he doesn't look it.

He doesn't act it.

Well, no, actually, he can see age sometimes.

He can see it in the prisoner's eyes when he's staring upwards, at the sky, the world he used to roam.

He can see it in the prisoner's movements, slow and steady, with nowhere to be, hobbled and stilted by his bad leg.

Can see it in his embarrassment, the humiliation in his face whenever he has to stop to relieve his bladder, still weak after all this time. His kidneys would probably never recover.

He sees age in all of these things.

It used to disturb him.

But not anymore.

The prisoner doesn't seem fazed by his own partial nudity.

His eyes are rather distant, as always, as he listens to the rain beating down overhead, stopping and hitting their tent in soothing, rhythmic tone. They're curiously devoid of any feeling as his mouth moves.

"I stood outside in the rain. Guarding the strategical tent. It was cold and wet and uncomfortable."

"I've never been in the army," the dissident says. His eye traces a line on the prisoner's upper thigh. But as it wanders further, he closes it, forcing himself not to go places he doesn't belong. "That sounds terrible."

"But I did it," the prisoner says.

"You followed orders, nothing wrong with it."

"Why?" The prisoner finally pushes his legs into his sleeping bag.

He turns to face him and the dissident stifles a laugh, feeling like he's a teenage girl and he and the prisoner are having a sleepover party in the backyard.

"Because… you had no choice," the dissident says.

"I didn't think so either," the prisoner says.

He wiggles further into his sleeping bag, then stops abruptly, and looks over to the dissident.

"Why do you make that choice?" he asks unexpectedly.

The dissident frowns.

"What choice?"

"To stay so far away. To…avoid contact with me at any opportunity. You never did that before," the prisoner says, without a hitch in his voice, not a hint of embarrassment.

The dissident lets out a breath of surprise.

"That-that's what you want, isn't it?"

The prisoner nods, but he looks unsure.

"But why is what I want more important than what you want?" he asks quietly.

The dissident feels like they're wandering into dangerous territory, but the question is too compelling not to answer. He blurts out, "It just is."

"It wasn't before."

The statement, said so casually, so matter-of-factly, makes him burn with shame.

He rolls over to the other side, feeling a mixture of panic and guilt.

He tenses as he feels a hand touching his shoulder, and not through the sleeping bag, but directly.

He jerks away, but the prisoner is stubborn and just touches him again, this time on his back.

"I'm sorry. I just want to understand what it is you wanted," he says softly, so softly that the dissident is filled with an irrational rage, a defensive need to lash out. He wants nothing more than to shove him away, force him out of the tent, make him sit out in the rain for a few hours.

But those thoughts, as soon as he thinks them, make him feel guilty as he considers what the prisoner is asking.

Of course he wants to understand.

He's not like you.

It must've confused him.

It scared him.

It's only fair, even if it seems painfully obvious to *him*.

"I was just very…restless from being cooped up. You were the only person I could take it out on. That was just the…I dunno. Boredom. Instinct," the dissident says. Feeling heat creeping up his neck and cheeks.

"It had nothing to do with procreation," the prisoner says.

"Of course not! You're not a-" the dissident lets out a huff of disbelief. "I mean, you know this!"

"I know. I just didn't know any other purpose for sex."

"Don't call it that."

"That's what it is."

"It makes me uncomfortable."

"Sex?"

"The word."

"Oh."

The dissident wonders if it's raining hard enough to drown himself. If he just poked his head out, looked directly up…

"I'm sorry. But I knew you had…intercourse for recreation. I just did not know…that it included…same-sex interactions."

"I mean, some people…but not me, not before…it was a weird situation, ok? I won't do it again, you…you made it clear that you weren't…"

"It didn't stop you before," the prisoner says, his cold, factual voice once again cutting him to the bone like an icy wind. "I told you I didn't want to have sex, but you kept going."

"Don't call it that. And I-I did stop!"

"Not because I asked."

"So what?"

"So I don't understand."

"Don't understand what?" the dissident near-shouts, very upset now. "Why I stopped?"

"No. Why you resist right now," the prisoner says solemnly.

His companion jerks upright, almost hitting the prisoner on the way up.

"Why I resist now?" the dissident demands, the irritation in his voice sharper, so electrified by disbelief that the lightning outside seems less dangerous. "What do you mean? Why I-?"

"Looked away," the prisoner finishes for him. "When you came in, you looked away, even though you didn't have to. This is your country, not mine. I don't belong here. I don't belong to the Empire anymore. I have nowhere to belong to, nothing to strive for, no one to serve, no one but you, that is."

His anger dissipates again.

The prisoner's face, blurry and indistinct, hovers out of his range of vision.

"The moment you saved me from destruction and took me under your care, brought me to your way of life, this body fell under your authority. I'm still a prisoner here. Perhaps not theirs, but yours. But as long as I live under…your rules, your power, then I still live under their rules, and their power, because you are a product of these things, having been born into and made by them. So your own rule over me is still theirs. And if sex is what you desire, if sex is how your culture and your rules manifest themselves, then I just…don't understand why you don't just take it from me. Cultural differences notwithstanding."

The dissident opens his mouth to say something, although he's not sure what, but the prisoner stands up abruptly, still almost completely naked.

He winces at the sight of his back as the prisoner walks over to the entrance of the tent.

Their rules. Their power. Your rules. Your power.

They gave him those scars. You gave him those scars.

You didn't mind them when you first saw them, save for their hideous aesthetic.

Why are you so upset seeing them now?

The prisoner bends down and unzips the flap.

He reaches out and pulls his backpack in.

205

He retrieves his water bottle and holds it out, gathering water droplets as they fall.

"It might be toxic," the dissident warns.

"I'll take a chance."

"And you're wrong."

The prisoner's hand trembles as he holds the water bottle.

The dissident can see it, even with his blurry, halved vision.

It's scarred from so many controlled breakages, from being crushed and cut up and twisted and pulled at.

He was the enemy.

Was.

What is he now that his pain causes you pain?

"You might be in my country, but you're still allowed to feel and think as a man from your own country. Maybe you don't belong here, maybe you didn't belong there. Why is it so hard for you to understand…that you don't need to belong to anyone? That you don't need to be…someone else's, you can just be you. Exist as you are, on your own."

The dissident feels a sense of hypocrisy, of wrongness, mixing with the sudden passion swelling up within him, but he can't stop.

"I'm sorry. I'm sorry for what I did. That was wrong of me, it was *wrong.* I never thought it was, but I see now. I felt how it felt, to be powerless, and weak, and at the mercy of something else, but you saved me when you could've let me die and been free. You saved my life and now I see you as you truly are, not as my enemy, not just some-some foreigner, but as a friend. And friends don't…they don't use each other when they're bored or-or just feeling restless. You *don't* want to have sex with me, you just feel obligated, because you think this is what my *culture* is like, but it isn't. Or maybe it is, I don't know, I don't know anymore, things have been confusing ever since I met you, ahahah, you damn foreigners, always so fucking confusing…"

He lets out a rattled laugh. Something dangerous is brewing in his throat, and he clamps his mouth shut, determined to keep it in.

The prisoner is staring at him.

He wants him to stop, yet he's strangely comforted by it at the same time. Those empty, mysterious eyes aren't so empty or mysterious anymore. In fact right now, they're full, almost full to bursting, and so transparent, so clear and open, that as painful as it is to meet them, he can't look away.

"A friend. You see me as a friend?" he asks.

The dissident feels like he's drowning in his eyes, which are suddenly much closer, because the prisoner is right in front of him, hands on either side of his hips, their faces mere inches apart.

"Yes. You are. God, yes, you are, I-I'm such an idiot, I'm-"

He falters as the prisoner gets closer, as it seems like he's going to-

But he closes his eyes and stills.

He sits back.

The dissident forces back his disappointment, then chides himself for feeling disappointed at all.

"If I don't belong to anyone, then you don't either," the prisoner says. The dissident gives him a strange look.

"I know I don't."

The prisoner stares at him long and hard, the rain beating overhead, lightning flashing outside and illuminating the walls of the tent with its brilliance.

"Are you sure?"

94

"Are you sure?"

"I can do it, sir."

"There's a lot of sensitive information in there. Your mission is to extract any and all information about their operatives both foreign and domestic. This is not a stealth mission, however. If you fail to do your first objective, then your second is to destroy that facility's staff and functionality. If you can, and if there are any left alive, release any prisoners you find there."

"Should I bring any back with me, sir?"

"No, if they're operatives of ours, then they were already compromised. And if they're foreign enemies, then they won't cooperate with us and are of very little use anyway. Just release them if you find them, the government could use a little havoc. Plus they might be more focused on finding them than you."

"Understood."

"This is your first mission. Don't make it your last."

The prisoner's hand is shaking so violently that it's beginning to draw attention.

The dissident, grinning painfully, seizes it.

"Stop it, you're making us look noteworthy. That's the last thing we want," he hisses in his ear. Smiling and kissing his neck as a curious couple stares at him.

The prisoner, not expecting it, flinches, but squeezes his hand tighter and relaxes just a fragment.

But still, he'd been jumpy ever since they'd finally left the wilderness, and made it to the last place he'd stopped before first beginning his journey.

Their first stop is the bank.

The prisoner's eyes dart around, taking in the small, dingy shops and dirty asphalt streets and old, mismatched architecture styles.

He's never seen anything quite so chaotic or disorganized.

People stumble about in every direction, obeying no law of traffic, walking in the road, trotting in opposing directions on the sidewalk, swerving to avoid people carrying packages, walking dogs, dragging along children, some of whom stare quite openly at him.

"Mom, that man walks funny-"

"Don't look at him."

"Mom! Look at his funny skin-!"

"Quiet!"

The prisoner shrinks away from the people, closer to the dissident, his side pressing into the machine the dissident is fiddling with.

"They're keeping an eye on my account, they'll see immediately where I am and what I'm doing," the dissident murmurs. "This is good, they'll know that I haven't died."

"What…what are we going to do?" the prisoner asks, feeling out of place and a little overwhelmed by the unfamiliar sights, sounds, smells, and people. It's not nearly as crowded as home, but it's more chaotic, less ordered. Just as he's thinking it, an old man walks right into him and begins to curse him out, whacking him in the bad leg with his stick. He catches himself, but his leg still stings, and the old man chortles as he hobbles away.

"Well. Good news is we can ditch the camping gear and the hunting and fishing. We can start eating in restaurants. God, I love the outdoors, but there's only so much I can take," the dissident laughs.

The prisoner uneasily grimaces back.

He would've preferred hunting.

And when the dissident lets out a joyous yell as he leaps into the hotel bed and puts his filthy hair on the pillow, hugging it close as he laughs from the excitement of being back in "civilization," he grimaces again.

"You couldn't have gotten more than one bed?" he asks.

"I couldn't withdraw too much, there's a limit on how much money you can get from banks. Besides, it would look suspicious buying a room for two, wouldn't it?"

"It looks suspicious anyway, I've been seen," the prisoner says.

"Well, sure, but people will assume…I mean, they'll assume we're…uh. You know." The dissident points between the two of them.

"What?"

The dissident looks nonplussed.

"Dating?"

The prisoner stares at him.

"Dating?"

95

The prisoner keeps his hands in his lap.

He's lost his ramrod posture and is slouching slightly, covertly glancing around.

"Stop looking like a convict," the dissident whispers. "No one will think anything of us if you just act normal."

"And how do I do that?" the prisoner asks, eyes still impulsively looking about.

In the evening, all of the activity had at least settled down, but there are still people around, milling about, walking arm-in-arm, sitting at tables, filling the air with quiet murmurs.

The prisoner's still on edge, because he's been around crowds, but they were strictly regimented crowds. Crowds that had a place to be and an order to their flow. They stayed to the right or left, did not touch one another, and made no attempt to make eye contact or smile.

These people are constantly smiling at him.

His face hurts from all of the grimacing back he's been doing.

He takes to avoiding eye contact now, but he can feel their gaze on him, and it makes him long for the days of isolation, when his greatest concern was his friend dying from horrific injuries.

"Put your hand on the table."

The prisoner obliges.

The dissident takes a hold of it, his palm covering the back of his hand.

The prisoner warily looks about, at all the other connected hands.

"I don't know how much this will help," he says. "We don't look like...I don't look natural-"

"Relax," the dissident interrupts him, squeezing his hand. "Just relax. These people won't hurt you. They're just curious about you is all. They won't ask you any questions, and if they do, I'll answer for you. Just trust me, ok, there's nothing here to be worried about. Even if they talk about you, it's all just chatter, they'll forget about you in a week. Nothing to worry so much about, ok?"

The prisoner lets out a breath and seems to relax, his shoulders not quite so taut with tension, his fist, tight and hard against the table cloth and underneath his hand, loosening slightly.

The dissident lets go of it, but when the waiter asks him a question and the prisoner is immediately flustered again, looking panicked, he reaches down quickly and grips his knee reassuringly.

He orders for the prisoner, realizing with a thrill that this is the prisoner's first time eating *his real* food, prepared just like it is at home, and being almost inordinately excited about that.

He spends maybe ten minutes talking about what he's ordered for the two of them before realizing that the prisoner has no idea what he's talking about and his eyes are only fixed on his because he's still rather nervous in the public setting and afraid to look away.

"You know…this is a lot like what dating is," he says, abruptly changing the subject of a decidedly one-sided conversation. The prisoner's eyes lose some of their fevered edge, softening into a gentler curiosity.

"Is it?"

"Yes. I mean, mostly. You take someone you like out to dinner, talk about things you care about, go, I dunno, on a walk, and then take them back home. Then, if it worked out, if you didn't argue, didn't have major ideological differences, major, irreconcilable differences in upbringing, if you two like each other and being together, then you keep going out. You go on a second date, and then a third date, and a fourth date. You keep spending time together. Then get married and…spend all your time together."

"So dating is a manner of choosing with whom you establish stronger, solidified economic and political ties?" the prisoner asks.

The dissident laughs.

"Yes. That. Exactly. A bit too exact, but-"

"You say that like it's bad." The prisoner frowns.

"It's not bad, that's just not what most people…think of first when they think of marriage," the dissident groans as he takes a swig of his beer. "Oh Christ, I was missing alcohol."

The prisoner blinks.

"Then what do they- do *you* think of first?" he asks.

The dissident doesn't answer for a moment, too enamored with drinking.

He finishes and immediately gestures at a waiter for more.

"Love. Companionship. Friendship. Sleepy mornings where you wake up next to someone with pale, early morning sunlight creeping under curtains and not a sound in the world, just the two of you breathing, and you wish you could live forever in that moment because there's no world outside of that one, with the two of you together, feeling safer than you felt when your mother first held you."

The dissident falters, first embarrassed that he said something so sappy aloud, and then horrified as he realizes that the prisoner had never felt such a thing.

The prisoner doesn't look upset, however.

Merely…frustrated?

"Our concept of marriage includes an archaic need for reproduction, the sharing of assets, and the maintenance of social, economic, and political ties formed through generations," he says. The dissident fiddles with the table cloth. "Its social function was disregarded decades ago."

"Well-" the dissident bites back the acidic comment he had in mind. It's unnecessarily malicious and it's not the prisoner's fault that his simple statement had immediately rubbed him the wrong way. Besides, they should be passed this anyway. "Why is that?"

"We share resources. Anyone who requires medical assistance, food, water, shelter, anything, to live is provided with it. There is no need to tie one's self to a single person. Only the Empire," the prisoner says. The dissident hates his voice when it's like this. He hasn't heard it like this in a long time, mechanical, automatic, as though he were stating a law of nature.

"No need to tie yourself to anyone? I guess. Sounds lonely, though," the dissident comments as lightly as he can.

"You don't take care of those in need, your modus operandi is...every man for himself, is it not? Those who need health care services are those who can afford to provide these things for themselves. Those who need them, but can't afford them, become nonpersons, correct? That sounds lonelier to me," the prisoner says smoothly.

The dissident gapes at him.

Now that voice he's never heard before.

He almost sounded...

"That is the snarkiest thing you've ever said to me," the dissident says slowly, disbelievingly. A wide grin spreads across his face. "Well, ok. I'll bite. You're right. We have limited resources. Those who have power and money have better access to them. That's just how the world has to work. We can't all be equal, there aren't enough resources for that."

"We manage just fine," the prisoner says.

"Because you don't want anything more than to survive. We need more. We need to feel alive."

"By wasting resources?" the prisoner asks dryly.

"By living. And wasting resources, sure, but think about how you've been quantified your whole life! Your food has been regulated, your water measured, your every breath counted! You've never done anything just for the hell of it! What point is there in being alive if you never feel that way?"

"You would allow lesser people to suffer in order to enjoy your life to the fullest? What about their happiness, their comfort?" the prisoner asks, quieter now.

"It's just luck of the draw. Some people are just unlucky. Life is unfair." The dissident shrugs.

"It doesn't have to be," the prisoner says.

A fire in his eyes.

The dissident marvels at it.

"Mysterious no more."

The prisoner frowns.

"Pardon?"

"Nothing."

96

"No second date, then," the prisoner says.

The dissident laughs at that.

"What?"

The prisoner, walking slowly beside him, his pace flagging as he stops to stare at the lights strung about all over the town, casting a warm orange glow on dark porches and smooth grass, hesitantly takes his arm. He's merely imitating the gesture of a nearby couple, but the dissident seems rather flustered. But he doesn't pull away.

"If that was a facsimile of a date, then I suppose we would not meet again to consider potential lifelong companionship. We argued," the prisoner says, stopping altogether, his eyes bright, reflecting the light of the town. The dissident, who's seen it all before, watches him rather than the lights.

"Well, sure. But I'd ask you out again," he chuckles.

The prisoner gives him a confused look.

"But we are not compatible."

"Maybe not."

"And you said we had to meet certain criterion: not have an argument, not have major ideological differences, and not have major irreconcilable differences in upbringing. We had, have, all of those things." The prisoner frowns. The dissident squeezes his arm and pulls him away from the light, off into a more isolated corner, a little behind a tackle shop.

"Well I like you," the dissident says patiently.

The prisoner seems almost affronted by the statement.

"Ok."

"So that's enough to warrant a second date," the dissident says.

"But the other preconditions-"

"It's as simple as just liking someone," the dissident says, patting his shoulder vigorously. "If that was our first date, I would've asked you out again, absolutely. Maybe we're not gonna get married, but that went well, I thought."

"If we hadn't gotten to know each other before now, I doubt you would have… 'liked' me," the prisoner says almost reproachfully.

"We'll never know." The dissident shrugs. "But with the evidence we can gather, I can honestly say, yes, this was a successful first date. I guess now I walk you to your car."

"I don't have a car."

"It's just an expression."

The dissident looks around the corner at the lights again.

"Say, let's go for a walk. See the things there are to see. I've been going bonkers, with nothing to do out in the middle of nowhere. It's so nice being somewhere."

The prisoner thinks privately that this place feels like nowhere to him, that the mountains, the lake, the cabin, the skylight and the view through the windows, felt more like *somewhere,* held more significance, more *weight* than here, but keeps it to himself as he allows the dissident to guide him.

"This place is a little more rustic than I'm used to, but it's still better than nowhere land, right? Electronics store, theater, restaurants, nice hotels with TVs, running water, bookstore, souvenir shop, antiques shop, a…wow, a museum? I haven't seen one of those since I was a boy. They don't bother with museums anymore, not since the government divided its land and gave the parcels to the highest bidding developers." The dissident squints at it.

He drags the prisoner to every store, holding his arm almost the entire time, smiling at the store owners and starting up an amicable chat with them, always telling the same story about how he and the prisoner are celebrating their honeymoon, to the prisoner's utter bewilderment. After he explains what a honeymoon is, the prisoner looks properly embarrassed.

"You told them we were married."

"It would look suspicious otherwise," the dissident insists.

"If you cared about looking suspicious anymore, you would've just taken me back to the hotel and foregone all of this," the prisoner says.

That sobers the dissident up almost immediately, but the prisoner has no idea why.

He almost regrets it, but then the dissident is smiling, having brushed off whatever it was that had been bothering him, and tugs him down an alley, through to the other side, which leads out to a hill overlooking the town. A bench sits at the top of the hill, a small wooden patio roof above it. The dissident sits down with no grace whatsoever. He folds his arms behind his head, stretching his long legs out as far as they can go.

"I wouldn't honeymoon here. It's nice, but it's too quaint. I would've taken you to a ski resort or a…a hot spring."

"Why a hot spring?"

The dissident blinks.

"Uh…never mind."

Completely out of the blue, the prisoner touches his neck. The dissident flinches in surprise, but relaxes as the prisoner moves his hand away quickly, taking his tension as a request to remove it. It still hovers near his chin, though, tentatively touching the collar of his shirt.

"What are you doing?"

"I thought you might be blushing," the prisoner says simply. "I can't see you so well in this light, I thought I would check."

If he wasn't blushing before, he is now. He swats the prisoner's probing hand away.

"Oh."

"You were thinking about sex, weren't you?" the prisoner asks evenly, almost apathetically. The dissident will never understand his complete disinterest in sex, or his ability to talk about it so casually, so detachedly. "What does sex have to do with hot springs?"

"Nothing, forget I said it."

He can just make out the prisoner's face in the darkness, slivers of it, lit only by the glow from the cheery little town and the moon rising overhead.

His hair takes on a silver-tinged glow, every strand a constellation, his face outlined by moonlight, his eyes brimming with stars, swimming with the colors of the sky.

The dissident wonders dimly how he could've ever thought the prisoner was plain.

Don't. Stop it. Stop it.
It's too late. It's too late now, idiot.
You let this happen.
And now what, now what, you fool?

The dissident opens his eyes just a crack, but shuts them almost immediately, afraid of what he'd see.

Pale, early morning sunlight creeping under curtains.

The prisoner, sleeping beside him, facing away from him, his waist, quietly inviting an arm around it. Or worse, he'll be facing him, he'll be asleep, and his face, calm, plain, but blindingly, achingly familiar, with beauty etched in every moment he ever woke up to it peering over him, making pain go away, easing his loneliness, will be nose to nose with his own ugly, mutilated one.

And worse, much worse, is the thought that the prisoner might be awake, that his eyes will be open, those weakening eyes, those softening eyes, insensitive and harsh and brutally honest and vulnerable too, and he will feel the irrevocable feeling, the damning desire to never leave this moment in time, because there's no world outside of this one.

"I hope you and your husband are enjoying your stay?"

The receptionist smiles politely at him, but the dissident gets the (totally ridiculous) feeling that she's mocking him, that she knows the truth, that they're not married or anything close, and she's secretly laughing at him for falling-

He shuts his mouth, nods tightly.

"And you'll be leaving tomorrow morning?"

He nods again and gives her a pained smile as he walks away from the counter.

The prisoner is sitting on the edge of the bed when he comes back to the room.

"Is this all that's left?" the prisoner asks.

"We can take a bus out of here. No more walking everywhere," the dissident sighs. "It's beautiful, isn't it? We'll be home in three days, maybe two."

But the word leaves a funny taste in his mouth, and it makes the prisoner pause too.

We'll be home?

No, *he'll* be home.

The *prisoner* will merely go to the resistance where they'll transfer him around, take him into the underground movement for study, interrogation, and eventually-

The dissident snaps his fingers.

"TV, on."

The prisoner turns away rather quickly.

For some reason, he has an aversion to the screen.

It might be that he's not used to the lights or the fast colors.

Either way, the dissident tells the TV to lower its brightness and volume.

But after a while, he finds that he can't even hear what any of the actors are saying, and he hasn't been able to, not this whole time.

Because the prisoner is sitting next to him, his back to him, idly staring out the window, fiddling with his knitting needles. He doesn't know how to knit, and the dissident hadn't had any material or inclination to teach him, but he seems to like tapping them lightly together, rubbing his thumbs up and down them, deep in thought.

The dissident has been watching him out of the corner of his eye the whole time.

Has been since yesterday.

He just can't seem to resist looking at him, seeing his reaction to the new, foreign world around him, watching his eyes widen as he sees children playing in the streets. Sees them narrow in cautious distrust as random passerby wave at him, then widen again in fear as a small dog tied to a post leaps on his leg.

He's seeing his whole, dull, familiar little world transformed by the prisoner's presence.

He's seeing the mundane as miraculous and new, through someone else's eyes.

The dissident's gaze might be on the TV, but his mind is on the prisoner, and he can't deny himself anymore, he can't.

He turns directly toward him, but the prisoner doesn't react, so lost is he in whatever world he's dreaming of.

"Hey."

The prisoner doesn't immediately respond, but after a moment, he blinks himself out of reverie and turns to the dissident, looking contrite.

The dissident completely loses track of whatever it is he was going to say.

He just stares dumbly at him for a moment, the prisoner much too close, his heart racing as he suddenly considers the possibilities.

The possibilities?

What possibilities.

There are no possibilities.

You idiot. You dumb idiot. What are you trying to do?

"Dinner?" he says weakly.

The prisoner nods once.

But he knows he's only postponed the inevitable.

The waitress, used to his ugly face by now, doesn't flinch this time, but she still politely looks downwards rather than directly at him.

It's something he'll have to get used to, the same as he'd gotten used to the missing half of his vision, the oppressive hovering darkness that taunts him with his loss every time he wakes up, opens both eyes, and only sees with one.

People avoid eye contact.

He knew they would, but seeing a little girl shriek and run away from him is still rather painful, no matter how he excuses it in his head. Even people who understand, adults who know accidents and horrific assaults and natural causes, will always have to repress their first initial disgust, rationalize away their irrational fear and distaste for the distortion, for the ripple in their beautiful, flawless, collective skin, smile to his face as they force their repulsion beneath still waters.

He tells himself he doesn't blame them. And he doesn't, he flinches when he sees it too, in the mirror.

But the prisoner…

The dissident closes his eyes, rubbing them hard.

You woke up face to face and before you could roll over, he opened his eyes and looked right at you.

You flinched and made to turn away because no one should have to wake up to that.

But he didn't seem disturbed.

He didn't see anything wrong.

He just smiled and said good morning and you wanted to hug him, didn't you?

He's the only one who's treating you like you're normal.

Like he doesn't see…

Like he can see passed…

The prisoner is looking directly at him now.

His eyes don't trace the lines of his face.

They don't get caught up in the ridges or the twists of the scars.

They merely watch him, looking concerned.

"You've been very distracted," he says.

The dissident, not hearing what he said, just blinks rather stupidly at him.

Of course he doesn't see the scars.

They don't care.

They're like robots, they had the pain and the joy and the compassion and everything else bred out of them.

But his attempts to demonize him, separate the prisoner from himself and his people, are failing miserably.

That face had hovered over his own, on the nights when he was drenched in his own sweat, in the snow, on the wooden floor, in the tent.

Those hands had tended to his skin, his muscles, his heart, his eyes, brought him back to life, dragged him all the way home.

Those feet had walked hundreds of miles with him; they had carried him and been carried by him.

He is not the man I met.

And...I am not the man he met.

"You're very quiet."

The dissident blinks again and they're outside of their room.

The prisoner's hand slips into his and pulls his dazed body into the room, pushing the door shut behind them.

He lets go.

The dissident still feels his fingers holding his, however, as he takes a shower, as he wipes off the grime of the day, as he slips into bed, only wearing his underpants and a thin shirt.

He's still thinking about it when the prisoner, sitting up straight on the edge of the bed, his hands around his knees as he stares out the window to his right, turns towards him slowly.

And just as slowly, languidly, the prisoner lets go of himself and crawls over to him.

The dissident, still in a state of contemplation, doesn't comprehend what exactly he's doing until it's too late.

He *doesn't know what he's doing.*

The dissident, tingling with warmth, with exhilaration, the prisoner's lips, chapped and rough, on his, ignores the voice, because his heart is begging, his entire body is thrumming with frustration, with bridled eagerness, just like when he was a little boy and the entire world was in his hands and only the thinnest of strings was still holding him back, *he's in your arms, you're holding his back, tracing his spine, the spine riddled with pain, the carved valley of his back, he's so solid, he's so real, so beautiful, his hand is on your chest, do you feel it, is it pushing you away-?*

No, no, no, his heart pumps. It's gripping your shirt, it's holding you tight, but it's not pushing you away.

It's pulling you closer.

He gladly accepts the offer and the prisoner makes a noise, a surprised, almost-hum as the dissident deepens their kiss and in his enthusiasm, he begins to push the prisoner down onto his back and he's eager, so eager, to feel his body underneath him-

The prisoner, his eyes fearful, panicked, confused.

The prisoner, going limp, blinking sluggishly.

His eyes as empty as when they first met, when the prisoner was so close to death that the first time he woke up, the dissident could see the afterlife glowing in his pupils.

The dissident recoils and rolls off of him immediately.

The prisoner's eyes burn with hurt.

217

But the dissident's throat hurts too.

He looks away.

"I'm sorry," he says. "I'm-this is wrong-"

"What's wrong?" the prisoner murmurs. "This time, I do...I do...want it."

The dissident's heart clenches as he hears that, and it drops with the last word.

"Don't say that. Please."

"You've been acting strange. Distant. I know we'll part soon. And I have accepted it, but I thought we could...that I could learn something...from you. Before we do. I can't imagine...trying it with anyone else." And there's something he's not saying too.

Something in his voice that the dissident immediately turns away from, shuts himself off from, because it makes his heart hurt and his muscles weak.

"That's why this is wrong," the dissident exclaims, painfully aware of the prisoner and his body, hovering too close to him in his limited peripheral vision, just begging-

No. Stop that. You're imagining it again.

"You can't imagine it with anyone else because you...you don't know anyone else. I'm the first person you've ever met and you think that I'm normal, that what we're doing is normal, but it's not, because you've just...you've just got nothing...no basis for comparison. It would be wrong of me to...when you've got a world full of opportunities. Of people to meet, to...love without being blinded by dependency and..." the dissident fumbles his words and curses, long and quiet, to himself.

The prisoner is watching him.

He won't watch him back.

He just closes his eyes and sighs, willing the fluttering in his stomach, the airy, light-headed feeling to subside into steely resolve.

"...Dependency?" the prisoner asks.

The dissident shudders. Something about the way he said it...but no, stay focused.

"It wouldn't be right. I would be taking advantage of your inexperience. Of the fact that you've never met a person like me and were basically thrown into a situation where you had no choice but to learn how to act and think like us. You need...time to adapt. Without me, I mean. See what you truly want, what you'll have when you're all by yourself, and have the entire world at your fingertips, not just...me. There are a million ways to live and millions of people living. I'm just the first way, the first person, you've experienced."

He buries his head in his pillow like a child and prays the prisoner stops asking.

And he does.

They both wait as the room gets darker and darker

A long time passes before the prisoner moves.

The dissident feels the weight in the bed shifting, then removing itself altogether.

He doesn't look up, merely breathing long and slow into his pillow as he hears the door open and shut quietly.

And when he's sure the prisoner is gone, he rolls over, onto his side of the bed, and breathes deeply.

A mistake, since the sheets still smell like him.

99

The prisoner expects him to be asleep when he comes back.

And he certainly seems like it, his body limp, his breathing slow, not a single reaction as he eases back into bed with him.

But as he settles in, his back to the dissident, he hears a hitch in breath.

"I owe you my life."

"No," the prisoner says back. "We're even. You saved mine first."

"No. I saved you because it was my…actually, it wasn't even my mission. My mission was never to rescue anyone I found there, it was to retrieve sensitive information. I failed to do that and you were…my second option. I took you against your will and preserved your life for my own interests. All I did was take you away from the world you knew. All I did was shatter it, and force you into mine."

The dissident's not facing him; they're back to back.

For some reason, this is comforting.

The prisoner cradles the wrist he'd broken, turning over in his sleep and smashing it against a table what feels like years ago.

"And I…can't give you over to them. I can't," he says it quickly, with surprise in his voice, as if he's just realized it himself. The prisoner stiffens. "I owe you more than a life, I owe you a world."

The words flare, bright red and hot, in the darkness, emblazoned. Reckless and impulsive, they shine bright as stars in the prisoner's mind, burning in his chest with a sudden passion, a desire like desperation, almost paradoxically like despair.

But perhaps not paradoxically, the prisoner thinks, shifting his pillow from his head to his stomach and holding it tightly there. He curls himself around it.

A double-edged sword.

That's what your compassion is.

I had nothing.

I never knew I had nothing.

I was content having nothing.

But then you gave me something.

And in your cruelty, you waited until I learned to live with it, grow accustomed to it, maybe even…love what you'd given me.

And right at that moment, just as I learned what it was like to have, *you take it away.*

So that I would know loss at its worst.

But almost as if he can't help himself, he's moving closer.

The prisoner relaxes.

And feels the dissident's arm over his waist.

It falls over his stomach.

His fingers brush against bare skin.

They're so warm he shivers.

I had an empty world.

The dissident breathes an apology into his ear, but he still pulls him closer.

And you decide to give me another. After showing me a world full to the brim.

Solid. Warm.

Every cold night he'd ever had, alone, in the darkness, crouching, sitting, standing, wishing he could find someplace warmer but knowing that even beside a fire, even beside his comrades, he would never find it.

The memories, cold and harsh, feel so distant they might not exist, they might be dreams.

And he's just been woken up.

How cruel.

How cruel your kindness is.

100

"Will you be in trouble?"

"For failing? No. I didn't betray them and I wasn't caught. I more or less succeeded in my second objective too."

"Are you sure?"

"I'll be demoted and never sent out again, but honestly, that's alright with me. But...I don't suppose you have any useful information?"

The dissident chuckles as he says it.

The prisoner smiles ruefully.

It almost feels like a parody of how they first met.

"I was being honest. I have no information. The Empire makes a habit of only telling us the bare minimum, the details needed to complete the mission."

The dissident looks surprised.

"How could they expect such commitment? Such blind faith in their decisions and orders?"

With a shadow of pride, or maybe nothing quite that strong, appreciation perhaps, the prisoner replies, "Faith is what keeps the Empire strong, faith in people to carry out their orders for the good of others. Faith in people. Not fate, not luck, not fortune. And certainly not gods."

He says it almost playfully, as close to humorous as he's ever gotten.

The dissident grins, remembering their earlier arguments, the rage he'd felt at the prisoner's beliefs.

"So you're a useless prisoner, huh?"

"...I suppose I am." The prisoner puts his head in his hand, looking at his companion from the bed, fondness lining every muscle of his face. Not that the dissident, packing separate bags with utmost concentration, notices.

"Well that makes *me* useless, for having rescued someone useless."

The prisoner slides off of the bed onto the floor.

He settles on his knees behind the dissident, who's still not looking at him, who's separating clothing he's taking with him and clothing he wants to give the prisoner.

He's being too generous.

The prisoner catches his hand.

"So why do I have to be useless *and* alone?" he asks softly.

The dissident freezes, now very aware of him.

The prisoner doesn't understand why he's so affected by him.

He's smaller, weaker, and much less attractive than the dissident.

He can think of no other reason for the dissident to be freezing up like this whenever he comes close.

"You won't...be alone. You'll find someone. There are a lot of people you've never met. Give them a chance."

The prisoner lets go of his hand. He resumes packing.

"Where would I go?"

"Stay here, if you want. Or leave. You can take care of yourself, you'll find somewhere to call home."

"What if I already did? And there's nowhere else I'd rather be?" the prisoner asks lightly, nonchalant as he presses his forehead against the dissident's back.

The dissident falters for a moment.

For a terrible, wonderful split second, the prisoner thinks he's convinced him. Persuaded him not to leave.

Not to cut him free, to leave him without an anchor, without anyone or anything, to hold him to the ground.

Just like you were before, pilot.

But now that he's ruined you, you're nothing like you were before.

He took everything away from you and gave you himself in return.

But now he'll take that away.

Leave you with nothing. Leaving you nothing.

Teacher never did anything quite this destructive, did he?

Even when he beat you to a bloody inhuman pulp, he never quite managed to break you.

He never left you defenseless.

Vulnerable.

The Empire was cold, but it was secure. It was safe.

Even far, far away from it, you still held it within your bones, within your very blood, an iron defense against pain and corruption.

You were willing to die for it.

Fearless. Noble. Blank.

Just think, you almost died pure.

Now look at you.

When he leaves you, he'll leave you weaker, emptier than you've ever been in your entire life, and you would thank him for it.

"You can't know that. You haven't explored all of your options yet, and until you do, you can't assume I'm your best one," the dissident finally, reluctantly, says. But something's changed in his voice, and he straightens a little, the taut, thick muscles of his shoulders loosening slightly. The prisoner moves his head back as the dissident straightens, then moves it even further back as he turns around and grips him by the shoulders. "But...after this, I'll be going back to management, I guess. I'll be home. If you decide, after a little while, that you...really do... miss me...and that it's not just that I was the first person you met...then why don't you come to me then?"

The dissident grips him rather excitedly, his eyes almost watery with his eagerness. He has the air of a child who's suddenly had an idea they find brilliant, a child who's realized some great truth, achieved some great understanding that he's never considered before, and which he recognizes will bring him one step closer to the world of adulthood.

"This doesn't have to be goodbye," the dissident presses.

The prisoner sways under his touch.

Will you ever be the same?

No.

How could you be?

You need him now.

Doesn't he know that?

Doesn't he care?

"If you never want to see me again, I'll understand. But I…really hope we can…be friends at least. I would hate for this to be goodbye forever. Especially since you're staying a while," the dissident chuckles.

The prisoner finally moves his head.

He begins to stand up, to walk away, but the dissident catches his hand and stops him.

"I don't know how you feel about me, and I don't know if you know how you feel about me either," he says, his voice humorous and regretful. "But when you figure it out… I just want you to know that my home is always open to you. I'll keep a fire going. And bandages in my nightstand."

The prisoner laughs.

The sound shocks them both.

They both stare at one another, bemused, before laughing again, this time together.

The dissident claps his shoulder, then boldly seizes his hand, squeezing it with his sturdy, amicable grip.

The prisoner squeezes back.

But he can't resist.

It's their last night together.

He wants to have one last flare of that feeling, something he can savor while he's still got it, hold tightly within his memories where he can replay it on cold, lonely nights that remind him of the years he spent without it. He had been alone, had been comfortable with it, and himself, for all of his life, but now the thought of it terrifies him, because now he is different. He never knew he was empty, and now that he knows, the knowledge offers him no comfort, nothing to fill in the hole it had dug out of him.

The dissident is close.

If he says no, he will back away immediately.

Whether he needs it or simply wants it, it's not something he will demand for.

He just wants something to remember for as long as it takes to find him again.

As long as it takes to live without him.

He hesitantly, deliberately, leans forward, giving the dissident time to push him away or tell him they need to go to bed.

But he need not have.

The dissident meets him three quarters of the way there.

The closer you pull him, the farther away he'll push you.

But that's alright.

I won't let him go so quickly.

As the dissident eases him onto his back, so keen, fervent, so *electrified* that the prisoner's own body almost hurts, twinges on contact, as though a charge is running through the dissident and merely touching him had passed it on through, the prisoner knows that he will not be dismissed so easily.

What makes a world worth living in?

What makes a life worth…saving? What makes a life worth…struggling to preserve?

Is it people? Comfort? Pride? God? This?

I don't know.

I don't care.

I've found something I never had before, something I never knew I needed, or wanted, and I would loathe to let it go so easily.

If he wishes for me to leave, I will leave.

But I won't go far.

101

When the dissident wakes, the prisoner's head is bent just under his chin, air from his nose tickling his throat.

Take him with you.

No.

No, he can't do that.

Take him.

No, he can't do that.

They would know.

The resistance would know who he was.

And he had already decided.

But you want to.

It doesn't mean he will have it.

Maybe someday.

The dissident will go away, perhaps.

Find somewhere else to live.

The resistance will keep tabs on him, but they won't keep a close eye on him, not after this screw up.

Then the prisoner will find him.

Or *he'll* find *him*.

This doesn't have to be goodbye.

What if it is?

The dissident doesn't let his mind linger on that question.

But he allows himself a fantasy.

He imagines letting the prisoner come with him.

He imagines, foolishly, introducing him to his friends.

Showing him his house, the lake, the mountains he grew up with.

The house, awfully lonely without his parents.

He imagines the prisoner in it, lying on his couch, sitting at his dining room table, eyes wide as he watches the dissident's TV, plays with his voice-interface, sees the library he'd inherited from his parents.

One day.

Not today.

One day.

The prisoner is utterly silent through breakfast.

The dissident hadn't been sure how he wanted to do this.

He'd withdrawn as much money as possible, giving himself only enough to pay for a bus ticket out of the town, and giving the prisoner the rest.

"Where should I go?" the prisoner asks lightly, disinterestedly, as though he's not really asking, but attempting to keep a conversation going.

They're sitting outside. The dissident has a map on his lap. He's waiting for a bus out of town. He tells the prisoner that he'll pay for him to stay here for a little longer, but the prisoner says he's not interested in staying here.

So the prisoner is waiting with him for the bus.

And the dissident writes down a list of cities.

He goes through a bus schedule and circles and underlines and traces routes.

The prisoner watches him without a flicker of comprehension. The dissident scribbles away, not aware of his companion's utter indifference, merely excitedly chattering away about places the prisoner could go, the jobs he could find in this sector or that.

In the end, he writes his address down.

"This is where I live," he says. The prisoner's eyes flicker to his pen, then to the address underneath. "Don't...Don't come right away. Take...a year or two. I'll be there for at least that long."

"...Is that where you're headed?" the prisoner asks.

"No. I'm going to stop...somewhere else first. I haven't been there in a long time and I want to site see while I'm passing through."

The prisoner folds the map carefully in his hands, stowing it in his jacket pocket.

"A year."

"You'll be ok," the dissident says. "Maybe you'll even meet someone you like better than me. And maybe you won't. Whatever happens, it'll be up to you. It'll be your decision and you'll be making it without me clouding your judgement or monopolizing your attention. It's...better this way. Trust me."

He covers the prisoner's hand with his own as they both watch the bus approaching out of the corner of their eyes.

"Do you trust me?"

The prisoner turns his hand over, brushing the underside of the dissident's palm with his fingers.

"Yes."

The dissident stands up, his whole arm tingling.

"Then...believe me when I say you'll be alright."

He hesitates, making an awkward motion, a strange half-lunge as though he were going to pull the prisoner into a hug, but then thought better of it. He merely gives him a sturdy handshake. The prisoner lets go easily enough, but as the dissident boards, as he puts his foot on the first stair, he feels a hand on his sleeve.

He looks back, traitorously, hypocritically hopeful.

The prisoner stares solemnly into his eyes as he holds him there.

"You never learned my name, did you?"

The dissident shakes his head.

The prisoner pulls him back, taking his foot off of the stair, and draws him close.

His hand holds the dissident's shoulder and he leans in close to his ear, so close the dissident almost reconsiders his decision. Almost.

He whispers it into his ear.

The dissident smiles.

"Now why didn't I call you that before?" he sighs.

It's only later that the dissident realizes that he never told the prisoner his name.

The prisoner whispers it to himself later that day, after retrieving it from the hotel clerk, who had also told him what destination his "husband's" ticket was bound for.

"Excuse me."

"How can I help you, sir?"

"My husband and I checked out this morning from room 23C. But I was wondering, he bought a bus ticket from you, did he not?"

"Correct, we are an affiliate of National Footholds and can provide you tickets at half-price to anywhere-"

"Yes, thank you, could I get the same ticket?"

"As your husband?"

"Yes."

"...forgive me if it's not my place, but why did you not go with him?"

"We were to...meet somewhere else. But...I'm not sure where he's going or...who he's meeting. So I..."

"Ah. Say no more. I understand. Nothing wrong with being careful. My own wife cheated on me three years ago. I would've loved to have caught her in the act instead of finding out from my current wife, her friend, Lily. Such a shame, she was so beautiful-"

"Please, sir."

"Oh, sorry! Yes, this is the ticket he bought, the destination..."

"And the name he put down?"

"Worried he used a different name to cover his tracks before he left? Such a shame, how complicated young love can be. You know, my wife would like you. You could give up on him, stay here for a bit, maybe join us for a private dinner-"

"His name, please."

He won't be able to catch up with the dissident immediately. But he at least knows where he's going. So he takes the same bus an hour later.

Saying the dissident's name slowly in his mind the entire trip, his eyes closed.

Several other passengers get on and off. Some glance curiously at him. Some don't even notice him, too intent on finding a seat before the bus gets moving again.

Some are fascinating, wearing elaborate clothing, fashionable threads, the newest and trendiest of brands, and some are subtler, wearing dignified, simple styles, with expensive glasses or antique pocket watches, giving off an air of arrogance and intrigue as they read classics. But he's blind to them all.

He doesn't see any of them, doesn't see the trees rolling passed, the ground flying beneath him, the farmlands slowly easing into congested traffic as the city comes into view.

His eyes are either closed. Or open and staring up at the sky.

His mind far away, in a cabin beside a lake, nestled within a haven of mountains.

"What are you looking for, kid?"

The prisoner startles, his first immediate feeling panic, since he wasn't expecting anyone to speak to him, and then mild irritation at being mistaken for an adolescent.

A young man comes up behind him, having just come from the information booth himself.

He peers over his shoulder and smiles at the map of the city the prisoner is perusing. "Tourist?"

"Something like that," the prisoner says dryly.

"What kind of tourist? There's a lot to see here, kid. You looking for art? History? Or are you the other kind of tourist?"

The prisoner feels a shiver dance up his spine as the man leans in too close and his arm drapes around his waist.

"I can help you find your way around. I come here every spring. If you're looking for a good time, you came to the right place, and how lucky of you, running into the right guy too-"

"I'm looking for someone," the prisoner says shortly, abruptly pulling himself out of his grip, wanting to get away from him as soon as possible. He's not afraid of him, because the man might be taller, but he has the looks and movements of a civilian. No training whatsoever. The prisoner could easily bring him to his knees, wrap his arms around his neck, and make quick work of him.

But he doesn't want to draw attention to himself.

And he derives no pleasure from killing others.

Nor would it be necessary in this case.

So he merely gives the stranger a polite nod, ignoring the slur that he spits at his back as the prisoner walks away.

There is indeed a lot to see.

The prisoner's eyes hurt after just minutes of staring at bright colorful images, the likes of which he's never seen before, and certainly not so large and imposing.

Huge screens planted on the sides of buildings besiege his eyes everywhere he looks. Some buildings have built in screens, windows and glass architecture colored by colorful projections every millisecond.

Music blares from speakers. Heavily-muscled, oiled-up men and skinny, doe-eyed women promote some product, some lifestyle, all dressed rather scantily as they fall all over one another or pose for an audience. Some of them wink directly at him; some casually side eye him; others merely dance across silver and blue screens, large and realistic and so life like that he flinches when one stops right next to him. She flips her hair and crouches down and shows him a card. On it is an address for what he assumes is a strip club, but he is later proven wrong by another variation of the ad with the same address, which includes a brief description of the location's acupuncture and massage services.

It gives him something of a headache to walk through the streets.

He blinks and waves crashing against a shore, waves far too clean to be real water, abruptly become bright city lights and sharp, meticulous urban landscapes dotted with points of illumination like stars. He sneezes and when he looks up again, it's a mountain, people are skiing, they're laughing and holding one another close and showing off their branded clothing, their custom boots and stylistic jackets with animal fur collars.

He tries to look away, but he can't.

They're everywhere.

And he's so distracted by the screens that he barely notices the people walking in front of him, behind him, who grunt with irritation every time he accidentally brushes against one of them.

He wishes he could close his eyes, but he can't.

The nearest hotel is three blocks down.

There are many hotels in the area, according to his map, but the closest one is where he might as well stop first.

He'll use the dissident's name at the front desk.

If they question him, he'll have to say something.

Perhaps he can claim he's his husband again.

Or that he's a friend, just looking for a friend.

He has a feeling these people might not even care enough to question him.

Because as he walks, he sees them.

He sees their carefree laughter, their expensive drinks and elaborate accessories, their shiny, polished gems glistening on their fingers, their small dogs perched on laps or dolefully on the ground, their purses undefended and unattended, left on their chairs.

They smile at one another, even at him, some very painted up women winking upon eye contact.

He gets the feeling that luxury has dulled any sense of suspicion or paranoia from these people.

But it's only a feeling.

The real test will be asking for the dissident and seeing if they deny him.

He'll have a good reason to say it aloud, he realizes with a flicker of unexpected, eager anticipation.

As he walks, he wonders what he will do if the dissident isn't there.

Go to the next hotel?

And the next one?

And the next one?

What if he can't find him?

It's too loud, too bright, too full of strangers, moving and talking and eyeing him. More incomprehensible and disorganized than the battlefield, almost as hostile too, and more baffling than anything he's ever encountered.

He doesn't belong here.

He doesn't like it here.

What if the dissident decided to stay here?

Would you stay then?

The prisoner grimaces, but concludes that he would.

He would adapt.

He walks right by the hotel at first, not seeing its unimpressive, bland architecture, white and boxlike and squished between two more classical, striking silver buildings.

But then, realizing he's come to the end of the street, he turns around and heads toward the lobby doors, mentally rehearsing what he'll say to the clerk when he gets in.

Later, he will recall seeing a woman, sitting on a couch to his right, wearing a short skirt and a hoodie.

And a man hovering near the elevator some distance to his left, wearing a long sleeved shirt even though it's warm out and sweatpants with a beige jacket tied around his waist.

But upon first viewing, they barely register in his mind as he makes his way to the desk.

All he's thinking about is what he's going to say.

The dissident's name repeats itself in his head, almost like a chant, almost like a melody reverberating within his skull, the two words trembling, poised, in his throat.

"What were you thinking?"

"I don't know what you're talking-?"

"We're passed that point. We know, son."

"I really don't… I'm telling you, you got the wrong guy."

"You almost lost us. If you'd had the sense to stay away from cities then we would have never found you. Did you really think that it would be that easy?"

"I have no idea what you're talking about."

"Every screen in this city is a two way mirror, son. Once we identified the assailant in the security cameras, although you did make that quite difficult, I will give you that, it was simply a waiting game. You might've thought you could get away with stealing government property, but we always find you in the end. There's nowhere to hide here. Nowhere to go. No escaping your punishment. Those who are impure stand out like ash smudged on a white table cloth. Even if we hadn't identified you, we would have had you eventually. The dissidents always reveal themselves, sooner or later."

"They're the squirmy ones, ain't they boss? Can't resist banging at the walls of their little cage, rattling to get out."

"Well, rat has a connotation I would like to avoid. I'd like to think the young gentleman here is not vermin, no, but simply misguided. Twisted and perverted by our insidious little resistance group. Encouraged to break laws just for the sake of breaking them. Next time, choose your cliques a little more carefully, son. I know what it's like, being so young and energetic and feeling restless, but you'll regret it in the long term."

"Where…where are we? What is this place?"

"Home. Your home. My home. Anywhere within these borderlines is your home, son. It's time you learned that. The borders are there to protect us. To give us a place where we know no fear. Where we can live in peace and work to achieve a better society. I know it's easy to forget, to take for granted, but that's ok. We'll remind you."

"What…what are you going to do?"

"Oh don't look so worried."

"He looks awfully pale."

"He does, doesn't he? Don't look so frightened."

"I'm not! I would gladly die for the cause."

"Would you really? I don't see that. In fact, it's rather bizarre, normally you look so ferocious, like some caged wild beast. But you're rather…docile. Tamed. Like something extinguished that fire within you, cooled it to a simmer. What happened out there, would you tell me? Why did it take you so long to get back to civilization? And most importantly…"

"…"

"Where is he? The prisoner you stole?"

"Whoa! This guy is strong!"

The prisoner hears something crack as he smashes the back of his head right into his assailant's nose.

The man howls.

"Be quiet, you idiot!" the woman hisses.

She lunges at the prisoner, but he shoves her aside, using her own weight to throw her off balance.

He lunges for the door, but someone catches him around the knees and takes him down before he gets anywhere close.

He tries to twist, to wiggle out of their grip, but they hold firm and the other two have time to regroup.

They haul him backwards, the woman and the man whose nose he might've broken grabbing both arms and forcing him into a chair.

The man holds him down while the woman ties his ankles and wrists to the chair's legs and arms respectively. He immediately tries to pull free, but is slapped for his troubles.

"Knock it off!" the man exclaims.

The prisoner gives him a disbelieving look.

His nose is bleeding profusely.

He snorts and then coughs, cursing as he goes looking for something to stem the bleeding.

The other two watch him distrustfully, the woman looking angry and the other man looking rather upset.

"This is the guy?" the man says.

"Definitely."

The prisoner says nothing.

"He's not saying anything."

"No, their people are quiet," the woman says authoritatively.

"And fucking crazy," the man with the bleeding nose complains. "Look what he did to me!"

"You should feel lucky that that's all he did. I saw our guy's face, he was fucked up. What did you do, try and tear his eye out?" the woman asks the prisoner.

The prisoner's eyes widen just barely.

But he still says nothing.

"Well I guess there's nothing we could do to get him to talk. I'm amazed he's even walking after being in the Blue Patrol's hands for so long. I'm amazed he's alive, actually, 231 did a damn good job…"

"No he didn't," the man interrupts. "He didn't get away with it, now did he? He was arrested and now he's fucked. And worse, he *lied.* He said this guy died. But he didn't, now did he?"

He kicks the prisoner in the shin.

But his victim doesn't make a sound.

"You don't look dead," the woman says. "Why would he lie?"

They all look at him, but the prisoner, tied to the chair and a true prisoner once again, just lowers his gaze and tries to think, his mind racing.

He had gone to the desk.

Asked for the dissident.

Been told his room number.

Perhaps it was foolish, perhaps it was merely impulsive, but he'd been compelled to go to it, even though the dissident had made it clear that he did not want them to be together (not yet, his mind whispers).

But instead of the dissident, he'd found an empty room.

And then these three, who'd crowded behind him and hastily shoved him inside of it.

He squints at them, mentally gauging their capabilities.

The man whose nose he'd bashed seemed like the strongest.

The other man hadn't wanted to get his hands dirty. He'd helped subdue him, but he wrings his hands anxiously and stays away from the struggle to get him into the chair. He stares at him now, his eyes calculating, but nervous, like a rat's.

The woman seems like a fighter.

She fidgets a lot, bounces vigorously on the balls of her feet, and had a great deal of arm and upper body strength when she'd attempted to get him into a headlock.

If he had to guess, he would say the man with the delicate hands was the leader, the woman his tactical advisor or second in command, and the man with the bleeding nose his muscle and enforcer.

But that hardly matters.

The most concerning thing on his mind is the news they had just presented to him.

The dissident had been arrested.

He had told his superiors (perhaps on arrival) that the prisoner had died.

But by following him to the city, he had inadvertently revealed the dissident's deception.

Which means they won't try to rescue him. He's a traitor.

And all he had to offer them was you, remember?

The person he wanted to protect.

He was willing to take the fall for failing his mission to let you live freely in this world, and now you've doomed both him and yourself.

How does freedom feel?

How does responsibility and making your own decisions feel, my boy?

"Why would he lie?" the woman repeats. "Did you threaten him? No, that doesn't make sense..."

"Do you know some secret about him? Did he do something dishonorable? Did you blackmail him?" the man who seems like the leader asks quietly. "Did you offer him something? Make some kind of trade?"

The prisoner wishes they would stop speaking.

It's hard to think while they're drilling him with questions he doesn't know how to answer.

They wouldn't believe the truth.

The prisoner has no doubt of that.

How could he explain in mere *words* what they had both been through?

Words felt insufficient.

Words were useless, powerless.

How could he explain in a simple sentence, a phrase, or even a story what had happened over these past few months, what had changed in both of them, perverting the values they had cherished since birth?

But what can you say?

If they know he is a traitor and let you free, they might assume he's better off dead.

"Well whatever it is that he offered you, he's dead now," the man with the bleeding nose says loudly.

The prisoner snaps out of his racing thoughts.

"He's dead?"

"He was arrested," the woman says.

"So he *is* dead."

"No. He's as good as dead."

"They've already killed him?" the prisoner asks.

"No! He was arrested, idiot. But he's a political dissident. Dissidents don't get released. They'll keep him locked up for the rest of his life. Which won't be horribly long." the woman says, "since there have been famines in the capital city and that's where they took him. Although, I think political prisoners will generally be fed before domestic terrorist prisoners, right?"

"That's assuming they see him as a political prisoner and not a domestic terrorist," the leading man says dryly.

"He won't be killed?" the prisoner asks.

"No?" the leading man says bemusedly. "Why, do they kill prisoners immediately in the Empire?"

"We do not...have prisons," the prisoner says shortly.

"How do you deal with criminals?" the woman asks interestedly.

"They are executed."

All three natives stare at him for a solid minute, disbelief and horror in their eyes.

They begin chattering about how fucked up that is, but he zones out, choosing instead to consider the information he's been given once again.

He's not dead.

Not yet.

But there's a chance.

There's hope.

If he had been born in the Empire, once his transgression had been discovered, he would have been shot immediately.

The prisoner eyes his passionate captors, now gesturing wildly as they talk about the pros and cons of the death penalty.

But luckily for him, he has a chance.

"Will you rescue him?" he interrupts.

The leading man slaps the other two on the shoulders, looking irritated as he restores order. "What?"

"When will you rescue him?" he repeats himself, looking slowly from face to face.

"Well never. He's there for life. He knew the consequences when he signed on."
The woman shrugs.

An ugly feeling begins to bubble in his stomach.

"You're not going to try to release one of your operatives?"

"An incompetent operative who not only failed his original mission but failed to achieve his secondary one. On top of that, he also *lied* to us. He told us you had died of your injuries. Even if we could save him, we wouldn't. There would be no point in it."

The woman bites her lip.

The prisoner zeroes in on her, interested in this reaction.

"No point? Did you know him at all?" he asks, watching her.

"I mean, he was new, I didn't know him," the man with the now-ebbing bleeding nose says just as the leading man shakes his head.

The woman says nothing.

The prisoner continues watching her as he speaks again.

"What will you do with me?" he asks.

"Take you back to base. Run some tests. Grill you for some information. If you fail to cooperate, well, you'll be terminated within sixty days. The environment shouldn't have to be burdened with any more useless weight," the leading man says.

"I won't cooperate," the prisoner says.

The man shrugs.

"We figured as mu-"

"Not unless you rescue him."

The leading man's mouth stops mid-word, hanging comically open as he gapes at the prisoner. The other two quickly turn to look at one another, so taken aback that they need to confirm that the other had indeed heard and seen what they had seen and heard.

The prisoner stares calmly back.

"What did you say?" the woman says cautiously.

"I said I won't cooperate unless you rescue him," the prisoner says slowly, thinking hard. "You asked if he offered me a trade, well he did. He let me go because…we were discovered by…the Blue Patrol. He…killed their agents, but realized that I would be captured if he was caught, so he told me to hide and wait for him while he went on to alert the resistance of his…success. He told you I was dead because…he was afraid he was being watched. And he was."

The prisoner hopes his voice isn't shaking.

He's never lied before.

He doesn't know how convincing he sounds, if he sounds convincing at all.

He keeps his face as neutral as possible and prays that any signs of dishonesty are dismissed as natural "foreign" habits.

"That's ridiculous. Why wouldn't he restrain you? Why would you just politely wait for your captor to come back and get you whenever he chose to?" the woman asks suspiciously.

The prisoner blanks for a split second.

He just stares at her, his head pounding with panic, his skin hot and uncomfortable with tension.

Trade. Deal.

"He…I mean, I…was intrigued by your world. I did not…want to be imprisoned any longer…by the Empire or by the Republic or…by your resistance group. He…"

These people are emotional are they not?

Play up the sympathy angle.

You could use friends.

Or at the very least, some pity.

"We…grew close on our journey."

This is true.

His voice becomes stronger as the lie, half lie, half-truth, begins to properly consolidate in his mind and on his lips.

"He wanted to take me directly to you, but I grew distracted. I wanted to see the world outside of my own. I had never seen your…entertainment, your…vibrant way of life. I was enchanted. He had pity on me. Before we were separated, I realized that the Empire was wrong. And evil. And I wanted to experience your world, not theirs, just for a little while. I pleaded with him. And when he killed the agents, he realized that we could strike a deal. I promised to stay in one place and wait for him, and be cooperative when the time came to be interrogated and he promised that I could…live for a while longer. Be free, just for a short while, before he came back for me. He did not betray you. He merely…saw the tactical use of a…cooperative prisoner."

The woman is nodding, looking almost touched.

The man looks a little less impressed.

He's still cradling his nose and looking rather agitated.

But his eyes are at least a little less harsh and he's frowning rather sympathetically as he listens. But the leading man isn't fooled, the prisoner can tell. He appeals directly to him.

"He…taught me another way of life. Another way to live. I accept my fate, my punishment, for being on your land, for breathing your air, and I will walk myself to your gallows when the time is right, but…I owe him. And I need him. I need him to convince his superiors to give me a chance."

"Because you think we're not capable of doing that ourselves?" the leading man asks suspiciously.

The prisoner doesn't even blink as he says, "Because I know you are not. He is different from all of you. He has more courage, compassion, and honesty than the three of you or even the entirety of your resistance combined. I trust him. I made a deal with him. I told him that I would wait for him. But he's waiting for me, for you, now. Please. If we save him, I will cooperate. But only if we save him, because…I owe him more than my life."

The prisoner cringes inwardly, but forces his face to remain earnest and pleading as he looks up at his three captors.

The woman is nodding, looking teary-eyed, while the man whose nose finally stopped bleeding looks rather touched now. The leading man has budged, just a little. He still looks stern, but more speculatively so.

"I'm not asking for freedom from you. I'm not asking you for *his* courage, compassion, or honesty. I'm not asking for a fair trial or a chance for redemption. All I ask is that we go to save him. Because he is the only one I trust to argue my case rightly and fairly. Because he is the only one who understands what I have been through, and how I have changed. Because…he is important to me. And I cannot bear the thought of leaving him to rot in a filthy cramped Republican prison when he rescued me from one, and gave me a new life, even if it was brief. So please. At least consider it."

The prisoner closes his eyes.

It feels wrong with all of these people staring at him. It makes him feel vulnerable, naked almost, but he keeps them closed as though accepting their judgment passively, submissively. Without opening his eyes, he knows they are exchanging glances, disbelieving or sympathetic.

"Even if we…wanted to," the woman says carefully. She sounds upset, her voice a little shaken. "We couldn't save him. He's in one of the most secure facilities on the continent."

"It's impossible," the man agrees.

The leading man is still evaluating the prisoner. His silence makes him nervous.

"But it might be possible. If you gathered your forces. Made a plan," the prisoner says without opening his eyes, feeling very much like he did when he first met the General.

"That would require going back to the resistance. They might not listen to a word you have to say. And without the dissident to explain himself, they'll assume you're a liar. Which you sound like to me," the leading man says slowly.

The prisoner's eyes slowly drift open.

"I think he screwed up," the leading man says slowly, belligerently. "I think you clawed his face to pieces and he lost you and panicked. He told us you died and got himself arrested."

"If I escaped him, then why am I here now?" the prisoner asks coldly. The woman whistles and the man shakes his head.

"Coincidence," the leading man says. "It's a city, perhaps you just came here to sight see, as you so passionately proclaimed."

"That's a rather unlikely coincidence," the prisoner retorts. "I came right to his hotel. Said his name. That's how you found me, remember? Why else would I come looking for *him*?"

"If he told you to stay, then why didn't you stay and wait for him to come back? Wasn't that your plan?" the leading man asks sharply.

Yes. Why couldn't you have stayed?

Why couldn't you have actually obeyed him-?

Not now.

"I was…worried. I thought he was my…only key to survival in an inhospitable place. Without him, I would be left in a strange world with no one and nothing. I wanted to…see him. Make sure he didn't…forget about me."

The prisoner feels the words, heavy and bitter on his tongue, and realizes that a lot of what he's said is true. It's just the context that's false.

The leading man frowns.

He doesn't want to believe him.

The prisoner's eyes dart swiftly to the woman.

She believes him.

The other man too.

Now just their leader, come on, come on, it's true, it's true…

"We are not mounting a rescue mission," he says sharply.

The prisoner's heart plummets. He slumps in his chair, feeling like his bones had been snapped by the dead weight of his sagging skin.

"At least…not until…we regroup… I'm not saying… I mean, for now…I believe you. But I would like to hear this from 231. And…I would also like a cooperative prisoner. After all, you'd be the first," the leading man says, giving him a hard look. "Which is why I have such a hard time trusting you, in fact. You're…I can tell you're from the Empire, but you're also…different. Completely different from any Empirean I've ever met. So parts of your story must be true. But you're still one of them, so neither I, nor any other members of our little resistance I'm sure, can take anything you say at face value. But…it's worth more…careful consideration by our superiors. We won't…go on any rescue mission, not immediately. But you'll come with us. Explain to them what you explained to us. And then, no matter what fate is decided for you…we will see what we can do about 231."

At first, the prisoner's chest feels like it's caving in.

He's failed.

Of course they won't try and save one of their own.

Even if they wanted to, they did not have the means.

The dissident is trapped.

A prisoner in his own country.

But hope, hard and glowing, is reborn in his chest, pushing outwards against the despairing pressures of his situation.

It didn't matter.

He had convinced these people that he would be cooperative.

He would play along.

Be obedient and eager to please. Perhaps escape them.

Find where the dissident was being kept and make his own plans to free him. Or perhaps meet their leaders, play "obedient and eager to please" with them. Gain their trust.

Keep an eye on the dissident's situation from the outside and mount a rescue, formal or informal, sanctioned by the resistance or not.

It might take time, but he could wait.

He had the patience.

He would not let the dissident remain a prisoner.

He would rescue him, no matter how long it took, no matter how many lies he would have to tell, no matter what humiliations or tortures he would have to endure.

No matter how much time had passed, either.

Even if it took these people decades to trust him, he would be waiting, patiently, busily, doing everything they asked of him.

And if it looked like they would not allow him to gain their trust?

Or if the dissident's life was in danger, and he could not afford to wait?

He would escape.

He would find others willing to help him. It was all a matter of persistence and endurance.

He would save the dissident's life at the cost of his own without a shred of remorse.

Perhaps he would not save his life from immediate death, perhaps only from longevity and suffering, from miserable incarceration, but he would risk his own freedom, his own longevity, dedication, and time to saving the dissident's.

"Thank you," he murmurs.

The woman gasps.

107

I will save you.

Because I don't believe in heaven.

And this is the only world I will get to know you in.

So even if it takes years.

Even if these people never truly trust me and I am miserable.

I would die to save your life, even though I deprive myself of the experience of getting to know you.

Because you gave me this life.

It seems only fair to give some of it back to you.

"The name's Monica," the woman whispers to him.

They sit in the lobby, the woman's two companions speaking furtively in the corner of the room behind a potted plant as the woman keeps an eye on him.

"I know 231 personally, we're old friends. I understand completely. I wish we could save him too. But it's really best that we let the resistance figure it out."

Will I attempt to escape before?

Or after I meet them?

"He's not... I mean, he's not top priority. He doesn't have sensitive information that he hasn't already shared with them. And he's not...I mean, it was his first mission, so they don't know just how much use he has, as an asset-"

Perhaps before.

"But there are other operatives in there! People who can help!"

Perhaps after.

No matter.

"Do you know...what we strive for? Truly?" Monica asks him.

The prisoner leans back in his chair.

"You must breach the southern border. Your people are dying. Expansion is the only solution."

He watches the chandelier swing merrily overhead.

"Exactly," she says with a smile. "Exactly. You understand the cause. Nothing wrong with making it a little personal. I get it. 231 is...really something, isn't he?"

Yes.

The prisoner lets his eyes slide out of focus.

I believe truly, that you must breach the border of the southern hemisphere.

Images of the dissident, sleeping, lying down, staring into the fire, staring at him, his eyes wide, his eyes narrow, horrified, delighted, scared, content, flash through his mind.

The bear, crouched over him.

The tent, where he stayed and kept watch.

The cabin, where they slept and tended to each other's wounds.

The sky, the wide blue and gray and red and purple and pink sky, a roof over the heads of all.

The distance between them, bridged by pain, dissolved by compassion, becoming nonexistent, superfluous, as they realized its true nature, its farce.

The distance, seemingly necessary, frigid and immovable, unchangeable, melted and easily thawed by reality.

Yes. The southern border will fall.

It must.

As must all the rest.

We will bring it down together.

`And perhaps one day, all of us, all of humanity, will come back together once more.

"What should we call you?" the leading man asks.

The prisoner hesitates.

His own name has never felt less relevant to his life, to his new purpose.

He starts to say it, but then stops.

He says something else instead, the first name he can think of.

Monica snorts.

"Amazing coincidence."

The prisoner smiles to himself.

"What? That...?"

"That you two would share a name," she giggles.

The dissident clasps his hands together, his manacles jangling obnoxiously against one another.

He will never see the prisoner again, that is assured.

But he prays, prays to a compassionate, merciful god, that the prisoner is no longer interested in him after a year.

That he finds someone else, something else.

Because he cannot bear the thought of the prisoner going to his house, smiling that small, rare smile of his, still loving him, wanting to share his life with him, and not because of proximity or out of a sense of obligation, but because he really, truly does want to be with him after a year or two of absence, and finding him gone.

Finding new tenants, without a single explanation why.

And living the rest of his life in this new world he promised him, a world he promised wouldn't be lonely, would be full of people, and places, and lovely experiences, alone.

The dissident prays the prisoner will forget about him.

But even though he's tempted to, he does not pray to God that *he* will forget about the prisoner.

No.

No, he does not want to forget.

The prisoner should move on, but *he* shouldn't.

He doesn't regret meeting him. Taking on this mission. Or saving his life, even though he wasn't supposed to, not really.

He doesn't regret letting him go. Or lying about his death.

His only regret is that they couldn't have had more time together.

As long as he's here, he will never move on from his past, but that's alright, because if there's one piece of his past that he would want to hold onto forever, it would be him.

What would you know about beautiful?
That it is always relevant.
That it has meaning.
That even the likes of myself can find meaning within it.

The next hotel they stop at is rustic, very traditional, offering an "authentic" cabin experience.

It has a fire, burning bright in the mantelpiece.

The prisoner, a captive and a prisoner, but still, somehow neither, sits beside it.

He blinks, sees its brilliance flare in the darkness of his closed eyes, and hopes that wherever the dissident is, whatever he's doing, he is warm tonight.